The Body in the Trees

RICHARD JAMES

For Izzy.

CONTENTS

SUMMER, 1892

"It is my belief... that the lowest and vilest alleys in London do not present a more dreadful record of sin than does the smiling and beautiful countryside."

The Adventure Of The Copper Beeches, Arthur Conan Doyle

Prologue

Detective Inspector George Bowman stood on Hanbury Street, blinking the dust from his bloodshot eyes. The sun had baked the road hard beneath his feet and a dusty film lay over everything and everyone. The very bricks of the buildings around him seemed to radiate heat. A collective lethargy had settled over the passersby as they shuffled in the harsh glare of the sun, their shoulders stooped. The wisest amongst them kept to the side of the street, hopping between arches and alcoves in pursuit of the cooler shade. A team of labourers struggled with their load, stopping at intervals to sit on their carts and catch their breath. A pawnbroker rested in the shade of the tatty awning before his shop and drew lazily on his pipe. A flower girl sat on the wall opposite to wipe her face with the hem of her skirts. The road was as busy as it ever was. Traders dragged their wares on rickety carts towards Commercial Road and the city. A workhorse pulled a dray of barrels from the brewery, the driver flicking his whip about its flanks in a vain attempt to provoke it. Swearing loudly, he swerved to avoid a drunken man who lay on his back in the middle of the road, his face obscured by a copy of the Evening Standard. Bowman was not in the least surprised to see that no one showed the slightest concern at his condition.

The inspector swung his hat from his head to smooth his hair with his fingers. There was a persistent throbbing at his temples and his mouth was dry. He had come to Hanbury Street in search of help, but now he doubted himself. Perhaps he was beyond rescue. Try as he might, he could not avert his eyes from the kerb. Shuffling slowly to the spot where she had stood, he was struck by the indifference with which people walked past. A ghost stood at the roadside and they paid it no heed. He felt suddenly aware of the very absence of her. Swallowing hard, he raised his eyes to the opposite side of the street.

The Women's Refuge stood back from the road, a red-bricked building with a plain frontage. It rose over three floors, its windows staring balefully out to the street below. A faded sign above the door proclaimed it to be under the auspices of The Salvation Army and a gaggle of women gathered beneath its chipped and peeling paintwork. Bowman smoothed his moustache between a forefinger and thumb as his eyes fell upon a board, hastily propped up by the low wall. "The Evils Of Drink!" it seemed to bellow into the street, "Be free from its pernicious bonds!" Some smaller text invited the curious to attend a meeting at two of the clock in the Booth Room. Bowman flicked open his fob watch and squinted to read the dial. He marvelled that he had arrived on time.

Truth be told, he had not passed the morning well. He had risen late to find the landlady at his door. She was a dour, Scottish lady who lived on the floor above. It being a Thursday, she was tasked with cleaning his rooms. Clearly surprised at finding him at home, she had offered her apologies with an insinuating tone and stood with her arms folded across her bosom, her eyebrows raised in admonishment. Bowman had grabbed a jacket and hat and stumbled from the building to leave her to her duties, thankful for once that he had slept in the clothes he had worn the day before. He knew that, with a fair wind, he might make it to the meeting in time, and so he walked the streets of Hampstead in search of a cab.

Now he stood before the Women's Refuge, the blood rushing in his ears. Taking a breath to calm himself, he took a step off the kerb just as she had done some fourteen months before. He fancied he felt her hand on his back, guiding him gently across the road to the building opposite. Oblivious even to the carts that rattled around him, he straightened the tie at his collar and fixed his eyes on the door before him. If he gave himself time to think, he would turn his heels from the building in search of the nearest public house. A pint or two of porter would numb the pain, he knew, and a couple more would numb it further.

The interior of the hall was appreciably darker than the street outside. The shutters were closed at the windows to thwart the sun's heat and Bowman could feel the tiled walls cooling the air about him. A crush of women was directed to a counter where they might pay a penny for a meal and a penny more for a bed, their harsh voices echoing to the ceiling as they clamoured for attention. Bowman dropped his eyes to the floor, the better to avoid the gaze of those around him. Some were older and

2

clearly in a state of some distress, others much younger but sad around the eyes. Three or four officers from the Salvation Army stood in their uniforms, directing the ladies to their dormitories or the refectory where their dinner might be taken. Bowman would not have been surprised to see William Booth himself conducting proceedings. Anna had mentioned once that he would often work at the refuge or give talks to its residents. A charismatic speaker, he had spurred her on to devote ever more of her time in helping others. The assistance offered by the Sally Army was entirely laudable. Bowman had never thought that he might himself be the recipient of it.

Turning off the reception hall, the inspector was confronted by a kindly-looking woman in a smart, black dress. The straw bonnet on her head was trimmed with a blue ribbon and marked her out as a Salvation Army officer. She regarded Bowman over her half-moon spectacles as she spoke.

"Are you here for the meeting?"

"Yes," Bowman nodded in response, his breath quickening at the admission.

"Then you are just in time. Brigadier Garrett is preparing himself." She gave the inspector a pitying look and directed him into a side room with a high ceiling and a table at its far end. Some wooden chairs had been placed in rows before it with an aisle between them. Bowman saw with a start that only two were occupied, and that he was the only man present. Had it not been for the officer at his elbow, he might well have effected a hasty retreat, but there was something about the look she gave that told him such a move would be frowned upon. Slowly, he sunk into a chair by the door, toying nervously with the rim of his hat. He was at least grateful to be given respite from the heat of the day.

Looking about him at the others present in the room, he saw an old lady who was already asleep. She sat slumped in a corner, a string of drool emanating from her lower lip to collect in a pool on her lap. Her shoulders heaved up and down as she took long, shuddering breaths, her head nodding onto her chest as she sank deeper into her slumber. A young girl, perhaps no more than fourteen years old, sat fidgeting on the front row, looking back at him with quick, furtive glances. She knotted and unknotted a handkerchief in her trembling hands. Every now and then she would gasp, as if suddenly cognisant of some knowledge that caused her distress. She was dressed in a plain grey dress, her hair collected and pinned beneath a creased mob cap. Bowman leaned back in his chair with a sigh, regretting his decision to come.

The door behind him was thrown open with a clatter and soon he heard the tapping of a cane on the parquet floor. Turning to the aisle, he saw an old man walking slowly along its length to a lectern. This must be Brigadier Garrett, Bowman surmised, though quite what he had done to attain his rank he could not guess. The lectern was placed before a large picture depicting a battlefield. Wounded soldiers lay face down in the mud, their fingers reaching up to the sky. A warrior on horseback shielded his eyes against the supernatural glow that radiated from an angel at the painting's centre. Suspended amongst the clouds, the angel's wings spread wide over the entire battlefield as if to provide a comfort to those below. He wore an expression of divine sorrow at the scene beneath, and beckoned with his hand that the wounded and dying might join him. The painting was too literal for Bowman's taste but, he reasoned, served well enough as an illustration of the power of salvation. "Come unto me," the angel seemed to say, "and leave your Earthly cares." Bowman snorted, audibly. If only it were that easy. Glancing to the lectern, he saw the old man had taken his position there. Brigadier Garrett was a curious creature, having the appearance of a character from a fairy tale such as one might read to a child. He was short of stature and ancient. The smart Salvation Army uniform he wore seemed the only thing holding him up as he hung his cane on the lectern. His shoes were polished to a perfection that was rivalled only by the shine of his buttons. Most startling of all, however, was the great, white beard that spread across the old man's chest and even across his shoulders. A pair of shrewd eyes peered from behind the foliage of his eyebrows as he balanced his pince-nez precariously at his nose to read. A peaked cap jutted from his head, from which there sprang a wiry thatch of white hair. Resting his hands at either

4

side of the lectern, the old man gazed with barely disguised disappointment at the few assembled before him. When he eventually spoke, he did so with a powerful voice quite at odds with the frail vessel from which it emerged.

"Woe to those who rise early in the morning," he proclaimed with a fierce Irish accent. "That they may pursue strong drink." He paused dramatically to survey the room. Suddenly even more uncomfortable under the man's gaze, Bowman shifted on his chair. "Woe to those," the Brigadier continued, "who stay up late in the evening that wine may inflame them!"

The old lady had been jolted awake by the force of his words. Wiping the drool from her chin, she looked about her as if unsure of her surroundings, blinking in confusion.

"There is, the Bible tells us, a place in Hell for those who succumb to drink." The young girl in the front row began to sob. Rather than offering her any comfort, the man at the lectern turned his full force upon her. "We read in Galatians that those who practice drunkenness and carousing will not inherit the Kingdom of God." He allowed himself a beatific smile. "The Good Book could not be any plainer." He let the longest pause settle over the room before he continued, confident that no one there would have the guile to get up and leave. Stroking his beard, he stepped from behind the lectern and pulled himself up to what passed for his full height. "God hates drinkers," he asserted, simply. "And there is none other to blame for that, than you." He turned to gaze at each of them in turn, reserving a special look of distaste for the girl in the front row. "Look around you at the world that He created. Man has made it a place of filth and degradation, of fornication and sin. Proverbs tells us the heavy drinker and the glutton will come to poverty, and it is so. The greatest cause of poverty is drink."

Bowman's eyes darted to the back of the room in search of an escape. The woman who had admitted him stood guarding the door, clearly in thrall to the Brigadier's rhetoric. Her eyes burned with admiration and her arms were folded proudly across her chest. In that moment, the inspector knew he should prepare himself to hear the entirety of Garrett's speech.

"There is but one way to sobriety," the man was intoning,

"and that is through God. Dedicate yourself to Him and His works and the Kingdom of God will be thine. Turn from him, and nothing but damnation awaits."

This was almost too much for the young girl in the mob cap. Her sobs were louder now, and she shook fearfully in her seat. Garrett seemed possessed with a sudden strength as he moved towards her, his hand outstretched. "Turn to God and be saved," he boomed, his powerful voice echoing from the ceiling. "Renounce him and burn!" His eyes gleaming with a ferocious light, he stood with a trembling finger outstretched towards the unfortunate child. The effect was immediate. With a howl of pain, she slid from her chair and to her knees. The old man placed his hand upon her head. "Turn from drink and turn to God!"

Bowman could contain himself no longer. Clearing his throat, he rose unsteadily to his feet, the action alone drawing the attention of the man at the front of the hall. "You would do well to leave her be," the inspector cautioned as he moved towards him. Bowman was surprised at the feeling in his voice.

"She is in sin," replied the Brigadier, as if it were explanation enough. The girl on the floor shook her head to be free of his hand. "I am the Lord," he thundered, "and there is no other. Besides me there is no God!"

Bowman was on his haunches now, holding the young girl gently by the elbow. "She needs help, not admonishment," he pleaded. "She has a sickness."

"She has a weakness," Garrett corrected him, his beard quivering in defiance. "And she needs saving!"

"She needs air," Bowman insisted.

"None shall come to God who drink."

The unfortunate child at Bowman's side was trembling uncontrollably now. He turned to plead with the woman at the door. "Will you help me lead this poor wretch from the room?"

Lifting the girl to her feet, Bowman held out a hand to keep the old man at a distance. Garrett's eyes blazed as he stood firm, muttering under his breath. "Behold, I am the Lord, the God of all flesh," he intoned over and over as if it were an incantation.

The woman from the door had joined them now. Obviously

embarrassed at the disturbance, her eyes pleaded with the old man for his forgiveness at the interruption. Garrett simply sighed and turned away, clearly disappointed at the turn of events.

It took both of them to lead the girl up the aisle and to the door. The old woman followed proceedings with a half-interested gaze then promptly fell asleep again where she sat. Looking over his shoulder, Bowman could see that Garrett had taken his cane from the lectern and, shaking his head, was shuffling towards a side door. The afternoon's performance over, his whole demeanour had changed. The Brigadier was once more the amiable looking character from a children's story, his previous persona discarded as easily as one might discard a coat.

Reaching the door, Bowman noticed the girl had got lighter with each step. By the time they reached the reception hall, they were barely supporting her at all. Finally, she straightened herself up and stood unaided. Wiping the tears from her eyes with a sleeve, she looked up at Bowman with a toothy grin.

"Thank you, sir," she said with a mocking curtsey. For the first time, Bowman fancied he could smell alcohol on her breath. "I couldn't stand his cant no longer." With that, she bent to lift up her skirts and ran for the door, her childish laughter echoing around the hall.

Aghast, Bowman looked to the woman beside him for an explanation. "Her name's Tillie," she sighed, haughtily. "She is well known to us." Bowman raised his eyebrows. "She comes to us for warmth and food, then takes to the streets again to earn her penny."

"The penny she needs for her bed?" Bowman asked.

The woman nodded. "On a good day she'll make tuppence and spend a penny of it on drink." She looked at Bowman, pointedly. "As she did this morning."

Bowman shook his head in disappointment and smoothed his clothes about him.

"And what of you, Inspector Bowman?" He was startled by the use of his name. Looking up at his companion, he saw all traces of severity had slipped from her face. Now she regarded him with kindly eyes. "I could not help but recognise you." Bowman shuffled uncomfortably where he stood. He was at a loss for words. "I was on duty on the day of the accident," the woman continued. Bowman's stomach lurched at the word. "And I followed your story in the papers." With a shudder, Bowman remembered the headlines in the Evening Standard. He wondered just how much she knew. The woman leaned in, earnestly. "You must know, inspector, that God has a plan for us all." Bowman's heart quickened. "You are but an instrument of His work."

The implication behind her words caused the inspector's stomach to turn. If that fateful day had seen Bowman working only as an instrument of God, then His plan was truly a dreadful one.

"Have you come for guidance?" the woman asked, peering condescendingly over her half-moon spectacles.

Bowman's gaze was drawn through the door to the street beyond. Drawn to the negative space where she had stood. "Perhaps," he whispered, almost to himself. "But I will not find it here." He had never felt so alone.

As he made for the door, Bowman felt his hand beginning to twitch. He feigned reaching for the watch in his waistcoat pocket to disguise the tremor, but fancied it was too late. The woman in the Salvation Army uniform shook her head sadly as he retreated through the door, his head bowed and his mind set on soothing his fevered brain at the nearest public house.

I

A Strange Harvest

Tom Cousins knew how to curse. For a boy of twelve he was extremely well versed in oaths of all colours. As the brambles scratched against his bare shins he let a few fly before him, mainly aimed at the hound that sprinted ahead, heedless to his calls. This dog was more trouble than he was worth. A hopeless rabbiter and even worse a fighter, he ran away daily. Perhaps he thought it a game, that he should be chased through the woods around Larton by his master. Or perhaps he thought it was for the boy's own good. Either way, Tom was tiring of the sport. As he reached a clearing, he stopped to catch his breath. He had climbed quite a height through the baked paths of the wood and now he stood, breathing hard and dripping sweat. He felt his skin tighten in the sun and blinked into the glare. There below him lay Larton, sprawling to his left and right. He could see the glint of the river as it snaked through the village, its progress punctuated by the new iron bridge and the tower of All Saints Church. A plume of steam rose from a locomotive on the line to his right while, directly below him, a gardener tended the lawns of the manor house. Tom could see a game of croquet was in progress and marvelled at how those with the most money seemed to do the least to earn it. Squinting into the sun, he could see the lord of the manor in white flannels and striped blazer, standing to take his turn at the hoops.

Cupping his hands to his mouth, Tom called again. "Duke! Come 'ere!" Stillness settled on the scene. Had he been of a mind to listen, Tom would have heard the joyful cry of the song thrush and the whistle of wheeling kites. As it was, all he heard was the thumping of his own heart in his ears. Sweat stung his eyes. Suddenly, there came a bark. It came from deeper in the wood, by the pond, Tom guessed. Puffing his cheeks in exasperation, he gave chase again.

The nettles were thicker the deeper into the wood he went. Several times he yelped in pain as they stung his bare arms and

9

ankles. Thorns and briars snatched at his clothes. Low twigs whipped at his face. Passing through the old chalk quarry, now temporary home to the travellers who had come to gather the cherries, he clutched at a young sycamore sapling for balance. Their caravans and tents huddled together amongst the bracken and brambles, and lines of dusty washing hung between the trees. The quarry had long since fallen from use, but its smudged white cliffs stood testament to ancient industry. Had he stopped to look, Tom would have seen the marks of Neolithic tools and graffiti. Piles of lumpen chalk had become part of the landscape, compacted by centuries of rain and wind into permanent features. The chalky soil had given rise to flowers that thrived in its seeming barrenness; cowslips and wild basil competed for space with lady's bedstraw and meadow buttercups. Still Tom clambered on, his feet struggling for purchase on the gnarled roots and exposed rock. The dappled shade of the wood gave him some relief from the cruel sun, but still his freckled face ran wet with sweat. His shirt was soaked. His skin was caked in the dry, red dust he kicked up as he ran. Waving away a cloud of flies that pursued him, Tom finally breasted a ridge and saw the pond before him.

Gummer's Pond was a fetid, stagnant pool of just a few feet deep, home only to mosquito larvae and the slimiest of pondweed. The hot summer months had seen it dwindle to little more than a large puddle. The caked mud around it was hard and unyielding. A cloud of insects buzzed at its centre, lit by shafts of sunlight as it broke through the canopy. There, on the other side of the pond, stood Duke. A large lurcher, he was handsome enough, although his sharp nose and beady eyes betrayed a character not to be entirely trusted. Tight muscles rippled along his flank and his tail twitched violently from side to side as he stood, otherwise still and alert, on the opposite bank.

"That's it, Duke," Tom soothed. "There's a boy." Slapping a fly from his neck, Tom inched closer to the hound. Duke stood panting at the water's edge, his long snout pointing up to the branches above his head. He had clearly seen something. Tom's words were greeted by a single bark but still the dog did not move. Just a few feet more and Tom would have him. Duke's tongue hung heavily from his mouth as he stood. "Tired, are you boy?" Tom had affected a singsong tone to appease his hound. "Well, maybe that'll teach you to run away on the hottest day of the year." He wiped the sweat from his forehead with a tattered sleeve. "And maybe it'll teach me to give chase after you." A low, guttural growl rolled from Duke's throat, his attention caught by whatever quarry he had seen in the boughs above. A squirrel perhaps, thought Tom as he crept ever closer, arms outstretched as if that alone would confound Duke's escape. Just as he had the dog within reach, he allowed himself the briefest of glances into the branches above. The shafts of light that pierced the canopy landed on a pair of booted feet, twisting slowly in the air. The sight was so incongruous that, at first, Tom could make no sense of it. His eyes rose upwards into the foliage. First he saw a pair of legs, then a torso. Suspended from a branch above him, was the body of a man. Tom's legs buckled beneath him. He hit the dirt hard, then scrambled back to his feet to look around. All was quiet. A sudden rush of panic overtook him, and he breathed hard against an impulse to vomit. Dragging his fingers through his damp and dusty hair, he tried to formulate a plan. The man was clearly dead. An irrational impulse took a hold of the boy. Rather than turn his heels to head for help, he felt he must get him down. Peering into the mess of foliage, he could just make out a bloated face, half obscured by the leaves. A dry retch caught in Tom's throat and his stomach heaved at the sight. Steadying his nerves, he traced the rope up. It was tied around a hefty branch some way up the tree. Walking to the trunk, Tom could see it was studded with nodules and branches. He gave the dog a pat on its head. "Good boy," he said. "You stay there now." Like every boy his age, Tom knew how to climb. His favourite trees to conquer were the cedars in the grounds of Larton Manor because of the wide, low branches that afforded excellent footholds. The prospect of capture at any moment gave the enterprise an extra thrill. Now, there was no such hurry. Tom chose his footings with care. Grabbing at a sturdy branch, he pulled himself up a full four feet and swung his legs into a cleft in the trunk. More than once he grazed his skin against the bark, even drawing blood on an errant twig. Seemingly immune to such cuts and scrapes, Tom climbed ever higher until the branch to which the rope was secured came into view. It stretched out from the main trunk some twelve feet or so. Taking hold of a higher limb, Tom swung himself onto it and sat with one leg hanging to either side. Shuffling along inch by inch, it took some moments to come to where the rope was hooped and tied. Reaching into his waistcoat pocket, he took out a penknife. Gifted him by his father, it was a prized possession. Now it was put to grim use. The rope was rough, the type he had seen about the farm. Within minutes he was through it and the body fell with a heavy thud onto the ground below, narrowly missing Duke who backed away with a yelp of surprise. Lowering himself gingerly from the tree, Tom approached the body with apprehension. There was something about its clothing that gave him pause. The tattered corduroy trousers were common enough, but there was something about the waistcoat that was distinctive. The embroidery around the lapels was particularly extravagant. Faded though it was, Tom could clearly make it out; a red, hand stitched double cherry on a stalk. He could remember his mother sitting at the fire one winter's evening to complete the work. He forced his eyes ever upwards until they rested upon the poor man's distorted face. The tongue protruded grotesquely from swollen lips and sightless eyes bulged from their sockets. A mop of dark, curly hair was plastered to the man's forehead. The strain of having hung from the tree for several hours had disfigured the man's features almost beyond recognition. But to Tom Cousins, there was now no doubt about it. He was staring into the face of his own father.

Maxwell Trevitt never tired of the view from his window. The farmhouse had stood for almost a hundred years already, occupied in all that time by his forebears. It gave Trevitt a feeling of belonging. As he was fond of telling anyone who'd listen, he was the farm and the farm was he. As he looked across the acres of cherry trees, *his* cherry trees, he felt an ancient stirring. Generations of Trevitts had tended those trees and gathered their crop. He half expected to turn and see his father looking out with him, and next to him his father and so on. As he thought on his lineage, Trevitt gained an inch in height. His chest puffed out to strain against the buttons on his patterned waistcoat. His head was held so high he could not help but look down his nose at the man in his parlour. It is a truism that those most lowly born are the most given to snobbery, and so it was with Maxwell Trevitt. To any observer, he was a formidable man. Barrel-chested and broad shouldered, one could imagine the ground shook as he walked. His wide face was ruddy with toil, his cheek bones shone. A thatch of jet-black hair was scraped back from the expanse of his forehead, parted in the middle to expose a length of clean, white skin that ran like a scar to his crown. His thick ears framed a face that was completed with a broken nose, the legacy of a bar room brawl some years since. A brawl that he had, most decisively, won. Turning back into the room, he slammed a clenched fist down hard on the wide, oak table, releasing a cloud of dust that danced in the light from the window.

"I will hear no terms!" he bellowed. "They have no right to withhold their labour. They have no right to make demands." Trevitt had a voice that was used to being heard. The man before him cleared his throat, daring to meet Trevitt's steely gaze. This was William Oats, Trevitt's foreman. He had about him the natural, quiet authority of a man well struck in years.

Oats sat with his hat in his lap, wiping the dust from the brim with a bony hand as he spoke. "We have a week to bring in the crop. Beyond that, it will spoil."

"They are holding me to ransom. Pay up, or else!" Flecks of spittle flew from Trevitt's mouth, catching Oats' eye as they arced through the sunlight.

"They are concerned about conditions."

"Conditions?" Trevitt's fist met oak again. "I'll give them conditions!" Trevitt knew they had him over a barrel. With so many fit young men sent to fight Her Majesty's wars abroad, labour was at a premium. The itinerant workers he employed each year to harvest his crop were emboldened. "Is it not enough that they have work?"

Oats spoke up, bravely. "They have threatened to withdraw their labour unless you agree to their terms."

"A farm has stood on this very spot for the best part of a thousand years. And for the best part of those years, cherry trees have grown here. And for the best part of those years, my forebears have grown them. These outcasts should be grateful for the work."

"They demand a morning off and an increase in their wage to fifteen shillings."

"So they may spend that morning getting drunk on the extra wage! Vermin!"

William Oats pushed back his stool to stand, clutching his hat. His nut-brown skin was burnished almost to a shine. "What shall I tell them?"

Trevitt sucked air in through his teeth, smoothing his hair with a hand in exasperation. "In God's name, where is Fletcher Cousins?"

"He has not been seen this morning."

"Not seen? He's one of 'em. Speaks their language. This is the third day those trees have not been picked. Why is he not here?"

Oats remained unmoved. The truth was he had never liked Fletcher Cousins and was rather pleased to see him fall from favour. For all his civilised ways, he was a traveller and Oats had never trusted travellers. Good for picking fruit and that was all.

Trevitt was seething now, and stomped back to the window. "My family have given much to this village over the years," he hissed. "Perhaps too much."

"You would do well to meet them face to face." Oats was the picture of calm. "When you have heard their grievance, there may be a compromise to be found."

He regretted the word as soon as it was out of his mouth. Trevitt seized on it like a dog with a bone.

"Compromise?" he roared, spinning back into the room. His chest rose and fell like a great pair of bellows. "I will not hear of it!" He pointed with a stubby finger to a portrait that hung on the wall above the fireplace. It was pitched at an unfortunate angle, its frame chipped and festooned with cobwebs. "Did Morton Trevitt compromise?"

Oats sat again, resigned to listening to another retelling of Trevitt's favourite story. Placing his hat on the table, he leaned back in his chair in a vain attempt to get comfortable. He noticed the plaster around the chimneybreast was cracked and falling away from the wall in places. He suspected the portrait of Morton Trevitt hid an even greater multitude of sins.

"That man came into the world with nothing," Trevitt was declaiming, a distinct tremor in his voice, "and left it a rich man. He was shunned by the villagers, obstructed at every turn, yet still he prevailed. He brought cherries to Larton Dean and proved them all wrong. Soon enough, they were beating at his door for work, and he delighted in turning them away."

Oats knew all this, of course. He was only in place because his grandfather had seen fit to invest in Morton's farm when all others had spurned him. The two families had been intimately entwined ever since. Oats' father had served Trevitt's father and now Oats served Trevitt. It was the way of things, as much as Oats would wish it otherwise.

"I will not hear of compromise, Oats. You would do well to remember it." Trevitt thrust out his lantern jaw in defiance.

"Then your harvest will be left to rot," Oats said, simply. "You cannot go to the village for help."

"Nor would I want to. If it's just me and the wife, we'll bring it in. There's enough hours in the day."

Oats sighed to himself. He knew that even Trevitt didn't believe that. There was a camp of travellers at least twenty strong in the old quarry at Chalk Wood, and they would all be needed to bring the fruit in on time. Trevitt would need many more hours in the day to bring it in with just his wife at his side.

"Is that what I must tell them?" Oats stood in readiness to leave, shaking his head in exasperation. He fixed his eyes on Trevitt in a gaze that gave the farmer to understand this was his last chance.

Trevitt knew the old man was right, of course. He always was. Oats had been in the right with the building of the new barns and with the draining of the lower fields. Trevitt had made a pretty penny from Oats' schemes and ideas. Never once had he asked for recompense, and therein lay his weakness. Therein, mused Trevitt as he looked the old man up and down, lay the reason why he, Trevitt, was the owner of the largest cherry orchard in the Thames Valley, whilst Oats had languished in a servile position all his life. However, whilst Trevitt knew him to be right, it didn't follow he had to agree with him. This dispute threatened the very existence of his farm. Give them an inch and those travellers would take a mile. And there was something else at threat too, something much more precious than the farm and its attendant income; Trevitt's pride. He would not be seen to buckle to a rabble of gypsies and vagabonds. They must be taught a lesson and kept in their place. The sooner the season was over and they disappeared back to their own filth, the better. Trevitt despised them. Not because they represented the worst of humanity but because, in truth, he was but a step, just a poor harvest away from falling to their level. Life on the farm, on any farm, was harsh. Two of the three hectares at Trevitt's disposal were given over to the growing of cherries in three orchards. To pay his rent, effect repairs and pay for the running of the farm, every cherry must be picked. This year even more so, as the purchase of nets to be thrown over the trees in defiance of the birds had set him back a small fortune. This year he would not only be dependent on the cherries, but the cutting of grass beneath the trees for sale as hay. He would not see his enterprise jeopardised by an unruly rag-tag of dissolutes.

"Tell 'em to go to Hell," rounded Trevitt, his chest heaving. "And pick the Devil's own cherries if they must!"

Oats opened his mouth to respond, but was interrupted by a flurry of activity at the door. Turning, he saw a woman in a torn dress and tatty shawl standing in the door, her face a picture of thunder.

"You've blood upon your hands, Maxwell Trevitt," she cried, "and a man's death upon your conscience!" She clutched a squealing baby to her bosom.

Oats could see a young boy grasping at her skirts, his freckled face caked with dust He recognised him as the woman's son,

Tom.

"What is it with the Cousins that they none of them keep a civil tongue in their mouths?" Trevitt spat. The woman's face was caked with the dust of the fields, and Oats could see where tears had streaked her cheeks. "What means this interruption?"

"He is dead! Murdered!" the woman wailed, raising a finger to point accusingly at Trevitt.

"Oats," spluttered Trevitt, turning away from the woman, "will you go find Fletcher Cousins and bid him keep a firmer hand on his wife?"

"He is found right enough, Maxwell Trevitt," the woman keened. "Found hanging from a tree. Driven to it by his treatment at your hands!"

A thick silence hung in the room. Trevitt blinked in confusion. "Boy," he commanded, "what is the truth of this?"

Tom slid into the room from behind his mother, his head bowed. Oats saw his face was flushed as much as from exertion as from his tears. His blond hair lay plastered to his forehead with sweat. His calves were raw with scratches and nettle stings and his breath came quick and short. He had clearly been running.

"He's to be found at the end of a rope," he panted. "I cut him down but left him there."

Oats glanced to the thickset man by the window. Trevitt looked taken aback by the news, but there was something about the curl of his lip that led Oats to believe he was not entirely displeased. Trevitt nodded curtly to Oats.

"Go with the boy," he barked. The old man took the lad by the shoulder and steered him through the door. "Pick up a cart from the orchards," Trevitt called at their retreating backs. Suddenly, the farmer was all concern. "Mrs Cousins," he soothed, "please take a seat."

"I will not sit with you," she returned, her eyes burning bright. "Nor will I rest until I see you hanged like my poor Fletcher!"

II

The Lie Of The Land

Detective Sergeant Anthony Graves knocked gingerly at the door, a frown creasing his usually cheery features. He had known Inspector Bowman for the best part of five years and had accompanied him on numerous investigations. He had been with the inspector through his darkest hours and had attempted, in his own inimitable fashion, to lighten his days when he could, for which he hoped Bowman might be grateful. He felt, through it all, that he had got to know the inspector well. So, it was with some surprise that he found, after bounding up the stairs two at a time, that the door to Bowman's office was shut and locked. Putting an ear to the polished oak, he fancied he could hear a scuffling movement from within and so knocked lightly. The movement ceased. Knocking again, Graves heard a sudden scurry and the closing of a cupboard door. There was a pause. Slowly, deliberately, the key turned in the lock and the door swung open. Graves could not help but gasp. The man before him bore little resemblance to the Bowman of old. He seemed a good six inches shorter. His skin was ashen and sickly looking, his hair limp and greasy. A pair of red eyes stared up at the young sergeant. They flicked furtively around the room as he motioned that Graves should enter. It was clear he had something to hide. Bowman flew to the shutters at his windows, throwing them open with a desperate display of energy with which he obviously hoped to convince the sergeant of his sobriety. He was fooling no one. As the morning light streamed into the office, Graves noticed that all was in disarray. Bowman's jacket had been thrown over his wing-backed chair with careless abandon and papers littered his desk. The second chair had been pulled over to a window, and Graves had the distinct impression Bowman had been using it to rest his feet.

"How may I help you, Sergeant Graves?" Bowman's moustache twitched almost comically.

"We have a case," Graves replied. "The commissioner has

entrusted me with the details."

Bowman was busy rearranging the furniture. The smaller chair was dragged before the desk that Graves might sit. The inspector draped his jacket more decorously on the back of his chair and sat opposite him, his elbows on the desk, picking nervously at his fingers.

"And what are they?"

Graves leaned forward, eager to impart the particulars of the case. "We are to journey to a village called Larton, east of Reading, where a man has been found hanged."

Bowman frowned. "Reading?"

Graves nodded. "One Fletcher Cousins, a gang master at a cherry orchard. There are suspicious circumstances, of course."

Bowman stood and turned to the window. Gazing across the river, he could see it was to be another hot day. Already, the heat was rippling off the wharves and builders' yards on the south bank. A smudge of smoke rose from a sawmill, lending a sickly, orange halo to the morning sun. Below him, the Victoria Embankment basked in the heat. Passersby paused to fan themselves with the brims of their hats or to rest against the river wall. A dog lay in the shade of a tree, lazily flicking his tail.

"What suspicious circumstances?" Bowman asked, slowly, his habitual frown cutting deep on his forehead. If truth be told, the throbbing at his temples had returned and he found the glare of the sun almost too much to bear. He fought the urge to fling the shutters across the windows once more.

"We are to learn more upon our arrival," Graves beamed, enigmatically. "The lord of the manor wants the thing wrapped up quick. The man was found on his land and there is much talk amongst the village which he cannot abide."

"That is his sole reason for calling Scotland Yard?"

Graves nodded. "That, and the fact that he dines with the commissioner at the Trafalgar Club on a regular basis." Bowman rolled his eyes. "They have been friends since Jaipur."

"So we are to go as a favour." Bowman shook his head.

"I suspect this is just what you need, George."

Bowman was brought up short by the use of his Christian name. Looking down at Graves, he saw the sergeant's face was clouded with concern. Bowman swallowed, unsure how to respond.

"It might do you good to get out of London, sir," Graves added.

Bowman's eyes turned to the map on the wall opposite. It spanned almost the room's entire length and showed, in detail, every road and alley, every wharf and bridge the city afforded. Several million lives were contained within its limits and perhaps, Bowman mused, a million crimes. He had once thought the map a useful device. Now, he thought as he let his eyes wander through its streets and lanes, it was a tyranny.

"In what way?" Bowman asked by way of a challenge. He noticed Graves shift awkwardly in his seat and immediately felt sorry for him.

"I just thought," Graves stammered, "that the clean air would do you good."

Bowman gnawed at his lip for a moment, then swung himself into his chair.

"Why did the commissioner not call me in to tell me of the case himself?"

Graves looked uncomfortable. "Perhaps he was busy, sir."

Bowman nodded. He understood. The commissioner was intent upon sending him as far away from Scotland Yard as possible. Out of sight, out of mind.

"Perhaps you're right, Graves," Bowman said with something approaching a smile. "It would be good to leave the stench of London behind us." The inspector's eyes swung across the map then, guiltily, to the bureau beneath. He snapped his head back in time to notice that Sergeant Graves had followed his gaze. He had plainly noticed that Bowman's decanter of brandy had disappeared from the tabletop. Ostensibly held for the use of visitors in need of fortification, Graves had noticed the level of brandy had been falling quicker of late. He saw now that the decanter had been locked away, and took it as an indication that his superior did not wish it to be known just how much was left in the bottle. Graves was struck with a sudden understanding. He had clearly interrupted Bowman at his drinking. No wonder the inspector had locked the door.

"Perhaps," Graves continued, his voice thick with meaning, "it would be best to leave much behind us."

Bowman swallowed again under the sergeant's gaze and cleared his throat. "I am puzzled, Graves," he began. "Just what can be so suspicious in a man hanging himself from a tree? Distressing though it is, it is a fact that many a man will take his own life in the course of a year, particularly in the country where life is harsh." He frowned. "Is there evidence of foul play in the matter?"

"We are to discover all upon our arrival," Graves said simply, his hands spreading wide.

The sizeable village of Larton had grown up within the confines of the Thames Valley, some thirty miles to the west of London. The river meandered lazily through the village, resting in quiet pools before seeing fit to join the race to the city. Its banks of reeds and rushes were home to kingfishers and dragonflies, and the patient observer might see water rats and voles scurrying for shelter. An ornate iron bridge raised through public subscription spanned its width, a tollbooth standing sentinel on its north side. Swifts and kites screamed in the cloudless skies, wheeling on the warm eddies that rose from the parched fields. The ground climbed on either side of the river, with Larton laying on its south bank, a ribbon of a road connecting its three constituent parts; Larton Village, Larton Rise and Larton Dean. In the centre of the village stood All Saints Church. One of three churches in Larton, its brick and flint walls stood on a sight where locals had worshipped since the Norman Invasion. The well-tended graveyard was final home to many a distinguished local family, but those more distinguished were laid beneath the flagstones in the church itself. Ornate memorials adorned the walls proclaiming their names to the Sunday congregations; the Burwells, Hedleys and Melvilles; all names well known in the village. An old wooden door on an outside wall stood locked against trespassers. Entry to the crypt beneath had been denied for decades. The church's proximity to the river had rendered the crypt unsafe over previous years and the decision had been taken to abandon it all together.

The High Street was a dusty track, home to a butcher, a general provisions store, several public houses and a hotel. After several hundred yards, the road snaked through open land with the Thames on its right. This tract of marshy common land, bisected by a causeway, divided the Village from Larton Rise. More than that, it marked a division between the people of Larton. Those in the Village felt superior to those in the Rise, the former populated by smart and attractive dwellings, the latter by worker's cottages and scrubby homesteads. The visitor could spot an inhabitant of the Rise with ease. Typically, he would be found in his work clothes and tatty hat, on his way to work the fields. The women could be seen in their aprons and mob caps, their only dress washed and hanging on the line to dry, their several children screaming to be fed or running, shoeless and feral, in the dusty streets. The residents of Larton Village were more likely to be found in their smarter clothes, catching the train to the nearby towns of a morning to practise the dark arts of accountancy. Their children were led in lines every morning to School Lane, there to be tutored and disciplined, made ready for a life amongst the professional classes. The open land between them was more than a geographical divide, it served to mark a border between them as stark as that between two distinct countries, as different in culture and aspiration as could be thought possible. Beyond the Rise and its scrappy cottages lay Larton Dean. From its vantage on the hill, Larton Dean delighted in looking down on everyone else. From its highest peak, the Thames could be seen, glistening in the sun. The trees of Chalk Wood hid much of the Rise and the Village from view, so it was possible to believe that Larton Dean stood aloof from the world or, in particular, from its neighbours. Even the houses had a haughty air. Here lived the bankers and speculators who had made their fortunes and yearned to breathe the country air without wishing to mix with those who were born to it. Their smart children were taught at home by fussy governesses who read them Shakespeare and Milton. Their wives commanded footmen and gardeners, cooks and maids of all work. Their grand houses were run with a fastidiousness borne of snobbery. Each household fought to outdo the other and much gossip was expended in the comparison of gardens, outlook and general appearance. If Larton was not one village but three, then Larton Dean was subdivided still further. To live near Trevitt's farm was considered to be near contempt. To have a house with a view across the valley, at the uppermost height of the hill, was considered the pinnacle of achievement. And so Larton was a village where each constituent was in a constant state of war with the other, where every citizen was regarded with suspicion and every resident was weighed in the balance of where in the village they lived and how they earned their living.

In the midst of it all stood Larton Manor. With its immaculate, manicured lawns and soaring towers it seemed a building out of time, an anachronism of impressive gravel paths, trimmed hedges and Tudor windows. It sprawled over several acres of well-kept grounds incorporating a stable block, sweeping land laid to pasture and, at its perimeter, a boathouse giving out onto a tributary of the Thames itself. It occupied the space as if by ancient rite, as much as the inhabitants that dwelt within its forbidding walls. The Melvilles had owned much of Larton for centuries. From the lowest reaches of the Village to Trevitt's farm in the Dean, Lord Melville and his family kept a jealous hold on the pasture, marshland and orchards of the valley, offering acres out for rent to tenant farmers.

Detective Inspector George Bowman stared forlornly from the carriage window at the unfolding countryside before him. His mouth drying in the heat, he had slipped off his jacket and folded it carefully on the seat next to him, his hat perched on top. The journey from Scotland Yard had been without incident, although he was concerned at the speed with which Graves had led him from his office to a waiting hansom cab and from there to Belsize Crescent to pack a suitcase of clothes. Bowman had demanded that the sergeant wait outside rather than be witness to the chaos of his rooms and had stuffed his case with such shirts as he could find. From there he had been spirited to Paddington Station. It smacked of a carefully planned intervention. A short wait later, and Bowman was bundled aboard the next train to Reading via Brunel's Great Western Railway. Famed as the 'Holiday Line', it proceeded to the West Country, Devon and Somerset. The great engine, painted in a sober Brunswick Green, had puffed cheerfully through Slough and Windsor, pausing briefly to allow knots of holidaymakers to board its distinctive chocolate and cream coaches. They did so with great excitement, the children clambering over the seats to their parents' amusement and Bowman's disdain. More than once Bowman had winced as the children's excited cries rang through the carriages, pressing his fingers to his throbbing temples for relief.

All the while, Sergeant Graves sat in the seat opposite him, his eyes alight at the displays of childish exuberance around him. He had delighted in winking and smiling at the children, even going so far as to ruffle the hair of a small, clearly delighted boy clutching a toy boat in his chubby fingers. Engaging him in conversation, Graves had chuckled and twinkled like a favourite uncle at the boy's responses, then settled back in his seat to gaze with Bowman at the changing landscape beyond the glass. Some three miles from Southall, the horizon had revealed itself beyond the skyline of gasworks, slums and tenements. Farms replaced factories and a great tapestry of fields spread to a horizon dotted with trees. Copses sprang up to give shade to farm workers and their horses, taking lunch on fallen logs and stretching their sore limbs to ease them. The sun glanced at intervals through the window, and Graves noticed Bowman wincing in the glare. As they slowed at Langley Marsh, the young sergeant leaned forward in his seat, eager to pose a question to which he doubted he would be furnished an answer.

"What was the upshot of your meeting with the commissioner, sir?"

Bowman's brow furrowed as he contemplated his response. For a moment he considered feigning not having heard the question, but Graves' enquiring gaze was impossible to ignore. Commissioner Bradford had been pleased enough with Bowman's conduct during the investigation at St. Saviour's

Dock, though he had raised questions as to the inspector's mental capacity. Bowman had his suspicions that Chief Inspector Callaghan had reported back none too favourably with regard to Bowman's erratic behaviour. The commissioner had sighed as he ran his fingers through his hair.

"Bowman," he had begun, "you place me in a difficult position." The commissioner had walked to gaze out of his office window at the streets below, his one remaining hand flexing in the small of his back as he spoke. "The Press have been asking questions concerning the ease with which the Kaiser was able to operate in Bermondsey." Bowman nodded. He had eventually apprehended the Kaiser on the banks of the River Thames, but too late to prevent the deaths of many innocent victims. "This has led to a wider discussion amongst our more..." the commissioner had searched for the word, "*Spirited* newspapers, concerning the number of inspectors at our disposal." Bradford had harrumphed as he turned to face the inspector. "A matter for the Home Office, of course, but I cannot be seen to be laying off inspectors of whose conduct I do not entirely approve." He had smoothed the empty sleeve of his jacket where it lay pinned against his chest. "In short, Inspector Bowman, I need numbers."

"I understand, sir," Bowman had replied, with something approaching gratitude.

"Make no mistake, if it were not for that, you would be out on your ear and back to Colney Hatch." Bowman had winced at the mention of the asylum where he had, only the year before, spent seven months. "I have been scrutinising the details of your previous cases." The commissioner had picked up a sheaf of papers from the desk and waved them before him. He then leant in closer to the inspector, his voice low. "I do not deny, George, that you are an asset to the Yard." Bowman blinked at the use of his Christian name. It seemed that, of late, too many people had been all too quick to employ it. "And it is that alone that has saved your skin." Bradford's white moustache had bristled. "For now."

"Thank you, sir," Bowman had heard himself reply.

"I am minded, however," the commissioner had continued,

"to place you in the care of one of your colleagues." Bowman had blanched at the phrase. "Sergeant Graves is, I believe, a man of good temperament and one who may be trusted to play a straight bat."

Bowman blinked. He resented being looked after like a child. "He is that, sir," he agreed, quietly.

"I shall put him in your way, Inspector Bowman. It will do you good. But in the meantime, I shall place you on intermittent leave."

A sigh had shuddered through Bowman's body, not unnoticed by the commissioner. "To be clear," Sir Edward Bradford had concluded, "you are only to work on those cases he brings to you, for he shall be doing so with my explicit authority." Bowman had nodded in understanding, lifting his fingers to his temples where a dreadful throbbing had returned.

Bowman stared across the carriage at his young colleague. Swaying with the motion of the train, he was leaning forward on his elbows, his blond curls swinging into his eyes. Bowman knew why Graves was here. Did Graves know he knew? The inspector had always had an unswerving admiration for his companion. He was ever dependable, with a constitution fit for his occupation. But now Bowman felt another emotion prick at him, like the prongs of a fork, and he did not like it. He felt resentment.

"He is satisfied," Bowman replied with masterful ambiguity. Graves held him in his gaze, a look of doubt clouding his usually cheerful features.

"Good," the sergeant replied, simply. An uneasy silence hung between them as the train pulled into Reading Station, a sharp whistle heralding its arrival.

As they stood on the platform awaiting a connecting train, Bowman raised his head to the sun and felt his skin tighten in the heat. The neck of his shirt was moist with sweat. Graves returned from a barrow at the station entrance and offered him an iced confection that he declined despite feeling hungry. Moving to stand in the shade of the waiting room, Bowman took a breath to steel himself. He could feel Graves' eyes upon him.

Guiltily, he began to wonder where and when he might find his next drink. The alcohol had quietened his dreams and stilled his visions. He hadn't seen Anna for weeks. It was only now, in the withering gaze of the sun, that he realised what a desperate void the visions had left. As dreadful as the apparitions had been, they had provided an unlikely comfort. Graves placed a hand lightly on his back.

"Here we are, sir."

The little locomotive was something of a celebrity in the area. Known as the Larton Donkey, it chuffed its way along the line from Reading to Larton every hour and had done so for nearly twenty years. Only two coaches were given over to passengers at this time of day. The rest of the train comprised carriages for farming equipment and supplies. The inspector could make out a ploughshare and several bales of straw slung onto a low, open truck. He guessed that, upon its return, it would be laden with produce from the many farms and orchards that nestled in the Thames Valley, destined for markets around the Home Counties and beyond. As the engine idled at the platform, the two men stepped aboard and took their seats, ready for the twenty two minute journey that would see them step, with dusty boots, onto the hard and sun-baked platform at Larton.

III

In Chalk Wood

William Oats ran his fingers through his hair. The travellers had made their home as usual in the quarry at Chalk Wood. On any ordinary day, it would be a short walk to find work in the orchards of Larton, most especially at Trevitt's farm. But today was not an ordinary day.

"Trevitt says he'll come himself and pull you from your wagons," Oats reported, a look of exasperation on his tired, lined face. He had the look about him of one worn down with years of care. The skin of his balding head shone like polished wood, and his deep-set eyes stared forlornly from beneath the promontory of his brow.

"Let 'im," came the response.

Jared Stoker sat on a fallen log, his legs swinging nonchalantly before him, the long stem of a pipe clamped between his teeth. He was a slim-hipped and stringy man of twenty-five, but had the worldly-wise demeanour of someone twice his age. The down of a moustache lay languidly on his upper lip, the only adornment on an otherwise youthful face. His eyes were so dark as to be almost black and of such unfathomable depth it was impossible to discern what thoughts lay beneath. In all, he was of a Bohemian disposition. If his hair had not been tied back beneath a kerchief, it would surely have hung down to his shoulders. A blowsy shirt hung loose beneath a corduroy waistcoat, and his neck and wrists were hung with mysterious emblems. A tattoo sprouted from beneath the collar of his shirt and up onto his neck. For all that Oats could see, it depicted the head of a bird, possibly a crow.

"Surely you'll miss the pay?"

"It's a worker's market, Oats," Stoker purred, drawing on his pipe. "Trevitt knows that."

Oats knew he was right. The recent campaigns waged in the name of Queen and country had depleted the numbers of young men fit for seasonal work. Stoker's services and those of his men were now at a premium. Having spent the early summer at a farm further up the valley, one happy to pay whatever Stoker had demanded, they could no doubt afford to wait.

Oats looked around him, wiping the sweat from his brow with a hand. Though now out of use, the chalk quarry had been worked for centuries. There were lines of cottages in the village that had sprung up specifically to house the quarry workers in the middle of the century, and many a local man, Oats among them, who could remember the feel of a pick in his hands. With larger and more profitable quarries opening up in more accessible parts of the valley, interest in Larton had waned. Now, the bright white escarpment that surrounded the hollow in which the travellers were camped was dotted with patches of green. Ferns and grasses had taken a hold of the chalk, their roots making their way with ease through the porous rock. Excepting the summer months, when the travellers" camp was pitched beneath the slopes, Oats thought the quarry a romantic place. He would often stand alone of an evening as the sun set over Chalk Wood, cocking an ear to hear again the tap of iron on chalk and the shouts and hollers of his fellow labourers. It was hard but honest work, and Oats could not help but feel a pang of guilt that his employment now consisted of pen pushing and the management of men.

"We only ask for fifteen shillings and a morning off in three," Stoker offered simply. "He knows the terms."

"That would break him," Oats insisted. He resented having to deal with Stoker face to face but, with Cousins dead, the task now fell to him. "How many men do you have?"

Stoker cast his eyes about the assembled camp. Four caravans were parked in a circle around the clearing, a vast pot bubbling and spitting from a fire that blazed between them. Beyond them, canvases were thrown across frames to provide yet more shelter. Naked or partially clothed children ran between them, squealing with delight. Lines of washing were hung between the trees. In a corner, half a dozen grazing horses flicked at the flies with their tails. Somewhere, some men were chopping wood. From a gap in the foliage came a woman with a brace of rabbits slung over her arm. Tossing her catch onto the ground by a caravan, she took the cheroot from her mouth and splashed her face in a pail of water. Three women gossiped as they worked near the fire, chopping and skinning a bird or two for dinner. Their eyes fell with suspicion on Trevitt's man. Yet more stood around the camp either engaged in chores or waiting vacantly in the heat of the day.

"There's a dozen men here at Trevitt's disposal," Stoker announced, tapping the ash from the bowl of his pipe. "If he pays for them." As if to suggest that he didn't care much either way, Stoker leaned back along the log, placed his hands behind his head and closed his eyes against the sun.

"There's two hectares of cherries to be gathered," thundered Oats.

"Then let him ask about the village for help."

Oats knew that was out of the question. Trevitt had, in his adult years, made himself an enemy to so many people in Larton that he was barely spoken to in the streets. If truth be told, Oats wasn't so much surprised by Stoker's response as filled with dread at the prospect of relating it back to Trevitt. Flinging his arms in the air with exasperation, William Oats turned to leave the camp to its business. Just as he stepped from the clearing, however, he was surprised to be met by a representative of Larton Police Station. Silas Corrigan was dressed in his full regulation uniform, even on this hottest of days. From the buckles on his boots to the buttons on his coat, he seemed nothing less than the perfect model of the local constabulary. Even his hat seemed placed at the regulation angle.

"Running errands, Mr Oats?" he leered, his thin face creasing into a smile. Police Constable Corrigan stood well over six feet tall, and would have been an intimidating presence were it not for his officious manner.

"I am here on Maxwell Trevitt's business," Oats blinked, his thin shoulders slumping at the sight of the policeman.

"There's no sign of intimidation, I would hope?"

"Not from our side," Stoker interjected from where he lay.

"You've got trouble enough to deal with, Jared Stoker." Corrigan stepped through the undergrowth and further into the camp as he spoke, his keen eyes flitting along the caravans and tents in search of trouble. The women who stood about the camp retreated to the shadows as he approached and Oats noticed those chopping by the fire had ceased their toil to watch. Only one person was brave enough to draw nearer; the woman whom Oats had seen throw the rabbits to the ground. She drew her skirts about her as she sat next to Stoker, a defiant look upon her face.

"There are those in the village," began Corrigan accusingly, "complaining of an increase in thefts and burglaries."

"Then they must look to their neighbours," the woman said, much to Stoker's amusement.

Corrigan was passing his eye along the lines of washing that hung from the trees. "There's many a petticoat gone missing on washing day, and many a silk handkerchief taken from an open window."

"If they're rich enough to afford a silk handkerchief," the woman purred, rolling a cheroot between her fingers, "they're rich enough to afford another."

Stoker barely bothered to hide his mirth. "I wouldn't trade words with Ida, constable. She's learned, don't you know?" This last was spoken with as refined an accent as Stoker could muster, and was rewarded with a thump to the stomach from the lady in question.

"If I was that learned, Jared Stoker," Ida teased, "I wouldn't be so stupid as to be your wife!"

Oats drew nearer. He could tell from Corrigan's demeanour that he was here on more important business than the theft of a petticoat.

"You may regret your involvement with him, madam," began the constable, "when Scotland Yard has finished with you."

The air felt more oppressive still. Ida's fingers came to rest in her lap, her cheroot unfinished in the palm of her hand. Oats raised his eyebrows involuntarily at Corrigan's words and even Stoker seemed to take a breath. "Scotland Yard?" he rasped from his supine position. The cry of a distant woodcock seemed to mock him as he swung his legs from the log and sat up straight, rubbing feeling back into his shoulder with a delicate hand.

Corrigan was pleased at the reaction. "Lord Melville is concerned at Fletcher Cousins' death. He wants to get to the bottom of it."

"Local constabulary not up to the job?" Stoker shared a look with his wife. Ida snorted with derision.

Corrigan resented the insinuation all the more because he knew Stoker was right. Drawing himself up to his full height, he determined to look more officious than ever. "Our resources are limited," he blustered.

"I thought Cousins had hanged himself." Oats was standing stock still beside the constable, keen to understand the situation.

"So it was believed," said Corrigan slyly. "But there are many features of interest." The constable leaned in, lowering his voice conspiratorially, "Not least the fact that he was hanged not a hundred yards from your camp." The constable had raised a pale hand to point into the trees beyond the quarry. Gummer's Pond, and the tree where Fletcher Cousins had been found hanged, lay just beyond the lip of the hill.

"A man may go about these woods unnoticed for hours," Stoker shrugged.

"Ay," agreed Corrigan. "But your men are all over them. They know every sound and call." He looked pointedly at the woman before him. "They know the best places to poach." Ida Stoker lifted a nonchalant eyebrow at the accusation. "You can't tell me a man could yomp up this hill with a length of rope and hang himself from a tree without you knowing." Corrigan stood with his hands on his hips.

"We must have been sleeping," Stoker shrugged, breezily.

"I know you set a watch at night," Corrigan spat back. "He would have heard or seen."

"I see what is happening here." Ida stood, arranging her skirts irritably about her. "The villagers suspect us, just as they always do. Something goes missing, it must be the gypsies," she threw her arms wide. "There's poaching in the woods, it must be the gypsies. A man hangs himself from a tree," she stood nose to nose with Corrigan, her nostrils flaring, "perhaps it was murder, and perhaps it was the gypsies." With that, she turned abruptly away, kicking a stray log into the fire as she passed.

"Sounds dangerously close to a confession to me," Corrigan chuckled after her.

"If you have anything to say, say it." Stoker held Corrigan's gaze.

"I have nothing to say," said Corrigan with a smile. "Except that you should watch your step. There's many in the village who would be happy to see you moved on for good." The policeman leaned in again, the better to make his point. "Whatever the reason."

"Is that a threat, Constable Corrigan?" Stoker's eyes blazed as he reached into his pocket for a liquorice root.

"You'd be surprised how easy it is to make things stick, Stoker. And you'd be surprised how quick word spreads in these parts." Corrigan spread his arms wide. "Where would you be if the work dried up?"

Stoker stood to object, but he was caught off guard as Corrigan raised a hand. Pushing hard against Stoker's chest, the constable pushed the man back to the dusty ground. "Just watch your step, Stoker," Corrigan hissed, "Or you and your sort will feel the heat." He cast a disdainful eye around the camp. Several men, roused by the commotion, stood at the doors to their makeshift tents. Seeing two of them brandish their tools with menace, Stoker raised a hand to calm them.

"If you've said all you came to say," he said, meeting Corrigan's gaze as he rose to his feet, "I would urge you to leave." Brushing the dust from his trousers, he stripped a little bark from the liquorice with his teeth and spat it at Corrigan's feet. "I am sure the whole of Larton will sleep easier in their beds knowing Constable Corrigan's on their side." Stoker chewed slowly on his liquorice root as Corrigan looked him up and down.

"Don't get too comfortable in yours," the constable breathed. Placing his hat back on his head, he cast his eyes at Oats and, with a nod, signalled that the interview was at an end. Oats could barely meet Stoker's eye as the two men turned away from the clearing, tramping nettles beneath their boots as they fought their way through the foliage back to the village beneath the hill. Jared Stoker watched them go with narrowing eyes. As they moved through the trees and beyond his sight, he motioned to his companions that the altercation was over and made his way to the fire. Bending to retrieve the brace of rabbits from the ground, he took a knife from his pocket. He flung them onto the stump of a tree near to the quarry wall. Breathing heavily now, he grit his teeth with a snarl and began to tear at the rabbits" skin with such ferocity that flecks of crimson spattered against the white of the chalk.

IV

Terminus

The first thing Bowman noticed was the horizon. From where he stood on the platform at Larton Station, he could turn a circle and trace it with his eyes, taut and sharp against the summer sky. Even in the heat he instinctively pulled his jacket tighter about him, missing already the taller buildings and monuments of the capital.

"Not a very popular spot, eh, sir?"

Graves was right. The two detectives were the only passengers to have alighted from the Larton Donkey. The great engine had heaved itself away from the platform with a complaining hiss, leaving the men to contemplate their predicament in near silence. Far from being a hotbed of murder and violence, mused Bowman, it didn't seem very much had happened here for quite some time. A line of red brick cottages stood tumbledown and forlorn beside the track, their patchy gardens overgrown with brambles and weeds. Bowman noticed barely any of them had glass panes to their windows. The door to one stood torn from its hinges, merely leaning against the jamb. Behind it, Bowman thought he caught sight of an old, toothless woman, peering from a ramshackle porch. He was about to call out to her to ask for directions to Trevitt's farm, when he noticed a figure striding along the platform towards them. He was a thin, severe looking man in the black livery of a driver. It was clear from his demeanour that he despised being made to wear his heavy woollen coat on such a day and, as he stopped before Sergeant Graves, the inspector saw him sweep his hat from his head with some relief.

"Inspector Bowman?" the man enquired with none of the customary warmth of a greeting. His voice was thick and fulsome, with the cadence of an accent approaching that of the West Country.

The sergeant laughed and pointed to his fellow detective. "A case of mistaken identity, I'm afraid," he chuckled. "Though I'll make an inspector yet." Graves' blue eyes shone with mischief and, not for the first time, Bowman envied him his alacrity of spirit.

The man's face fell as he turned to the shadow of a man before him and it was clear from his expression that, for a moment, he doubted Graves' word. Faltering slightly, he gave a curt nod to cover his discomfort before continuing. "I am to take you to Larton Manor, there to meet with Lord Melville."

"Not to the orchard?" Bowman's eyebrows rose at the news.

"Lord Melville thinks there is little to be gained there for now."

Graves raised his eyebrows as he turned to the inspector. "Ours is not to reason why," he said with a shrug.

Taking the two men's cases, the driver led them both past the dilapidated ticket office to a dusty yard beyond. There stood the grandest carriage the inspector had seen for some time. It seemed to gleam with pride, its glossy, black paintwork shining in the sun. The wooden trim had been polished almost zealously so the whole contraption looked as though it had just been delivered, fresh from the workshop. As the driver heaved the cases aboard, he took a cloth from his pocket to wipe the dust from the wheels. Two smart, black horses stood, impatient in their harnesses.

"It seems we have something of a welcome after all." Bowman turned to follow Graves' gaze. Above the entrance to the ticket office, he saw a line of bunting hanging limp from the wooden soffit above the door.

"That'll be for tomorrow's regatta," the driver explained wearily. "It passes for entertainment in these parts."

Bowman looked around him. Apart from the driver and the shady figure behind the broken door, he had yet to see another soul.

"There will be people enough," the driver continued, reading Bowman's expression. "It's about the only day Larton comes together. Ten to one it'll end in a fight on the causeway." The man was heaving himself up onto his perch. "It always does." He sat stock still at the reins, the pretence at conversation clearly over.

Bowman shared a look with Graves, who was plainly enjoying every moment. Rubbing his hands together, the young sergeant sprang to open the carriage door and, snapping to attention, he raised his hand in a stiff salute. "His Lordship awaits," he grinned, and Bowman couldn't help but smile in return.

Tom Cousins skulked by the river in his favourite spot along the causeway. Where the road rose over the little tributary, the young lad had made a den for himself. There, beneath the bridge, he had tramped down the nettles and slung a blanket over a tree root that rose from the mud. Weighting each side down with stones from the riverbed, he had fashioned himself a tent from which he could observe the heron and the stickleback and keep a watch on those who passed over the bridge to the village.

Tom knew his life had changed. Where once he had kept company with the other children of Larton, now they shunned him, regarding him with suspicious eyes. That Fletcher Cousins had been found hanged in Chalk Wood disturbed them enough. That he had been found by his own son filled them with a preternatural dread. As he walked alone through the village, he would see children and adults alike gather together to nod and point, their voices hushed in whispered insinuations. Where he might once have expected sympathy, he received nothing but cold indifference. Those richer men from Larton Dean who he might once have relied upon for a ha'penny, now turned away as he approached. The friendliest of villagers crossed the road to avoid an awkward meeting. As a consequence, just when he should have been listened to the most, Tom was ignored. With his father gone, and his meagre wage from Trevitt's farm with him, there would be less food on the table. Life was precarious in Larton and he had already lost two brothers to scarlet fever. What chance did his family have now, teetering between life and death?

Throwing himself to the ground in his den beneath the bridge, Tom scooped up a handful of stones to throw into the river. Duke waded in after them, shaking the water from his snout as he fished them from the riverbed. Duke was Tom's only joy. He felt a kinship with the hound. Together they had been witness to an extraordinary event beyond the comprehension of others. Duke nuzzled against the boy's face, causing Tom to rock back with a giggle, wiping his face on the back of his hands. Soon he would have to go home. With a pocket full of apples from old Thornhill's tree and a loaf of bread taken from the bakery shelves, he might feed the family for one more night. If he climbed the hill to the Dean tomorrow he might well find an open window and, from the proceeds, feed them for another. As he settled back to the sound of the babbling water, Tom took a breath. He had once snuck into All Saints Church on a Sunday to hear the vicar give a sermon. He had stood amazed at the scene as the villagers filed in, their heads bowed. There stood Albert Padley the pharmacist, whom Tom knew to be an adulterer. In the pew behind him, Vincent McGonigle gave lusty voice to 'Guide Me, O, Thou Great Jehovah', despite the fact that everyone in the village knew he had stolen from school funds. Even Mrs Thewlis who, it was commonly known, had starved and beaten her own children, could happily let her eye wander unaffected across the carving to her left. There a representation of Christ himself, arms outstretched, head inclined in a gesture of gentle entreaty, stood above the inscription; 'Suffer the little children to come unto me.' Each of the worshippers seemed content to join in with the great pretence, that God had reserved for each of them a special place in Heaven. Tom's eyes had been drawn to the vaulted roof where the congregation's voices resounded as one song. Standing in his rags amongst the villagers in their Sunday best, their eyes fixed upon the altar before them, he could be certain of one thing; that God had no care for him or his family. The vicar, a forbidding man with the face of a drinker and the breath to match, had taken his place at the pulpit to read from Corinthians.

"When I was a child," he had intoned, "I spoke as a child, I understood as a child, I thought as a child." Tom saw him grip the sides of the lectern for support. "But when I became a man, I put away childish things."

The phrase had puzzled the boy. He could not then imagine how such a thing might feel. Now, as he plucked at the grass on the riverbank, Tom fancied he understood. He would have to put away childish things and become a man. At the age of just twelve, it was a daunting prospect. Without the presence of a father, Tom knew he was destined for the workhouse, his mother and baby sister with him. He leaned back in the shade of the bridge, scratching Duke about the ears for comfort. As the dog fell asleep amongst the bulrushes, Tom heard the rattle of an approaching carriage. Scampering into the light to investigate, he peered through the tall grass that grew along the bank and saw a smart, black landau passing over the bridge. The paintwork glinted in the sun. His eyes seemed to lock with those of one of the passengers, a lean, forlorn-looking man with a limp moustache and a troubled countenance. Dipping below the line of the bridge, Tom crouched to watch the carriage turn off the road and into the sweeping drive leading to Larton Manor.

V

By Appointment

Bowman stared from the coach as it passed through Larton to the manor house. Occasionally, the scrubby trees and hedges beside the road had fallen away to reveal dry plots of land before lonely farmsteads and cottages. Every building they passed seemed in a state of disrepair. Evidence of industry presented itself at regular intervals; a blacksmith at his anvil, dripping sweat as the chime of his hammer rang out across the road, a woman dressed in little more than a filthy apron casting seed before her scraggy chickens, a team of labourers put to work to gather hay in a field. Beyond a line of trees he glimpsed the river. The canvas of a marquee hung limp and unsecured and several trestle tables had been arranged along the bank; the site, no doubt, of the impending regatta. Bowman saw several men at work to erect a tent and hammering posts into the ground. As they passed from Larton Rise into the Village, he noticed a change. The houses were at once smarter and better tended. For all that they presented a cheerier aspect, however, Bowman couldn't help but notice that every window on the lower floors was adorned with bars to prevent intrusion. Now and then he would catch sight of suspicious eyes peering through curtains. Two men in overalls paused in their work repointing a wall along the roadside to watch the carriage pass, their eyes narrowing as they tried to peer at the passengers within. From their wary demeanour, Bowman guessed strangers were rarely seen in Larton. Catching sight of a small boy beneath the bridge on the causeway, Bowman lifted his eyes to see the chimneys of Larton Manor rising in between a knot of poplar trees in the distance.

"Why do you think we are expected at the manor?" he asked of his companion, the smell of polished leather pricking at his nose.

Graves leaned his chin on a hand to watch as the countryside rolled by. Bowman mused that the sergeant seemed to be regarding the whole excursion as little more than a jolly adventure.

"Beats me, sir," Graves offered, cheerily. "Perhaps there's more to know before we begin."

Bowman nodded, slowly. He couldn't quite shake the feeling that, somehow, he was being tested. If so, he was determined not to be found wanting, though how exactly he could prove himself to the commissioner some thirty miles from London was, he felt, something of a mystery.

The two men were flung to one side as the landau swung off the road. Bowman cursed the driver and threw a look of apology to Graves as he straightened his hat upon his head. Soon they were travelling over a gravelled drive, and it was possible to believe that they had entered another world and time entirely. A manicured lawn stretched before them towards what Bowman could see had originally been a squat, Tudor manor house. Several alterations over successive generations had left the house with something of a hotchpotch appearance, but none the less impressive for it. A whole new wing stretched out to the left, home to two storeys of rooms, their casements thrown open to admit such air as they could. To the right, the original house sprawled into the grounds beyond. A patchwork of wooden beams and whitewashed loam peered between the ivy that encroached across much of the house. The gardens beyond were obscured by a rolling topiary, swooping and diving in abstract shapes.

A set of wrought iron gates was shut behind them as the coach passed through, the gatekeeper standing for a moment to consider the carriage's occupants. Ahead, Bowman saw a pair of peacocks scatter from the road at their approach, a flurry of indignant feathers flying from the oncoming clatter of hooves and wheels. Squawking noisily at the retreating carriage, they scratched at the ground as if to express their annoyance.

Finally, the carriage came to a halt before the grand entrance. Peering from the window, Bowman could see the porch had been added some time after the original building. It was far too big for the small wooden door that stood in its shade. Two rampant lions, carved in stone and at least eight feet high, stood to either side, their claws reared and their teeth bared. The whole effect was to give the house the appearance of having ideas above its station. Perhaps, mused Bowman, it spoke volumes as to the character of its current occupant.

The two detectives had been sitting for quite some time before it dawned upon the pair of them that they had been left alone to disembark. The driver had descended from his lofty height and now stood to one side, his arms folded, in deep conversation with a gardener. Every now and then, Bowman saw the two men glance his way. He and his companion were undoubtedly the subject of much discussion. With a sigh and a look of resignation, Graves lowered the window and reached out to the handle. The door swung open with ease, and Bowman followed the sergeant out and onto the gravel drive. Bowman cleared his throat to get the attention of the driver, but the man in the heavy coat turned away, clearly believing his conversation with the gardener to be of greater import. Rolling his eyes, the inspector walked to the front door and reached for the bell pull.

"Quite the welcome," scoffed Graves, his hands behind his back.

"Indeed," Bowman agreed, feeling none too comfortable in these forbidding surroundings.

Just as they had given up hope of ever gaining entry, the door was pulled part way open. Scraping against the uneven floor, it plainly took some effort to open further. There, in the doorway, stood a man of indeterminate age. Indeed, it would not have surprised Bowman if the man was as old as the house. His skin was as lined and dry as the wood in the porch around him. Barely five and a half feet tall, he was dwarfed by the lions that stood to either side. Bowman was doubtful he was even aware of them. The ancient footman, blinking in the light, stepped bravely across the threshold to address them.

"Yes?" he croaked. As the man stood in the full glare of the sun, Bowman could see he was attired as if from another age. A pair of breeches hung loose around his skinny legs, revealing wrinkled hose tucked into a pair of shiny black shoes, each adorned with a silver buckle. A long, mustard-coloured waistcoat hung almost to his knees, a silk scarf tucked into the collar from which protruded a pale, scrawny neck. Finally, a delicate pince-nez balanced precariously on his pointed nose, though what use they were Bowman could only guess. The whole effect was of a child who had been let loose at the dressing up box, or of a small ape who had been dressed in the accoutrements of a man for amusement.

"We have been called by Lord Melville." Bowman tried hard to stifle his mirth. "I am Detective Inspector Bowman from Scotland Yard," he gestured to his left, suddenly feeling the need to speak up. "This is Sergeant Graves."

The diminutive footman had to crane his neck to take both men in. Seemingly satisfied at Bowman's introduction, he gave a smart nod and turned back into the house.

The hallway, at least, gave some respite from the heat. The ivy creeping at the window conspired to obstruct the sun's rays entirely, so much so that Bowman paused mid step so that his eyes might adjust to the gloom. Looking about him, he saw an array of stuffed animals in various intimidating poses. Here a tiger skulked amongst some potted ferns, there a brown bear reared to its full height. Fowl of various kinds were presented in glass cases or, he noticed, even strung from the ceiling as if in flight. Clearly bemused by the spectacle, Sergeant Graves nodded towards a polar bear, poised to strike from behind an ornate marble pillar. It really was the most singular thing he had seen for quite some time. Their footsteps echoing off the tiled floor, the two men were led into the older parts of the house. Graves had to duck to save his head from the low beams and Bowman found himself having to breathe hard against the damp air. Here, the windows gave out to the grounds behind the house. Ducking his head, Bowman could see several children playing croquet with an older lady he took to be their mother. She was smartly dressed in a sparkling white crinoline dress, a fashionable hat pinned to her hair.

At last, they were led into a more open space, dominated by a large, brick fireplace. Here, tattered rugs were thrown about the floor, rucking here and there so as to prove hazardous to the unwary. A suit of armour stood to attention by the door, a halberd raised in its gloved hand. All around the room, a haphazard collection of furniture groaned beneath the weight of books, charts and papers. Even to Bowman's eye, there was no uniformity of intent here, no uniting principle of design. Finally, his eyes alighted upon a carved bas-relief above the fireplace. Two rearing horses stood either side of a globe which itself rested upon a pair of crossed swords. Beneath the carving lay the words; 'Absolutum Dominion'. If ever there was a phrase that might apply most precisely to the man who stood at the fireplace, this was surely it. He was no taller than Bowman, yet he had about him an air of absolute entitlement. His face seemed carved from granite, his sharp eyes clear and probing. A mane of thick, curly hair was arranged over his forehead, giving him a countenance and profile, mused Bowman, such as one might see on an old Roman coin. The man stood, solid and immovable, hands on hips and feet planted on the floor, displaying the easy air of one for whom nothing in life had been unattainable.

"Detective Inspector Bowman and Sergeant Graves," announced the footman with a sharp bow, his thin, rasping voice devoid of anything but a weary indifference.

"Thank you, Jewson," returned the man at the fireplace. His voice was clear and sonorous as a bell.

As the footman turned away from the room, Bowman saw him look Sergeant Graves up and down, clearly displeased at the lack of gravity with which the young sergeant was approaching the situation. Graves returned the look with his usual, cheery smile, then turned his attention to the man by the fireplace.

"Inspector Bowman, you are welcome." Lord Melville took a step from the fireplace towards the sergeant. Now in the light, Bowman could see the man was dressed in a formal coat, waistcoat and trousers. A silk stock was tied at his throat and the chain of a fob watch hung from his pocket. He walked with a cane and presented himself with a limp that Bowman recognised as a symptom of gout. Seeing the man's eyes on his companion, the inspector stepped forward, eager to dispel any confusion as to who was who.

"This is Sergeant Graves," he explained. The man at the fireplace raised his eyebrows. "I believe you are expecting us?"

"Expecting you?" Lord Melville boomed. "You are here at my behest, Inspector Bowman!"

Bowman swallowed hard. Lord Melville clearly fancied himself as a force to be reckoned with.

"I do hope Prescott wasn't short with you?"

"Prescott?"

"My driver. I'm afraid he finds the company of horses more appealing than that of people."

Graves smiled, mischievously. "He clearly spends a lot of time in the care of his carriage."

"We are here in connection with the death of a Mr Fletcher Cousins," Bowman coughed, irritably. "We understand he was found on your land." As if in response to some unspoken command, Sergeant Graves reached into his pocket for his notebook.

Melville regarded the inspector with an almost Olympian detachment, as a learned man might regard a child. "He was found in Chalk Wood," he intoned. "Along with half of Larton, it has been in my family since Domesday." He fixed Bowman in his gaze. "On your journey from the station, inspector, you will have no doubt observed many a farmstead, field and smithy. They all pay rent to me. Anything that occurs upon my land reflects upon my family as much as the village. If Larton thrives, then so does Larton Manor." He smiled. "And, of course, vice versa."

"It seems a rather singular village."

"Larton is a village in three minds, inspector. The Dean, the Rise and the Village have always been at odds. The only time we come together is for the regatta, and only then to beat each other in competition."

"And the manor's place in all this?"

"I like to think it provides a certain continuity. Perhaps a reminder that all in Larton are one."

"Under the yoke of the Lord of the Manor?" Bowman's moustache twitched.

"If that is how you wish to see it, yes." Melville gave a slight smile.

The inspector nodded. "Might we have the details?"

At this, the man sighed, as if already bored of the story. "Fletcher Cousins was found some three days ago at eleven of the clock in the morning, hanging from a tree in Chalk Wood. There were no signs of foul play."

"Yet you are convinced it was murder?"

Melville was silent.

"Who found the poor man?" Graves asked, the stub of a pencil poised between his fingers.

"His son," retorted Melville. Bowman winced at the news.

"Has he been questioned?"

Lord Melville shrugged. "You should direct that question to the local constabulary."

Bowman sighed. "I should think the one person you would wish to interview would be the one who discovered the body."

"He's just a boy," Lord Melville scoffed. "You'll get nought from him but flights of fancy."

Bowman sighed. "Why have you called upon Scotland Yard?"

"Because, Inspector Bowman," began Lord Melville, "Fletcher Cousins is not the first."

Bowman heard Graves' pencil come to a halt on the page. Lord Melville nodded. "Not by a long chalk."

Bowman shared a look with his companion as Lord Melville walked across the room to a large sideboard by the far wall. As with everything in the room, it was completely out of place with the rest of the furniture. There was something Oriental in its design that was wholly out of keeping with the Tudor beams in the walls around it. Opening a drawer, he retrieved a bundle of newspapers, gesturing that the inspector should join him at a low table that stood in the light by a window. As Melville laid the newspapers flat upon the tabletop, Bowman could see they were copies of The Berkshire Chronicle. Graves leaned in, the better to read the headlines.

"May the Fourteenth," began Melville, jabbing at the paper with a finger, "War Hero Dead At Larton." He turned to Bowman. "The unfortunate man shot himself in the head." He picked up another newspaper to lay over the first. "June the Eleventh," he read from the masthead. "Railwayman Falls From

Larton Church Tower."

Graves scratched furiously at his notebook, desperately transposing the information beneath each of the lurid headlines.

"In both cases," Melville asserted with a stab of his finger, "the verdict returned by the coroner was one of self-murder."

"Did you know these men?" Bowman enquired, gently.

"By sight, at least," Melville confirmed.

Graves looked up from his notes. "Were they from the same part of Larton?" he enquired, his pencil poised.

Melville bent over the table again, indicating each headline with a finger as he spoke. "The railwayman was from the Village." He flipped to the next edition. "The soldier lived in Larton Dean." Melville thought. "Is that pertinent, do you think?"

"Perhaps," the inspector allowed, gnawing at his lip. "But what of the latest? Fletcher Cousins?"

"He's not local at all," insisted Melville. "Or at least he wouldn't be considered so." He turned to the fireplace and walked to the mantel to retrieve a pouch of tobacco and a pipe. "You would have to direct all your questions concerning Cousins to Maxwell Trevitt, the farmer in Larton Dean."

Bowman heard Graves scratch at his notebook.

"May we take these newspapers from you, Lord Melville? The information they contain might well prove invaluable."

Melville gave a shrug. "As you wish." He turned at the fireplace to regard the inspector with an unblinking gaze. "Detective Inspector Bowman," he began, tamping down the tobacco in his pipe, "would you think it usual for a small village such as Larton to have such a high incidence of self-murder in so short a time?"

Bowman's frown cut deep at his forehead. Fletcher Cousins was the third man to take his own life in just eight weeks.

"On the contrary, Lord Melville," the inspector demurred, "I would think it most unusual indeed."

"And that," Melville concluded with a nod, "is why I prevailed upon Scotland Yard."

VI

Checking In

The King's Head was a public house and hotel standing halfway along the high street in Larton Village. Originally an old coaching inn, it stood close enough to the street that its lower courses of brick were caked in detritus from the road and the windows with a skein of dust. Even at this early hour of the evening, the steps up to the entrance were crowded with a throng of locals. Fresh from the fields, they lifted their drafts to their lips almost in unison, whenever there was a convenient lull in their conversation. The building rose over three floors to an ancient, thatched roof through which rose a pair of impressive chimneys. An ornate sign hung listless in the still air above the door. An obviously hurried likeness of King Charles II stared out with a censorious expression, seemingly in judgement at the drinkers beneath. In truth, as was often pointed out, the Stuart king had been guilty of far worse in his time. The entrance to a courtyard lay between the inn and a small butcher's shop. A narrow passage led between them to a square cobbled space, big enough to accommodate half a dozen horses and their carts. Much of the original Georgian architecture survived within, from the thick walls and tall windows to the wide, sweeping staircase that rose to the higher floors.

Having been dropped at the inn by Prescott, Melville's rather terse driver, Bowman and Graves were left to carry their cases up the few steps to the door themselves. The gaggle of drinkers in their path fell into an awkward, suspicious silence as they passed, their eyes narrowing in their scrutiny of the strangers in their midst. Bowman had to physically barge past one with his shoulder in order to clear a way to the door. The man met Bowman's gaze with a steely stare, his beery breath almost causing the inspector's eyes to water. He wondered how wise he had been to accept Melville's invitation to be quartered at the inn for the duration of the investigation. As he entered the public bar to the rear of the building, Bowman could feel the fingers of his right hand twitch in anticipation of a drink. The room about him had begun to sway. The tremor increased. Thinking fast, he passed the case from his left to his right hand, the better to quell the shaking. As his mouth dried, he felt a strange sense of detachment. His body felt light, as if the weight of the case alone was keeping him on the ground. There was a pressure at his temples and an awful buzzing sound in his ears. His mind felt restless and Bowman struggled to make sense of his thoughts. Reaching out, he clutched at the low bar for support, sweeping aside three or four empty tankards as he fumbled for purchase.

"You alright, sir?" Graves enquired, concerned. Bowman's tongue felt thick in his mouth. The words choked in his throat. He nodded, trying to focus on the sergeant at his side. The walls were closing in, the ceiling pressing down upon him. That was it, he realised. That was what he was feeling. Pressure. It bore down upon him, blocking his ears and pressing at his temples. The building itself seemed to have a heavy presence, malevolent and brooding.

"I need - " Bowman began, struggling for breath. "I need... to sit down." To the evident surprise of the woman who had even now appeared to provide assistance to the new arrivals, Bowman collapsed to the floor, his eyes rolling back in his head, his right hand twitching in its strange, irregular rhythm, as if possessed of a life of its own.

The seat beneath him felt hard and unyielding. He was thrown left and right as he bounced over the cobbles, struggling for purchase wherever he could find it. Bowman fought to understand. Strange yet familiar smells assailed his senses. As if from far off, a cacophony of voices came to his ears. Incongruously, Bowman had a sudden memory of swimming in the river as a child. As his head dipped below the water with each stroke, the voices from the bank became muffled and distant. Was he under water? Bowman shook his head to clear it. There was something ahead of him, just out of reach. Two blurred, indistinct shapes, they rose and fell with a regular rhythm. Bowman narrowed his eyes to make sense of the vision. Suddenly, his ears cleared and the inspector was assailed by a wall of sound; people screaming, the sound of hooves. A cold wind assaulted him, buffeting him as he fought to remain seated. He made fists of his hands in a desperate attempt to maintain his balance, only to find he was clutching at something. Looking down, he saw he held a length of leather between his hands, stretching before him towards the diffuse shapes ahead. His chest was rising and falling in an effort to breathe. He tried to blink away his confusion and as he did so, there, before him, the shapes coalesced. Horses. He was at the helm of a carriage. Bowman felt a cold fear rise within him. His breathing quickened. Casting his eyes about him, he saw familiar buildings flashing past. He knew exactly where he was. As if to confirm his dreadful suspicions, Bowman's eyes alighted on a street sign affixed to the wall. The scene around him froze, as if the universe itself was conspiring to give him time to read the words; 'Hanbury Street'.

Bowman let go the reins. A dreadful inevitability had asserted itself. He felt like an actor in a play, scripted, prepared and rehearsed. Even with his hands at his side, the carriage rattled on. This time, he realised with a start, he was to be the driver.

Behind him, as he knew he would, as he had a thousand times before, he heard a crack. The bullet had snapped through the canopy of the carriage and would soon lodge itself in his shoulder, cold and deadly. Ahead of him, a woman pushed her child from the carriage's path. He could see the flanks of the horses steaming with their exertions, spittle flying from their gaping mouths. People shouted as he passed, some in anger, some in sheer surprise at his approach. One threw a stone that caught a horse on its rump, goading it to even greater speed.

Suddenly, he felt it. Tearing into his flesh, the bullet passed through bone and sinew to lodge just behind his breastbone, burning with a ferocious heat. He clutched at his chest despite feeling no pain at all. He knew exactly what would happen next. The carriage would veer violently to the right, into Old Montague Street and Queen Street before rejoining Hanbury Street to the east. There, Bowman saw the Women's Refuge. Looking again, he noticed the woman he had met at the meeting he had attended just seven days before. She stood, frozen in an attitude of horror, seemingly aghast at the events unfolding before her. Bowman met her gaze, her eyes burning into him with fierce accusation. He opened his mouth to speak, to implore or explain, when suddenly he saw her. There, stepping off the curb before him, just as she always must, was Anna. Her head was tilted away from him so that he could not see her face, but he knew it would be her. Looking beyond her, where Bowman had expected to see a representation of his past self, standing in sudden realisation of the horror before him, he saw nothing. It was as if the world had ceased to exist beyond her. A mist descended, holding them distinct from the world. The two of them, held in suspension. The moment seemed an eternity. He tried to scream a warning, but no sound came. The horses thundered on, their dread hooves sparking on the road. And suddenly, they stopped and all was quiet.

The silence was so thick, Bowman fancied he could taste it. The road and its attendant buildings were gone. More than that, they had never even been. Bowman felt a profound absence. A void where the world had been. A tangible and eternal nothing. He had always existed here and now, within this bubble of a moment, the horses suspended in mid air, the carriage beneath him solid and unmoving. The very air seemed pregnant with the dreadful knowledge of what must happen next. Slowly, almost imperceptibly, she turned her head towards him. Bowman's breath caught in his throat. Where he should have seen her face, her beautiful beguiling face, he saw... *nothing*. He felt his gorge begin to rise. Where Anna's face should have been, there was a ghastly, horrific absence of features. Her skin was smooth and stretched across her skull, devoid of any aspect. He tipped forward in his seat. A scream filled the air like the whistle of a train, hurting his ears. She turned fully towards him, her dreadful face seeing yet unseeing as he pitched towards her. He fell into its blankness, into the void of her face, his fingers clawing before him.

"Sir!" a voice exclaimed. "Be careful there!"

Bowman's eyes snapped open. Graves' face hung before him, his eyes wide with concern. The inspector's clothes clung to his skin, hot and damp. Looking about him, he tried to gauge his surroundings.

"We got you upstairs, sir," Graves was explaining, "to your room. We thought it best to lie you down."

Bowman realised he was reclining on a simple, wooden framed bed, a pillow propped beneath his head. The room was square and sparsely furnished. A rickety chest of drawers stood between the two, high windows that gave out onto the High Street. On the opposite wall, a small table held a jug of water and a chipped ceramic basin beneath which, Bowman saw, his suitcase had been stowed.

"A doctor has been called," Graves said, softly. "He will be with us straight."

Bowman struggled to prop himself up on his elbows. "No," he slurred, "I'll need no doctor." Swinging his legs from the bed, he pressed the heels of his hands against his forehead in an effort to quell the throbbing.

The scene was interrupted by the arrival of a young woman dressed in a simple cotton smock. A stained apron was tied about her waist and a dishrag thrown over her shoulder.

"Is he quite well?" she enquired of Graves. She spoke with the same, soft burr as the driver who had collected them from the station just a few hours before. Bowman recognised her as the last person he had seen before he had succumbed to his mania. Perhaps she had even helped Graves carry him to his room.

"He is well enough to talk," Graves glared at his colleague pointedly. "Though he will not see the doctor."

"I can send him away as quickly as I called him," the girl confirmed.

Graves turned to her, his handsome face aglow in the golden light of the afternoon. "Thank you, Maude," he smiled. "You have been more than helpful."

Bowman noticed the girl blush at his words. "I do what I can, Sergeant Graves," she giggled. An age seemed to pass between them as they held each other in an easy gaze then, finally, she turned to go.

"Oh, blast, almost forgot," she checked herself. "You are

invited to Trevitt's farm, Inspector Bowman."

So, Graves had told her his name.

"How did he know I was here?" Bowman's moustache twitched on his upper lip.

"There's little that happens here that goes unnoticed," Maude said, innocently.

Bowman nodded.

"I'm not sure he's quite well enough for that," Graves began.

"What time does he expect me?" Bowman was doing his best to feign normality.

"Seven of the clock," Maude answered. "The lad is still at the door if you wish to send a reply."

Bowman rose unsteadily to his feet and shuffled to one of the large, rectangular windows that looked out over the high street. Looking down to his left, he saw a young boy with a large dog playing absently in the street. The lad seemed to sense the inspector's gaze and turned to glare up at his window. Bowman fancied he noticed a look of recognition in the boy's expression.

"Tell him I will be there."

"But, sir - " Graves began in protest.

"Do you know Cousins' widow?" Bowman had turned to Maude.

"Florrie?" The young girl shrugged. "Of course."

"And could you furnish Sergeant Graves with her address?"

Maude seemed glad to turn her attention to the sergeant again. "Reckon so," she confirmed with a smile.

"Question her, Graves," Bowman began. "We need to know the circumstances leading up to her husband's death. We must discover why Cousins might have hanged himself."

"But sir," Graves objected. "Are you sure – "

"Sergeant Graves, we are here to investigate an important matter." Fancying the whole of Larton knew of the detectives" purpose by now, he saw no reason not to be explicit in Maude's presence. "And that is what we shall do."

VII

Articles Of Faith

As Senior Steward, it fell to William Oats to dress the Temple and the Chamber of Reflection for the initiation. He was diligent in his duties and renowned for despatching them with a solemn attention to the details. Dressed in a formal black suit and waistcoat, Oats had tied a pristine, white leather apron at his waist, as was required for all when in the Temple. The candles lit, he blew out the taper and walked slowly across the flagstones to the west wall. Pausing briefly, he cast his eyes up to the painting that hung there. It was a depiction of two pillars flanking a stone altar upon which was laid a red cloth and a copy of the Holy Bible. A golden goblet, a representation of the Holy Grail itself hung, somewhat improbably, in the air some six inches from the altar cloth. A figure concealed behind one of the pillars was visible from the shoulder only, his hand stretched out to point to the chalice with a delicate finger. The eye was led to this sombre scene, heavy with symbolism, via a chequered black and white tiled floor. At the steps to the altar lay a canvas in a frame, a picture within a picture, depicting a square and set of compasses. The whole was framed with a border of black and white triangular shapes, each side marked with the cardinal points of the compass. Though an old man, Oats had only recently begun his journey through the Brotherhood, but he knew enough to recognise the meaning behind the images. The two, free standing copper pillars that dominated the piece were Boaz and Jachin. They had stood sentinel on the porch of Solomon's Temple, the first in Jerusalem. Oats let his eyes rest on the square and compasses, the tools of the Great Architect. Almost as a reflex, he intoned the appropriate passage from the many books he had been obliged to study.

"The square to square our actions, the compass to keep us within our bounds."

Oats understood this as a warning to any brother not to

overreach himself, but rather to know his place in the Great Design. He could think of one or two in the Lodge who would do well to reflect upon the words. Between the compasses sat a sheaf of corn, picked out in gold. Peculiar to the Larton Lodge, it represented the labours of the farm workers in the fields but also the charity that each brother was expected to show to another.

"When thou cuttest down thine harvest in the field," Oats uttered solemnly, "And hast forgot a sheaf in the field, thou shalt not go again to fetch it: it shall be for the stranger, for the fatherless, and for the widow."

The words gave Oats pause and brought to mind those that Fletcher Cousins had left behind. His boy, in particular, Oats felt the most sorry for. Perhaps he should make a deposition to the Grand Master that provision might be made to secure his future.

Leaning before the picture, Oats lifted the lid on a great chest that stood beneath it. Moving a cloth to one side to reveal a large ornate box, Oats let his fingers caress the carved motifs that ran along its outside. The All Seeing Eye stared unblinking from the wood, its benevolent beams radiating outwards and over the lid of the box.

"The eyes of the Lord are in every place," intoned Oats, almost unconsciously, "Beholding the evil and the good."

Grasping the handles at either side, he lifted the box carefully from the chest. Slowly and with great reverence, he carried it across the floor of the Temple. Resting the heavy box on the floor, he reached up to pull a curtain to one side, revealing the Chamber of Reflection beyond.

A small anteroom to the Temple, the Chamber was of a hexagonal design and held no furniture beyond a table covered in a black velvet cloth. It stood upon a mosaic of black and white tiles, like those depicted in the picture on the Temple wall. Here, in the Chamber of Reflection, the All Seeing Eye was given prominence, gazing down from the ceiling with a benign stare. Aside from the points of the compass marking the north, south, east and west, the walls were bare so that the initiate might more readily fix his contemplation on the Holy Artefacts. Reaching for the box, Oats took each one in turn and placed them in their prescribed position on the table. A human skull was placed at the exact centre, a sickle blade and hourglass arranged with care to each side. A silver plate was loaded with bread from a pouch that hung from a loop on Oats' belt, a small jug filled with water from a stone basin by the door. A single candle was placed in readiness to be lit at a corner of the tabletop. Oats took the time to measure the exact distances with the span of his hand before resting each object in its place, stopping occasionally to measure them again. Finally, taking a handful of salt from a bottle and forming a fist with his hand, he let the substance fall to the table in a steady stream. Moving his hand from left to right, he carefully spelt out the letters "V.I.T.R.I.O.L." across the leading edge of the tablecloth.

Clapping his hands together to be rid of the residue, William Oats stood back to admire his handiwork. Everything was in its place. All that was required now was the convening of the Lodge, the presence of the Grand Master, his officers and the keen initiate himself, eager to learn the secrets of the Craft.

VIII

The Scene Of The Crime

The walk to Trevitt's farm gave Bowman the chance to clear his head. The throbbing in his temples had subsided now, but he was left with a feeling of acute agitation. As horrific as they always were, Bowman derived a sort of comfort from the fact that he would always see her in his visions. Now, it seemed, even that would be denied him. He did not know how he would cope without her.

There was still a great deal of heat in the evening sun. The air was still and close, and Bowman felt himself breaking into a sweat as he crossed the causeway from the Village to Larton Rise. Crossing the bridge over the little tributary, he stepped to one side to avoid a gang of labourers coming back from the fields. Their faces were caked in dust and dirt, their shirtsleeves and collars grimy from their toil. No doubt heading to The King's Head for the evening, they had about them that lightness of spirit common to all with a day's work behind them. Bowman had left Graves to conduct his interview with Florrie Cousins, then settle at the hotel for the evening. He was sure the eager sergeant would spend the rest of his night gleaning what he could from the locals regarding Cousins' death. No doubt these labourers would have a tale to share if prompted, particularly if they were plied with a draft or two to loosen their tongues. As they passed, Bowman noticed them sharing looks between themselves. One even nudged his neighbour, none too subtly, nodding in Bowman's direction. A visitor to Larton was a rare thing indeed, the inspector mused, sure that word must have spread of his investigation. Giving him a wide berth, the men skirted round him, but not before one of them had cleared his throat noisily and spat the resultant mucus at the inspector's feet. Bowman heard the word "filth" uttered as they retreated behind him.

Head down, he walked on. The streets in the Rise were busier and Bowman was greeted with cooking smells from the open doors of the cottages by the road. An old man leaned on a gate, puffing at a cheroot, his beady eyes watching as the inspector passed. Seeing him from her window, a mother ran to the path to gather up her children as they played on the road, ushering them before her through the garden gate. Her eyes flicked back to the inspector as she fled indoors, and Bowman thought he saw fear in her expression. He wondered if there was always such suspicion in the air.

Crossing over the railway line where the bunting for the regatta hung forlorn and lifeless, Bowman found himself on steeper ground. As the houses fell away behind him, so the road rose quickly to a substantial height. Soon, he was looking back on Larton Rise and the Village in the distance. The houses here were grander and fewer and further between. There were great distances between them and most were set back from the road behind grand iron gates or towering yew hedges. Larton Dean had a rarefied atmosphere. The village green was immaculate, home to a pretty duck pond and well kept beds of pink hydrangeas. A proud oak stood at its centre where, Bowman noticed, a rope swing had been tied for the entertainment of the local children. He paused mid-step to catch his breath. The furthest half of the green had been given over to a profusion of wild flowers. The tall grass seemed to shimmer in the heat, ephemeral. Tall poppies bobbed their heads in warning to the ox eye daisies that competed with them for space. Bees and butterflies flitted between them, and Bowman caught a flash of a dragonfly by the pond. In the still of the evening air, before such a display of life in all its splendour, it was impossible to believe that death had so decisively come to Larton. What secrets lurked behind these tall yew hedges, Bowman wondered, or behind the rickety doors of the cottages in the Rise or in the streets of the Village, that could result in three of its inhabitants taking their own lives within the space of eight weeks?

Turning off the road he saw, as Maude had said he would, a sign to Trevitt's farm nailed to a tree.

"Reckon you'll want to see Gummer's Pond first, inspector?" Bowman turned to see a barrel of a man in a patterned waistcoat walking at speed down the hill towards him. His red face was aglow in the evening sun, marred only by the broken nose that seemed to veer at an alarming angle. His black hair hung limp at either side of a wide parting from front to back. Stopping at the tree, the man hooked his thumbs in his waistcoat pockets to regard the man before him. "Lord Melville told me to expect you." Bowman sensed the man was somehow disappointed. "Though heaven only knows what further light can be shed on the matter." His accent was thicker than Bowman had yet heard, all stretched vowels and rising cadences.

"I am Detective Inspector Bowman of Scotland Yard," Bowman asserted.

"Trevitt," the man panted, "Maxwell Trevitt." He tapped the sign on the tree for effect, as if he were an actor pointing to his billing on a poster. He looked Bowman up and down. "We ain't never had a detective inspector in Larton," he sneered, "And I can't see as how we need one now."

"Time will tell," Bowman replied, carefully.

Trevitt took a breath, his chest straining against the buttons of his waistcoat. He seemed to make up his mind. "Well then," he said, decisively, "Let me take you to the tree, then you will join me for dinner."

At least it was cooler beneath the canopy. The air however, suffused with a woody scent, was closer still. As the two men stood before Gummer's Pond, Bowman felt a trickle of sweat run cold beneath his shirt. The ground had been uneven as they climbed and several times the inspector had tripped on an errant tree root, or found himself ensnared on some particularly persistent brambles. Clumps of nettles sprung up at regular intervals. As they stopped in the clearing before the pond, Bowman bent to scratch at a particularly nasty sting on his ankle. His forearm, he noticed, was marked with scars where branches and twigs had sought to impede his progress through the wood.

"That's where he was found." Trevitt was pointing with a fat finger to a large tree by the pond's edge. "Hanging from that there lower branch."

Following Trevitt's gaze, Bowman stared up into the canopy. The branch was perhaps ten feet from the ground. He could even see where a loop of rope was still wound round its girth. Striding through the undergrowth, he stood directly beneath the tree and looked around. Suddenly, he was conscious of being watched. A shadowy figure was lurking against a tree, pressing itself against the trunk in an effort to remain hidden. As Bowman peered into the woods, it seemed the figure had disappeared entirely.

"He could have hoist himself up easily enough," Bowman said thoughtfully, turning his attention back to the tree, 'standing on one of those old logs there." He gestured towards a heap of jumbled logs some feet away. "He might well have stood upon it to tie the rope, then kicked it away."

Trevitt nodded, thoughtfully. "The gypsies cut and collect the wood for their camp," he said. Bowman thought he caught a note of disdain in his voice. "I'm surprised they haven"t yet scrambled up to get that bit of rope." He nodded up into the branches of the tree. "Nothin's safe when they're about. Nor no one, neither. There was bad blood between Cousins and them." He nodded into the trees. "I dare say it might have flared into something deadly."

"Gypsies?" Bowman raised his eyebrows.

Trevitt sighed and spat at the ground. "We passed their camp just a few hundred yards up the track." Bowman was surprised. He had been too intent on avoiding the clumps of nettles and weeds to look about him as they walked. "Probably watching us now for all I know," the farmer raised his voice, pointedly, "Or care!"

Bowman tried to peer through the undergrowth. "Is this the only path to the pond?"

"It is," Trevitt confirmed, "You may take any course you wish, but that's the least obstructed."

"Then it's almost certain Cousins would have come this way," Bowman mused.

Trevitt shrugged. "As you say," he mumbled.

"You will know, Mr Trevitt, that I am here at Lord Melville's request. Do you share his conviction that this might be murder?"

"A man has died within feet of a gypsy camp," spat Trevitt in exasperation. "Why would you think otherwise?"

Bowman picked his way carefully back through the clearing to gaze up at the tree again. As things stood, he couldn"t help but disagree.

On the way back down the track, he made a point of stopping by the travellers" camp. Peering through the nettles, he saw a haphazard collection of tents and caravans nestling in a natural amphitheatre surrounded by an escarpment of chalk.

"They come every year for employment," breathed Trevitt at his side. Bowman could see several men and women lounging about the place. Two or three children ran naked around the camp, chasing one another with sticks for swords.

"They don't look very employed," he remarked.

Trevitt harrumphed. "They should be picking cherries from my trees," he said, "But their leader, Stoker, has ideas above his station." The farmer flexed his fingers as he spoke.

Bowman noticed a tall, youthful looking man, his hair tied back beneath a kerchief, standing in the centre of the camp. He seemed to be directing those about him as he drew on a long clay pipe, some to collect wood, others to clear areas of the undergrowth.

"They pitched their price too high," Trevitt continued off Bowman's questioning look. "And so my cherries rot as they enjoy their leisure."

With that, the farmer barrelled off through the bracken in a sulk, seemingly impervious to the thorns and briars that snatched at his clothes. Turning to follow him, Bowman was suddenly aware of a pair of eyes staring at him through the undergrowth. As he stepped towards them, however, there was a rustle of activity and the unseen observer made his escape through a tangle of bracken.

Trevitt's farmhouse had clearly seen better days. Bowman noticed the wood of the doorframe crumbling and peeling away as he followed Trevitt through the porch and into the hallway beyond. The tiles on the floor were obscured by dust that, kicked up as they walked, danced in the light from the windows. It hung in the air like mist, lending a diffuse murkiness to the interior of the house. Spiders" webs hung from every corner, festooned with the miniature carcasses of trapped flies and beetles, some twisting idly in suspended threads that hung from the intricate structures above them. Two dogs ran to greet the men as they stepped through the door. Trevitt shouted at them both angrily that they should "leave go," and they retreated whence they came, their tales shivering between their hind legs.

Turning into the parlour, Bowman was met by a sorry sight indeed. A woman stood by the window, ashen faced and dejected. She cast her eyes to the floor as Trevitt entered, and Bowman had the distinct impression that she was afraid of him.

"This is the detective, Bowman," Trevitt announced. "He's staying at The King's Head, but I dare say he'll get a better meal with us." It occurred to Bowman that the poor woman had not been informed he would be joining them. 'see to it there's a place set at the table, won"t you?"

The woman almost curtsied in response before she moved to leave the room. As she squeezed past the inspector, Bowman fancied he noticed the skin beneath her left eye was bruised, and she rubbed at her wrists as if in pain. All the while her eyes avoided his, as if the action alone would mean she could pass unnoticed. It was rather telling, Bowman thought, that Trevitt had neglected to introduce the woman by name. He guessed she was his wife, although there was nothing in his attitude towards her that would naturally lead to such a conclusion; no tenderness between them or looks of easy familiarity. Not for the first time, Bowman mused on how the glory of marriage was often wasted on those who least appreciated it.

When he turned back into the room, he saw that Trevitt had taken a seat. He waved in the direction of a cabinet by the door on which stood a dusty decanter and some cracked and mismatched glasses. "Help yourself," he grumbled as he lifted his own glass as if in a toast. "After a day among the trees, there's greater welcome in a glass than from a wife." Trevitt chuckled at his own joke; a lazy, throaty laugh that Bowman found most distasteful. So, she was his wife after all.

Bowman stood for a time, eyeing the decanter on the shelf. He felt a cold sweat prickle on his back and his heart beat faster in his chest. Brandy. Swallowing hard, he tweaked his moustache in agitation, fighting hard against an almost primal urge that threatened to engulf him.

"What was Cousins to you?" Bowman hoped the momentum of a conversation would steer him from his impulses.

"Gang master," Trevitt belched from the chair. He shifted his weight as he sat, and for a moment, Bowman feared the chair could not contain him. It creaked and popped as the man sought to make himself more comfortable. Legs spread wide and chin on his chest, he looked for all the world like a bloated king on his throne, sovereign of all he saw before him. "But he used to be one of them."

"Them?" Bowman was still eyeing the decanter.

"The gypsies. Which is why he was so useful to me." He sipped again at his drink and smacked his lips in such a way as to break Bowman's resolve.

With studied nonchalance, the inspector sidled to the cabinet and selected the biggest glass. Blowing dust from the rim, he uncorked the decanter. The stopper slid from the mouth of the bottle with an easy action, releasing the heady sweetness trapped within. Bowman stood to welcome the scent, his nostrils wide in invitation.

"He was one of them you see, when they first came to Larton," Trevitt continued, oblivious to the battle taking place by the cabinet. Bowman was holding the decanter up to the light, losing himself in the swirling, swilling golden glow. His tongue was thick in his mouth, his lips drying in anticipation. Casting a look at the farmer to see he was not observed, he poured himself a glass, filling it to the brim. Downing it at once before Trevitt could notice, he refilled it half way and replaced the stopper in the decanter. The brandy was of inferior quality and burned at his throat. A beautiful pain, harsh and astringent.

"They fell out. There's been bad blood between them ever since." Trevitt's voice was thick with lethargy. Bowman was certain he would soon be asleep if left to his own devices.

"What was the cause of the enmity between them?"

"You'd have to ask Stoker," Trevitt replied, haughtily. "Cousins is in no position now to tell us."

Bowman sipped at his brandy again, savouring the drink as it slipped from the rim of the glass to his lips. "Is there anyone in Larton who would wish to see Cousins dead, Mr Trevitt?"

Trevitt gave a dry laugh. "Just about everyone in Larton is another man's enemy, Inspector Bowman," he smirked, "And Fletcher Cousins was a master at making them. I should say you couldn"t count on the fingers of both hands just how many might have wanted him dead." Bowman raised his eyebrows at the admission. "But I dare say the same would apply to me, too." Trevitt turned his eyes on the inspector. "Life is hard in the countryside, inspector. And so we live by different rules."

"Not the rule of law, then?"

Trevitt sensed the trap. "Ay, when we can. But the law of nature has a greater hold upon us. We live by the seasons here. The crops don't go in by the spring, we don't eat come the autumn." Trevitt heaved himself forward in his chair to make a point. "London is a monster. A heaving, gorging monster. It takes everything we throw at it, leaving us precious little to ourselves. The whole of the Empire exists to feed it. It's a spoilt child, inspector, and I dare say those that live there know nothing of real life."

Bowman pressed the point. "And what is real life, Mr Trevitt?"

Trevitt sniffed. "We scratch a living, that is all. Not for us a night at the theatre or walks in the park. There's barely a house in the whole village got running water save the toffs in the Dean." He turned to face Bowman square on, his great chest heaving. 'death is commonplace here, Inspector Bowman. There needs no detectives from Scotland Yard to tell us that. We live side by side with it. That's the way it always has been and, I dare say, how it always shall be."

Bowman blinked. The brandy was already dulling his nerves. 'surely Cousins' death must be investigated?"

At this, Trevitt heaved himself to his feet. It took, Bowman noticed, all his effort to do so.

"You would do well to leave alone, inspector," he boomed,

"Go back to London and leave us to our ways."

"I am here at the express invitation of Lord Melville," Bowman stuttered. He felt the skin on his neck burn beneath his collar. In truth, he wasn't sure why he was here at all, beyond the fact that the commissioner seemed intent on keeping a distance between them. If it weren"t for one particular detail in the newspaper reports of the men's deaths, he would surely have been on the first train back to London. "It is my duty as an officer of the Metropolitan Police Force to investigate."

"You'll kow tow to his will then, will you?" Trevitt seethed. "You'll get few friends through bowin" and scrapin" to his lordship."

"I am not here to make friends, Mr Trevitt," Bowman rejoindered, "But rather to investigate a man's death."

From the look that Trevitt shot him from beneath his beetle brows, Bowman saw that that was just as well.

Following Trevitt's outburst, dinner was an awkward affair. Barely a word was spoken as Bowman was ushered into the dilapidated dining room to be served a meal of boiled potatoes and rabbit. The inspector had been surprised to see that Trevitt's wife had no intention to join them, but rather kept herself to the kitchen and the rooms to the back of the house. Once or twice throughout the meal, Bowman was certain he could hear her crying. As the poor woman's sobs filtered through the walls, Trevitt brazenly held Bowman's gaze, almost daring him to comment upon it. He had thought better of it, concentrating instead on downing his meal as quickly as possible, the sooner to be away and back to The King's Head. He had been struck by Trevitt's belligerence in the parlour. Now the farmer sat at the dining table, gravy dripping from his chin.

"What do you know of the other men who took their life?" Bowman dared to ask.

Trevitt paused at his meal, a forkful of food halfway between plate and mouth. He seemed to consider whether the question was worthy of response. "I knew old Sharples by sight," he said at last. "He had only lately come to the village.

"The old soldier?" Bowman remembered the papers having

made mention of him having shot himself.

Trevitt nodded, resuming his meal. "He was a Trooper in the Royal Horse Guards." He looked, mused Bowman, like some gruff beast chewing the cud. It was quite enough to put the inspector off his meal. "He had one of the almshouses by St. Luke's in the Dean." Trevitt slapped at his lips with his tongue. "You see, inspector, we even have our own churches so we don't have to mix."

"Why might he have shot himself?"

Trevitt paused again, unblinking. "They say a man's wits may retreat in response to some dreadful event." Bowman swallowed. Trevitt regarded the inspector carefully. Was he expecting a response? "He was never the same after his time in the army," he continued at last. 'saw some things, no doubt."

With that, Trevitt fell silent for the remainder of the meal. Bowman wondered at the man's remarks. Did Trevitt know of his history? Had Bowman left London only to have his reputation travel with him? He thought back to the nudges and glances he had seen from the men on the bridge. Perhaps there was more to it than a suspicion of strangers. As Trevitt cleared his plate, Bowman chose the moment to stand and push his chair back from the table.

"You must excuse me, Mr Trevitt. You have been most helpful. Will you give my thanks to Mrs Trevitt for an excellent meal?" He attempted a smile.

"That I will," said the farmer as he rested his hands upon his belly. "When I see her." Within moments, he was asleep, leaving Bowman to make his way from the farmer's cottage alone.

IX

Initiation

Prescott knelt before the table in the Chamber of Reflection, eager to take the First Degree. He had been flattered when approached to take his place among the Fraternity. He had, of course, heard rumours of the Larton Lodge but had never truly believed in such a thing. He had never achieved much in his life. Being the driver to Lord Melville was not a particularly high achievement for one his age but, in Larton, the prospect of advancement was slim. Cooper, the groom, was seemingly determined to stay in post forever, leaving little room for Prescott to progress. Here, amongst the Brotherhood, he felt he stood a chance. Progression through the Degrees had offered him a challenge. Perhaps here he would be granted the respect he felt was denied him in the village. Though he had served Lord Melville for much of his adult life, Prescott had never felt he had received the recognition he deserved. He was frequently ridiculed and often ignored. The invitation to join the Lodge would change all that, he was certain. Perhaps he would even rise through the ranks to sit in the east as Grand Master.

The sound of a discordant chanting from the Temple served as a reminder to turn his mind to higher things. He had been led blindfold to the Chamber of Reflection by William Oats. Only when the curtain had been drawn behind him had the Hoodwink been untied. Prescott had fought to hide his disappointment as he looked about him. Save for the odd shape of the room and the table of strange objects that stood before him, there was little to inspire him. He recognised the collection of ephemera arranged on the tablecloth. In the literature he had been given to prepare for the ceremony, he had read of the skull and the hourglass and of their meaning in the Ritual. They were set before him as a reminder of his own mortality and the futility of all things. The bread and water symbolised the simplicity of an initiate's life. However, he struggled to remember the meaning behind the letters of salt on the tablecloth. "V.I.T.R.I.O.L."

Prescott whispered under his breath as Oats fussed around him, tying a leather apron about his waist. "Visita Interiora Terrae," he began, 'rectificandoque…'" Here he stopped, unable to recall the next few words. "Visita Interiora Terrae," he began again, then paused. He could not for the life of him remember the rest.

The apron tied, Prescott felt a gentle pressure on his shoulder. Oats was pushing him down to kneel before the table. His knees cracking in complaint, Prescott relented. The tiled floor was cold and hard, and he hoped he would not have to stay there long.

Oats bowed long and low before the table then turned wordlessly to exit through the curtain into the Temple beyond. He was careful to draw it smartly back behind him so that Prescott was denied even the briefest glimpse of what lay beyond. The driver puffed out his cheeks and turned back to the table. He was now required to spend some time in solemn contemplation of the Craft. As the blood drained from his legs, however, the only thing he could solemnly contemplate was the state of his knees. Forcing his mind to higher things, he returned again to the phrase that had eluded him.

"Visita Interiora Terrae," he muttered beneath his breath. What was it? He struggled to remember the meaning in hopes that it would prompt his mind to recall the Latin. "Visit the interior of the earth", he intoned to himself, "And, purifying it, you will find the hidden stone." It was an elaborate way of saying, look within yourself for the truth. Too elaborate, Prescott thought to himself, rolling his eyes as he struggled with the translation. This time he approached it at speed, as if sheer momentum would carry him to the end of the sentence.

"Visita Interiora Terrae," he repeated, 'rectificandoque, Invenies Occultum Lapidem." That was it. He raised his hands to rub at his face in relief, just as Oats returned to the room to collect him. Finding Prescott with his hands raised before him, he confused the gesture with that of prayerful introspection, and smiled at his acolyte's piety.

Oats had been appointed Prescott's mentor and it was apparent he took his duties seriously. With a sombre air, he reached across to the table and pinched some salt between a forefinger and thumb. Letting it go over each shoulder, he muttered something under his breath before helping Prescott to his feet. The driver was grateful for the opportunity to stretch his legs, although he was cautioned by a look not to say a word. He knew he must not speak unprompted until the ceremony was over and so he nodded in understanding as Oats led him to the curtain.

Prescott's heart beat just a little bit faster. Here he stood, a lowly driver, on the threshold of a sacred and secret knowledge. At last, perhaps, all things would be known to him and he would have a place in the world, or at least in Larton which amounted to much the same thing.

After a dramatic pause, Oats drew back the curtain with a flourish and Prescott saw the Temple before him. It was lit by at least a hundred flickering candles of differing sizes. They stood on every surface and sill, lending a warm glow to proceedings. An altar table lay beyond. Around the room, the Officers of the Lodge stood, intoning their psalms with lusty voices. Prescott recognised many of them from the village. The butcher, the landlord of The Kings Head and the headmaster of Larton School were among them, though he was forbidden to show them any signs of acknowledgment.

Treading exactly in Oats' footsteps as he had been tutored, Prescott made his way into the temple. The air was still and damp in the windowless room with no hint of a draught. Prescott remembered the hard, stone steps he had been led down while in his Hoodwink and guessed he was underground. Having been collected and blindfolded from a pre-arranged location in the woods around Larton, he couldn''t even be sure which part of the village he was in. The twelve Officers were stood in a circle around the room, chanting in unison. Ornate wooden chairs had been placed in the corners of the room, set back from the Temple in alcoves. All but one of them was occupied. Prescott racked his brains to remember those who were seated. The Junior Warden was sat in the south, he remembered, and the Senior Warden in the west. Directly opposite, in the direction of the rising sun, the Grand Master sat in the east. All their faces were obscured in the shadow of the alcoves. The chair in the north corner was empty, as Prescott knew it always was, although the symbolism eluded him for now. He reprimanded himself and made a mental note to get back to his studies just as soon as time allowed.

As the volume of the chanting increased, Oats turned to Prescott with his palm open before him. With a nod of his head, Prescott turned up the hem of his apron as was expected. Turning from him, Oats then started on his course around the room, Prescott following slavishly in his footsteps. Beginning in the east towards the west by way of the south, they circled the room about the altar. The very act of walking the circle about the Temple served to link him to each and every man who had, since the dawn of recorded time, sought communion with the Great Architect. Prescott allowed himself to feel humbled by the thought.

Finally, they came to a stop and Oats took his position with the Officers. Prescott judged himself in the northeast corner of the room, as scripture dictated. Just as the first stone of the Jerusalem Temple was historically laid at the northeast corner, so Prescott was placed to signify the beginning of a true and correct foundation.

As the chanting fell away, a silence descended. Prescott flicked his eyes around the room. Suddenly, he heard the rapping of wood on wood. The Grand Master had risen, banging the gavel on the arm of his chair. It was a signal that those seated in the room should rise. Prescott strained to see into the gloom, but the shadow defeated him and the Grand Master remained unseen.

"Circumambulation teaches us that no single man is alone," the Master intoned with a sonorous voice, "But that, with a true and trusted friend in whom he can confide, he can always, unfailingly, find his way home. We live and walk by faith."

The gathered Officers around the room took up the final phrase in response. "We live and walk by faith," they chanted, as one.

Each of the Wardens, now standing before their chairs, pointed wordlessly before the altar table in a sign that Prescott should advance there. He made his way slowly to the altar and prostrated himself. Spreading his arms to make the sign of the cross, he felt his cheek pressing against the cold black mosaic tiles on the floor.

The Junior Warden opened his mouth to speak. "Have you come to the Lodge of your own free will?"

"I have," Prescott replied, conscious that his neck was held at an awkward angle.

"The Lodge represents the world," said the Senior Warden from his place in the west. "Are you sure of your place in it?"

"I am," Prescott squeaked.

Finally, the Grand Master himself completed the verse. "Where does the square lie?"

"On top of the compass." Prescott blinked the dust from his eyes.

"In life, as in the Lodge," the Grand Master continued from the shadows, "We must prostrate ourselves in humble submission, trust our Guide, learn His ways, follow Him and fear no danger."

The gathered Officers chanted in their sombre chorus. "Behold, how good and how pleasant it is for brethren to dwell together in unity!"

The Junior Warden answered them, his voice quivering with emotion. "It is like the precious ointment upon the head, that ran down upon the beard, even Aaron's beard: that went down to the skirts of his garments."

Now the Senior Warden played his part. "It was the dew of Hermon, and as the dew that descended upon the mountains of Zion: for there the Lord commanded the blessing." Daring to lift his eyes to the assembled throng, Prescott saw his mentor, William Oats, standing with a look of pride upon his face. His thoughts were interrupted by the Grand Master, his words echoing portentously around the Temple as if they were the Word of God Himself.

"By letters four and science five, this G aright doth stand, in due Art and Proportion." Prescott saw the Grand Master point with an outstretched arm to the altar table. There stood an open copy of the Holy Bible and a goblet engraved with the single letter, G. "By the Scriptures, Square and Compass, you have your answer, friend."

As the Officers again took up their chanting, Prescott rose from his prone position. Cursing his stiff knees under his breath, he advanced upon the table to drink from the goblet. The wine was tart and unpleasant to the taste. Thankfully, only a sip was required before Prescott was permitted to turn where he stood and take his first steps as an Entered Apprentice Of The First Degree.

X

Changing Tack

Inspector Bowman was at a loss. As he walked down the track from Trevitt's farm, he had to admit to himself that he was no further along in his investigation into Fletcher Cousins' death. There seemed to be no indication at all that it was anything other than self-murder. He had seen for himself how easy it would have been for Cousins to loop the rope around the limb of the tree, stand upon a stump of wood then kick it away once it was secure around his neck. As he had made his way through the farm on his way out, he had even seen coils of rope similar to the fragment left in the tree. Certainly there was no love lost between Trevitt and his gang master but, as far as Bowman could see, there was no motive for murder. He could only hope that Graves' interview with Cousins' widow would throw some light where now there was only darkness.

Squinting into the low sun, Bowman marvelled that there could still be such heat in the day at so late an hour. He could feel the baked ground beneath him radiating warmth through the soles of his shoes. As he left the track from Trevitt's farm to Larton Dean, Bowman turned his feet to St Luke's Church.Stopping for a moment beneath the oak tree near the pond, Bowman placed a hand upon the ancient bark. There was something about its resolute solidity that gave him pause. If he stood there long enough, he fancied, he might well feel it breathe. Judging from its enormous size, the great oak might have stood for five hundred years and, for all he knew, might live a hundred more. The village of Larton, and perhaps the whole of humanity, might rise and fall within its lifetime, yet still the oak would stand, implacable and knowing.

The sun was dropping below the tree as Bowman approached the church, and much of the road was finally in shade. St Luke's was a pretty building, perfectly in keeping with the neat lawns and trim hedgerows of the houses to either side. Its brick and flint walls were well maintained so as to be free from the ivy that Bowman could see had taken a hold of the tombs and gravestones around it. Passing by the thatched lychgate that was adorned with intricate carvings of holy figures and sacred text, Bowman followed a gravel drive that led to the back of the church. There, nestling against the perimeter wall, he saw a line of almshouses. There were ten in all, separated from the track by a strip of manicured lawn. Each had its own path leading to a low front door set beneath a stone lintel. Bowman noticed that each lintel bore a word, carved in an ornate script by an expert mason. Standing back from the houses so that each front door was within his view, he saw that each word, when read one after the other from left to right, spelled out a complete inscription;

"HE - THAT - GIVETH - TO - THE - POOR - LENDETH - TO - THE - LORD."

Provided and maintained by charitable trusts, almshouses were typically gifted for the use of those in a community who were the most vulnerable. Often they had been of a particular employment or station. Knowing that Trooper Sharples had been resident here, Bowman guessed they were primarily for the use of old soldiers. Often, they returned from the wars with nothing but the clothes they wore. Many found it difficult to find work or to adapt to civilian life after military service. Others still had injuries that precluded them from living a full and useful life. Unable to find their place in society, they often had no option but to throw themselves upon the mercy of local charities and trusts for support. The luckier among them were saved from a life of poverty and given shelter. Trooper Sharples had evidently been one such a man.

The dwellings before him were simple and yet, thought Bowman, sufficient to allow any man to live a life of comfort. Many of the plain red brick frontages were adorned with blooms. Roses had been trailed over one or two of the doors, and Bowman stood for a while to admire their scent. Two or three of the gardens had been subdivided into plots for the cultivation of vegetables. At the end of the row, Bowman saw an old man leaning over a spade, bending every now and then to shake the earth from a clump of waxy looking potatoes and set them aside upon the grass. As he approached the man, Bowman saw that, rather incongruously for one at work at so lowly a chore, a line of medals was pinned to his chest.

The old soldier looked up as he felt the inspector draw near.

"Are ye lost?" he asked, warily.

Bowman could tell at once that he was, or had at least once been, a proud man. His back as he stood was ramrod straight, his shoulders pushed back so that his chest puffed out before him. He had a narrow face with a clean-shaven jaw. His shrewd eyes peered out between a pair of trim, white eyebrows, his snowy white hair was parted meticulously above his right ear. Despite his exertions, Bowman noticed, the man had not a single hair out of place.

"Which of these was home to Trooper Sharples?" Bowman asked, knowing the question in itself would be enough to rouse the man's suspicions further.

'depends who would be asking." The man chewed at his tongue.

'scotland Yard would be asking," Bowman answered, carefully. "I'm Detective Inspector Bowman." Bowman reached instinctively to his inside jacket pocket for his papers, only to realise he had left them in his coat at The King's Head. Suddenly awkward, he endeavoured to turn the movement into an attempt to scratch at an itch. He let his hand fall.

The man frowned. It was clear he was not impressed. "Kreegan," he announced by way of introduction, "James Kreegan." He looked Bowman up and down. "Are you what passes for an inspector?"

From his position on the man's path, Bowman caught his reflection in a mullioned window. It was true he was looking far from his best. His face was flushed with the exertion of his walk and he was alarmed to see his eyes were swollen, his skin clammy and blotched. Ashamed at the man he had become, Bowman cleared his throat.

"You are a military man?" he asked, keen to change the subject.

"Captain in the Grenadiers." Kreegan snapped almost to

attention as he spoke. Bowman could see it took all his effort not to salute.

"Which of these belonged to Sharples?" the inspector repeated, letting his eyes wander up the line of pretty dwellings.

The old man relented. "Number Nine," he announced, "Just next door here. He was only there three months, come from Windsor in the spring."

"But he must have had some connection to Larton to be granted an almshouse?" Bowman mused aloud.

"An estranged brother, he said. Long dead now."

With a strained nod of gratitude, Bowman walked across the grass to the house next door. It was the same exactly to every other house in the terrace. Pushing at the door, the inspector found it locked as expected.

"Is it occupied?"

"Not yet," growled the old man, leaning on his shovel.

"There must be plenty in the village who would be grateful of such a house."

"Ah, but there's not many have given so much for their country."

Bowman turned to see the old soldier's chest was puffed out further still, his chin jutting higher into the air. "Jedediah Sharples served his Queen and country well. It was an honour to have him as a neighbour, if only for a short while."

"Where did he fight?"

"Last saw action at El Teb in the Sudan in Eighty Four." Bowman could swear he saw the old man's eyes grow misty with pride. "Terrible mess, it was. He spent three days alone in the desert, terribly injured. Heatstroke and some disease or other put paid to front line work," he mumbled. "He told me he was never the same again."

Bowman was thoughtful. 'did he suffer all the rest of his life?"

"He did," said Kreegan, sadly.

"Enough to end it?"

The question seemed to hang in the air. The man held Bowman's gaze. "It would seem so." he said. 'sharples spent the intervening years in one dosshouse after another before finally being offered an almshouse."

"Is there no way in?" Bowman gestured to the front door beside him.

"There's a door front and back, just like all the rest."

Bowman sighed. Looking in at the window, he could see a sparsely furnished parlour with one or two pictures on the walls.

"They've not been for his belongings yet." Bowman was surprised to find the old soldier suddenly at his shoulder. For a moment, he looked the inspector up and down, as if considering whether to be of further assistance. "Walk to the end of the terrace," he said at last. "The path leads round to the gardens."

Bowman was not surprised to find the back door locked. He stood in the shade of the back garden. It was bordered with a neat yew hedge to all sides, with gates left and right into the neighbouring gardens. As he glanced to his right, he saw a curtain twitching in the next-door property. Certain he was being watched, Bowman ducked back to the door. Steeling himself to put a shoulder against it, he was startled to see Kreegan standing next to him, a key in his hand.

"We're all getting old in these houses," he explained, "We know one day we'll be found by a neighbour. So each one holds another's key." He held it before him. "Old soldiers always look out for their pals."

With a lean hand, he reached for the lock and opened it with a soft click, pushing the door ajar before him with a wink.

Stepping gingerly inside, Bowman was immediately struck by the smell.

'damp," explained the old man beside him, pointing at the furthest wall. There, Bowman saw a slick of black mould around the contours of the windows. The floor beneath was clearly wet and here and there, covered with a silvery film. Slugs clung to the wall around a hole in the window frame, their slimy trails tracing their paths over the glass. An imposing sideboard was the largest piece of furniture in the room. Too big for so small a house, it rose almost to the ceiling and held a few plates and a cracked glass on a tarnished silver tray. It was stained with some unknown substance that had hardened on the wood. Aside from a threadbare chaise longue and a small stove in the corner, there was little else to see. The bare wooden floor had been exposed by the removal of a carpet, and Bowman saw colonies of beetles and ants creeping between the wooden planks. It was a home of course, and provided shelter of sorts, but it seemed hardly befitting of one who had served his country with such valour.

"That's where I found him." Kreegan had walked on ahead and stood in the middle of the room, nodding down to the floor before the chaise longue. "With his brains blown out."

Bowman's eyes widened in surprise. "*You* found him?"

"I came as soon as I heard the shot. I knew there was something wrong." Bowman was crouching on his haunches, imagining the body before him. "I heard the shot and then the smashing of glass, just as I told the constable." The man's voice had affected a weary tone.

Peering closer at the floor, Bowman noticed a dark stain on the wood. "Then, this is where he lay."

"Blood everywhere," the old soldier confirmed, 'spattered up the wall there, too."

Bowman followed his gaze to the wall opposite. There were indeed flecks of blood on the painted brickwork and the picture rail. The inspector stood and stretched his legs. "You say you heard the sound of smashing glass after the shot?"

Kreegan nodded. "They say it was from when he fell into this." Stepping to one side, the man indicated a wooden case that had been placed on the sideboard. It was fashioned from a dark wood, polished so highly that the grain shone through. The lid was made of glass and Bowman could plainly see that, though still locked, it had been broken. Walking carefully to the sideboard so as not to disturb anything further, Bowman looked inside the box. It was trimmed with a faded, velvet lining and contained a collection of medals, old coins and memorabilia of a life spent in the army. Bowman noticed the old man had recovered a picture from a pile of papers on the shelf and was holding it up before him in the light of the window. It showed a man standing tall in full military uniform, his bayoneted rifle by his side. A set of luxurious moustaches adorned his face and his eyes seemed to burn with a patriotic fervour.

"Trooper Sharples?" Bowman asked as he took the portrait.

"The very same," said Kreegan, quietly. "He was proud of his service and kept a few mementos of his time in the Sudan."

"In here?" Bowman was looking closer at the box. A strange, geometric design was inlaid just below the lock, but had been almost rubbed away with use. Holding the box to the light from the window, he could just make out the shape of an instrument of navigation, somewhat like a compass, carved into the wood. Inside, he noticed a shell casing or two amongst the ephemera.

"Along with his service revolver."

Bowman raised his eyes.

'don't worry, inspector, it was always under lock and key." Kreegan pointed at the lid, still locked in position.

"So, he smashed the glass as he fell?"

"So they say."

"They?"

The soldier shrugged. "It was in the coroner's report," he stammered. "I was called as a witness."

Bowman turned to the window, gnawing at his lower lip. The room felt suddenly very small, the air oppressive.

"So, are we to believe," he began, slowly, "That Trooper Sharples, his mind in a sufficient turmoil to contemplate the taking of his own life, unlocked his box of keepsakes, drew out his revolver, loaded it, then calmly locked the lid again before blowing himself to Kingdom come?"

'seems so," Kreegan shrugged.

"And that," Bowman continued, turning back into the room, "Instead of falling backwards from the momentum of the shot, as the blood-stained wall behind him would suggest, he first fell *forwards* upon the box, breaking the glass as he did so?"

The old soldier was silent.

"Where is the gun now?" Bowman demanded.

"Taken," Kreegan shrugged, "For evidence."

Bowman nodded. Here at last was a mystery. "Who did you call upon when you found the body?"

"Constable Corrigan from the police station in the Rise," the old soldier blinked, struggling to recall the sequence of events, "I called upon the curate at the church, and he sent a boy to the police station. Constable Corrigan came at once." As he turned to face the inspector, he suddenly realised he was alone. Confused, he walked to the window and pulled aside the rag that hung in the place of a curtain. There, striding along the gravel drive that ran past the church and back to the main road, he saw Inspector Bowman, his hands in his pockets and his chin on his chest, clearly deep in thought.

XI

Last Orders

Anthony Graves was struggling. He was used to winning people over but had to admit that, on this occasion at least, he had failed. The King's Head was a riot of noise. There was a queue at the bar at least a half a dozen deep and the air was full of the aromas of tobacco, sweat and beer. It being a Friday, Graves guessed the workers in the fields had been paid and had come to spend their evening divesting themselves of their hard earned wages. Save one old lady who sat alone at a corner table nursing a glass of gin, the clientele was exclusively male. They were all in a competition, it seemed to the young sergeant as he sat by the piano, to be louder and ruder than each other and he could barely hear himself think above the jeering, shouting and cursing that filled the room. The crowd spilled out into the street. Young men brawled in the road, others argued at the tops of their voices. From where he sat, Graves could see one old man urinating up against the pharmacy door on the other side of the street. He rolled his eyes at the prospect of trying to get a decent night's sleep.

"Not going to give us a tune?"

Graves turned to see Maude at his side, collecting glasses and tankards from the tables about him. She was jostled as she spoke and Graves noticed several drinkers feasting their eyes upon her over the brims of their glasses. She nodded to the piano as she added more glasses to her tray.

"I could," Graves smiled, "But I don't think I'd be heard above the din, much less appreciated. Is it always this busy?"

"On a Friday, it is. There's three pubs in Larton, but still you'd think there wasn't enough beer to go round. These men are all from the fields and orchards around the place. The folk from the Village won"t dare set foot in here tonight."

'really?"

Maude bent to pick up some more glasses from the table. "Never the twain shall meet," she winked.

"We don't just come "ere for the beer, dearie!" A man in a battered bowler hat leaned in to squeeze the woman on the hip. Squirming out of his way, Maude delivered a resounding slap to his cheek. A cheer rose up from the surrounding mob, and they each pressed nearer for a better view of proceedings.

"Is that what you come for, Jenks?" Maude retorted, sharply, ""Cos there's plenty more where that came from."

"It's a start, ain"t it, Jenks!" The shout elicited a burst of laughter from the crowd. Jenks was staggering where he stood, more the result of his night on the beer than Maude's expert backhand.

"I'll see you in your dreams," Maude leaned in closer to the man, playfully tweaking at his bulbous nose, "P"raps you'll have better luck with me in your sleep."

Jenks fell back against the table in a parody of a swoon, his arms spread wide in an invitation to the barmaid to join him.

"He's love struck!" came the voice again.

"Worse than that," another added, "He's Maude-struck!" Those in hearing collapsed with laughter and there was much clapping of Jenks" back as he staggered away into the fray. Miraculously, Graves noticed, he had kept a tight hold of his beer throughout, and had not spilled a single drop. Seeing him retreat, Maude turned back to the sergeant with a twinkle in her eye. Leaning in to his ear, she revealed perhaps a bit too much of her ample bosom.

"How's the inspector?" she asked, her voice lowered to a conspiratorial whisper.

Graves' eyes flicked to the front door, suddenly guilty, where an agitated Inspector Bowman stood with his hands deep in his pockets. "Ask him yourself," he said as he rose, "He won"t bite you."

Everyone in the room seemed to follow Graves' gaze to the door. Almost at once, as their eyes settled on the inspector, their conversations ceased. An awkward silence settled on the room. Bowman looked about him, suddenly aware that he was the object of everyone's interest. Glasses and tankards were held part way to the drinkers" mouths as they scrutinised the man before them. Bowman was being sized up. Swallowing hard, he walked towards Graves, painfully aware of every footstep. A hundred pairs of eyes seemed to follow him across the room and Bowman was sure he heard sniggering as he walked. Daring to lift his eyes to the crowd, he was met with disdainful looks and sneers. He could see men nudging each other in sport and nodding in his direction. Several of them swayed from their drink, trying in vain to focus on the spectacle before them. Suddenly, there came a snort of derision and one man dared to speak his mind.

"Oh look," he shouted, "It's the *defective* inspector!"

The room erupted into a roar. Stung by the remark, Bowman stopped in his tracks. Casting his eyes at the approaching Sergeant Graves, he saw his companion shoot a look of reprimand to the young barmaid by his side. Bowman recognised her as the woman who had helped him to his room. So, she had spread the word.

"Been fraternising with the locals, Graves?"

Even the usually cheery sergeant looked downcast. "Hardly," he scoffed, "I've barely been spoken to all night. They're all of them rather backward in coming forward."

"All but one," Bowman replied pointedly, catching the barmaid's eye. As she looked to the ground to avoid his gaze, Bowman felt a pang of guilt. Of course she would talk. In a village such as Larton the appearance of two detectives from Scotland Yard was news enough, let alone the fact that one of them had promptly collapsed into a mania upon arrival.

"Where's yer handcuffs, detective?" leered Jenks from the crowd. "Tie me up with Maude for the night and I'll confess to anything!" There was much laughter at the remark and Bowman saw that even the barmaid in question fought to hide a smile.

'don't take Jenks back to Scotland Yard," called a voice from the bar, "Who would we have to polish our fists on?" Another man found the courage to stagger across the floor. He stood nose to nose with the inspector, his breath hot and beery.

"We don't welcome strangers to Larton," he breathed, "Poking their noses into other peoples" business. Get your arses back behind your desks in London and leave us to our work." His head nodded furiously as if to punctuate his words, and

Bowman felt hot flecks of spittle land on his face as he spoke.

"Alright, Murphy," the barmaid interjected, "Let's leave the gentlemen be, shall we?" Hooking the man by the arm, she steered him back to the bar, throwing a look of apology over her shoulder to Graves as she did so.

"Come to my room, Graves," Bowman said quietly as the crowd about them thinned, "We have much to discuss."

"It is best to trust no one, Sergeant Graves." Bowman was trying hard to contain his temper.

"I realise that now, sir." The young sergeant stood by the door as Bowman paced restlessly about the room. His habitual frown cut all the deeper on his forehead and, once or twice, Graves thought he could see the trembling had returned to the inspector's right hand. "But you seemed happy enough to let her into your confidence when asking for the Cousins' address," he said, boldly.

"You've compromised my authority in the midst of an investigation." Bowman clutched his hands before him in an effort to still the tremor.

"*I* have, sir?"

There was a note in Graves' voice that Bowman did not care for. "The last thing we need, Sergeant Graves, is the whole of Larton turned against us." The inspector felt a muscle spasm beneath his left eye and turned to the window to hide it. His skin felt clammy. Taking a breath to settle his racing heart, he cleared his throat to continue. "We may need to question some of these people with regard to the deaths in the village. We must command respect amongst them or we'll get nowhere. It'll be Smithfield Market all over again."

Graves cast his mind back to their investigation at Smithfield. When one of their number had been found swinging dead from a meat hook, the entire market had closed ranks in a conspiracy of silence. The detectives had needed all their wits to expose the black market in tainted meat and the dead man's wish to expose it. Wits that Graves feared had since deserted his superior.

'did you find anything of use in the woods?" the sergeant asked, gently.

Bowman stood in silence for a while, gathering his thoughts by the window.

"I saw a piece of rope tied to a tree," he sighed, "And Maxwell Trevitt was far from the perfect host. What did you learn from Florrie Cousins?"

Graves drew his notebook from his pocket and flicked through its pages. "It seems Fletcher was in debt. Trevitt is none too reliable when it comes to paying wages. Seems the final straw came when he promised to pay Cousins a wage only if he got the gypsies to work." Graves saw Bowman twitch at the window. "They're refusing to pick the crop unless Trevitt ups their wage."

Graves saw the inspector nodding. "Trevitt mentioned to me that there was bad blood between Cousins and the gypsies in the wood."

"Florrie Cousins remains convinced that Trevitt drove her husband to hang himself," the sergeant continued, "Leaving her with two young children to feed."

"I am struggling to see how Fletcher Cousins' death could be explained as anything other than self-murder."

"Then I'll book our ticket home for tomorrow morning, shall I, sir?"

Bowman turned to see his companion's eyes twinkling, gently. Graves was indeed a clever man, he mused. With one quip, he had disarmed the inspector.

"Not quite, Sergeant Graves," he said with a half-smile.

Bowman walked to retrieve his suitcase from beneath the washstand and hoisted it onto the bed with some effort. Sliding the catches to the left and right, he carefully slid his clothes to one side as if concealing something of import from his companion, before lifting out a bundle of newspapers. Graves recognised them as the copies of The Berkshire Chronicle he had seen at Larton Manor.

Bowman carried them to the chest of drawers between the windows, the better to be read in the light.

"There is a uniting factor to the deaths in Larton, Graves," Bowman said slowly, leaning against the chest for support. "Take a look."

Standing beside him now, Graves peered closer at the reports. "Trooper Sharples," he summarised, "Found with a gunshot wound to the head following discharge from the Royal Horse Guards. Seems it was his own gun." He read on, "A verdict of suicide was entered by the coroner." He slid the newspaper to one side to reveal the next. "Erasmus Finch," he read, leaning in closer, "Thirty five years old, jumped from the tower at All Saints Church." He scanned the text. "A verdict of suicide was returned by the coroner." The sergeant looked up to see Bowman was waiting expectantly at his side.

"The coroner has been a busy man these last few weeks. Wire his office," Bowman commanded of his companion, "And have him meet us at Larton Police Station first thing tomorrow." The inspector stared out the window. There was a drunken altercation in progress in the High Street, much to the delight of a sizable crowd of onlookers. "He and Corrigan might at least be able to spread a little more light on proceedings."

"Corrigan, sir?"

"The constable here at Larton. He investigated Trooper Sharple's death and, I dare say, the others, too. I would be willing to wager that Constable Corrigan *is* the local police force."

Graves nodded. The Metropolitan Police Force had been established as the first professional police force in the world. Its codes and practices had yet to be fully embraced in the shires.

There was a pause as Graves mulled the details of the cases over in his mind. Turning back to the newspapers, he began to scan the details once more.

"There's something else, sir," he volunteered, suddenly. Bowman turned to face him at once. He knew the tone in Graves' voice well enough and had learned over the years to pay good heed to it.

"What is it, sergeant?"

"The dates that each of the bodies were found." Graves was flicking between the pages now, his usually cheery features knotted into an expression of concentration. 'sharples was found on May the Fourteenth."

"He had killed himself just moments before," Bowman

confirmed. Graves shot his superior a questioning look. "I paid a visit to his lodgings on my way back from Trevitt's farm," the inspector explained. "The almshouses by the church. And he'd not been in Larton long."

Graves nodded, then continued. "Erasmus Finch jumped from the tower at All Saints Church a month later, on the Eleventh of June."

Bowman was gnawing at his lower lip. "Exactly four weeks after Sharples," he said, quietly. "That's certainly some coincidence for so random an act."

"Or the beginning of a pattern," said Graves, meaningfully.

Bowman leaned back against the chest of drawers, a hand to his forehead, his chin sunk onto his chest. "And yet Fletcher Cousins hanged himself on this Tuesday past, the Fifth of July."

"Both of the other deaths occurred on the same day of the week, sir." Graves stabbed at the newspapers with a finger. "If there is a pattern, then Cousins isn"t a part of it. And let's hope it isn"t repeated."

"Why?"

Graves held up the front pages by way of illustration. "Each of the previous two men died on the second Saturday of the month."

Bowman fought to clear his head. He would never have wished it known to his companion, but much of his recent life had been a blur. Days had merged, and sometimes weeks. At last, pitifully, he gave in.

"What is the day, Graves?"

"It's Friday, sir." Bowman looked none the wiser. "If this pattern is to be repeated," Graves clarified for the inspector's benefit, "There might well be another Larton man found dead tomorrow, the second Saturday of July."

The two men's eyes widened almost together.

"The regatta," they said, as one.

XII

Night And Day

The pillow felt like stone beneath his head. Bowman lay on his bed, the sheets twisted about him damp with sweat. He had faced a difficult choice; keep the windows open and be kept awake by the mayhem in the streets below, or keep them shut and suffer the inordinate heat. He had elected for the latter. With the windows shut against any movement in the air, the room had become even more uncomfortable. At least the light was fading. Creeping from his bed to the washstand by the door, he lit the lamp that stood there. Shaking the flame from the match, he poured a little water from the jug into the cracked china bowl. Hoping to feel refreshed as he splashed it onto his face, he was disappointed to find that even the water was warm. He looked up into the small mirror that hung above the table, his mind transported to another, sparse cell he had once occupied. Then, the air had been biting cold. The memory formed, sharp and clear. It surprised him with its intensity. He could smell the carbolic in the air.

Bowman dried his face on the hard towel that hung from the washstand and stood before the mirror. His limbs looked scrawny and weak, his shoulders sloped. There was a definite bow to his back. His eyes flicked to his suitcase. Bowman knew that deliverance lay within. He knew a temporary yet sweet oblivion could be his if he chose. He gazed back up at the mirror, willing her to appear.

Even in death, she had once been so tangible. He had feared her appearances at first but, as they had dwindled, he had missed them. His latest vision had panicked him. How could he not remember her face? He had held it a thousand times, fixed it in his gaze. Now he could not recall so much as the slope of her nose or the dimple in her cheek. How was it, he railed, that he could remember the grinning loon in the asylum, yet not remember her? Burying his face in his hands, Bowman tried to stifle a heavy sob, his shoulders heaving at the effort. Rubbing at his eyes, he stared again into the mirror. Tears streaked his sallow cheeks. He felt numb. He couldn't even bring himself to feel pity for the man in the glass. He felt nothing. Without her, he *was* nothing. He was a hollow man.

Turning almost mechanically to the bed, he bent to lift his suitcase onto the chest of drawers. Slowly, deliberately, he slid the catches and opened the case. Moving the bundle of shirts to one side, he reached for his comfort. He found it, as he knew he would, in the smooth, rounded glass of the bottle. He found it in the golden glow of the candle through the liquid as he held it up to the light. He found it in the blessed release it promised.

Prescott felt light as air. As he tripped through the empty streets back to Larton Manor, he reflected on how his life might change. No longer for him the drudgery of servitude. In time, he would rise. For now, though, he must hold his thoughts and bide his time. Circumspection must be his watchword. He could do nothing to impugn the Brotherhood. Turning into the drive to the manor and keen to avoid the gatehouse, Prescott sloped round by the large leathery magnolia that sat brooding by the perimeter wall and ducked beneath the drooping branches of an ancient plane tree. From there, he could see a light still burning in the stable block. Cursing that the groom should still be awake, he climbed a lower part of the wall and jumped into the manor grounds. In no fear of discovery, he walked across the lawn to the stables. The groundskeeper's dogs were left to roam at night, but he knew that if they scented him, they knew him well enough to leave him be.

Just as Prescott reached the squat, red brick building that housed the stables, he saw a door open onto the yard. Pressing himself up against the wall, he watched as Nokes the gardener strode purposefully from the building. He looked once or twice around him to check that he had not been observed before turning off the main path to the cottage provided for him in the grounds. Waiting a moment to be certain he had gone, Prescott walked carefully on.

Pushing at the door, he slipped into the stables. The stable boys were in their bunks, fully clothed as usual. Prescott knew they'd be up a full two hours earlier than him and so was surprised to see them playing jacks by the light of the moon on an old pallet placed between them.

"Boys," he called from the end of the stalls, "Did you see Nokes come in here?"

"No," replied one of the lads sleepily. "I was too busy beating Adlam." His opponent punched him playfully in the shoulder, but still there was sufficient force to send the boy reeling back from his bunk into a pile of hay. The commotion disturbed the horses in the stalls nearest to them, with one particularly handsome gelding neighing and shaking his head with the surprise.

"Alright, Chester," moaned Adlam. "Keep yer fists to yerself."

Prescott smiled to himself and reached out to stroke Magnus, his favourite of his master's horses. Standing seventeen hands to his withers, he had a pleasant disposition, without so much as a hint of the contrary about him. The driver looked around him, deep in thought. What had Nokes been up to? Magnus was nuzzling his hand. "Don't be late now boys," Prescott said at last, wiping his fingers on his shirt tails. "I don't want you keeping me up with your brawls."

The lads nodded their assent as they settled back to their game, with Adlam attempting a smart salute at Prescott's retreating back.

He could hear the sound already as he climbed the stairs to the loft above. The one reason he resented sharing quarters with the groom, was that he snored something dreadful. As he alighted the last step into the loft, the throaty, fleshy sound of Cooper's snore became louder still.

A single lamp burned on the table by the window, surrounded by the detritus of an evening meal and several empty beer bottles. The room was large enough for the two of them but had no dividing walls. Consequently, privacy was at a premium. Sheets and blankets had been slung up between various areas of the room, most notably between the two beds in the corner. They were comfortable enough but, with nothing more than a length of material hanging between them, very little was sacred.

Prescott leaned against the wall to kick off his boots, refraining from throwing one of them at Cooper to rouse him from his sleep. Instead, he swore beneath his breath as he stripped to his underclothes in preparation for bed. He was due to help with preparations for the next day's regatta, so wished to be up early to complete his errands first. With the walls rattling with Cooper's snoring, a good night's sleep seemed an impossible prospect. Just as Prescott bent to extinguish the lamp on the table, he noticed an envelope propped up against it. The design on the front caused Prescott to catch his breath. It was a geometric design, familiar from his recent studies and the ceremony in which he'd just played a leading role. A square and compass with a sheaf of corn between them.

His heart racing in his chest, Prescott grabbed both the envelope and lamp and crept across the room to the farthest wall, thankful he had not sought to rouse Cooper after all. Lowering himself quietly on the sill to the window, Prescott opened the envelope with care. Nokes must have left the missive without waking Cooper. He was at once concerned that a man could enter his quarters at night with such ease, but then reasoned that the estate's gardener would hardly arouse suspicion if spotted. Prescott took gulps of air to steady his nerves. Reaching inside the envelope, his fingers closed around a single piece of stiff card. As he pulled it into the light, he narrowed his eyes to read the instructions printed there. The words digested, Prescott replaced the card in its envelope and carried it back to the table with the lamp, careful not to disturb the snoring groom. Holding the envelope to the flame, he watched it catch light before dropping it gently onto a plate to gutter and fade. Soon, all that was left was a pile of ash, ready to be discarded with the last of Cooper's dinner. Prescott nodded to himself, slowly. If this was to be his first test, he must not be found wanting.

For the second time in a week, Sergeant Graves had found a locked door between himself and his superior. After knocking furiously for several minutes, he had admitted defeat and gone in search of Maude to enlist her help. Seduced at once by the look of concern on the sergeant's face, Maude had acquiesced, accompanying him back upstairs with a spare key to Bowman's room.

"Sir!" Graves called as Maude turned the key in the lock. "Sir, it's Graves!" Gaining entry at last, he stepped carefully inside, unsure of what he might find. The room was still in darkness, the curtains drawn. The air was ripe with the unmistakable tang of alcohol and sweat. Walking to the window, he pulled open the curtains and opened the casement to let in some air. Looking about him, he saw the room was in disarray. The newspapers he had read the night before were scattered about the floor along with several shirts and effects from Bowman's suitcase. An empty bottle with no label lay on the hearth by the fireplace. Graves winced as he held it up to smell what dregs were left in the bottom. Madeira. Turning slowly from the hearth, he looked in sadness at the crumpled form lying sprawled on the bed. Bowman lay in a twist of wet sheets, his head buried beneath a pillow. Casting a warning glance at Maude standing wide eyed by the door, Graves advanced to shake the inspector carefully by the shoulder.

"Sir?" he soothed, trying to keep his voice steady.

He was answered with a low, guttural grunt and Bowman tried to swing a heavy leg from the bed.

"Sir, it's Graves." The young sergeant's face was creased with concern. "We're due at the police station."

Bowman struggled to sit up. Throwing the pillow to the floor, he grabbed at Graves' arm for support. He rubbed at his aching eyes as he struggled to focus on his companion. His head was pounding, his mouth so dry he could barely speak.

"Police station?" he rasped.

"Maude," Graves turned, suddenly galvanised. "Get some hot water in that jug, will you? And not a word of this to anyone, do you understand?"

Maude nodded, darting to the washstand to collect the jug. Before she left the room she paused in the doorway, seemingly unable to tear her eyes from the wretched figure on the bed.

"Don't worry," Graves soothed. "He'll be alright." The inspector was staring about him, as if trying to get his bearings.

Maude smiled weakly then closed the door behind her with a soft click.

"Come on, sir, we need to get you up."

Bowman grunted again as Graves swung his legs from the bed.

"Maude has gone for hot water. You must get dressed and ready." Reaching down, Graves grabbed Bowman by the hands and pulled him upright. He swayed for a moment where he stood, blinking furiously as if to clear an image from his eyes. With that, he broke free of the sergeant's grasp, ran for the chipped ceramic bowl on the washstand and relieved his stomach of the burden of drink he had consumed the night before.

Graves sat at a table, staring idly through the window to the street beyond. He had watched as the shopkeepers had arrived to unlock their stores, sluice their doorways with water and pull down their awnings. A man with a cart had swept the road with something approaching a mild enthusiasm, leaning on his broom to stand and stare whenever the fancy took him. The chemist stood at his door, arms crossed, a pipe clamped between his teeth. Next door, a baker carried baskets of freshly baked bread to display in his window, eager for a good day's revenue for the results of his early morning labours. A young lad in a butcher's apron and jaunty hat sauntered past with a barrow. It groaned under the weight of several cuts of meat, each wrapped in paper and tied with string. Every now and then, a wheel would snag in a rut on the road and the boy would put his weight to the handle to shift it. For all the bustle of activity in the street outside, Graves was puzzled to see that no one man turned to acknowledge another. Rather, they regarded one another with suspicious eyes and sideways glances.

Alerted to his approach by a creek on the stair, Graves turned to see Inspector Bowman standing by the bannister, his eyes cast down to the floor. He looked for all the world, thought Graves, like a penitent child. His hands ran restlessly up and down his sides, and he could barely find the strength to meet the sergeant's gaze. Freshly shaved, an unsteady grip on the razor had left him with several cuts and nicks to the skin, most noticeably on his neck where specks of blood were apparent upon his collar. His hair had been wetted with a comb to lay flat upon his head, his moustache trimmed and tamed with a little wax. He was trying to present as normal a countenance to the world as possible. The tragedy was, Graves noted, that he was quite plainly failing in that intent.

"I am sorry, Graves," Bowman whispered.

Graves nodded, gesturing that the inspector should join him at his table. Bowman cut a brittle figure as he shuffled across the room, his shoes scuffing on the floor. Every movement seemed to require a Herculean effort. Sliding a chair from beneath the table, Bowman grit his teeth against the noise as its legs rasped along the wooden floor. If the situation was not so dire and the effect upon Bowman's reputation so damaging, Graves had no doubt he would have found the whole situation most comical. As it was, he sat with his arms folded across his chest, a look of stern disapproval playing upon his usually cheery face.

"I am at a loss, sir," he said as Bowman settled into his chair.

"I know."

"You have placed me in a most invidious position."

Bowman nodded painfully. "You must do what you must," he said. An uneasy silence passed between them. Bowman winced in irritation as a fly banged lazily against the window.

"I do not believe it is for me to do anything," Graves said at last. "It is for you to act."

Bowman winced. That seemed unfair. "What would you have me do?" His voice rose as he spoke, and Graves noticed a vein standing out upon his forehead. "Scuttle back to Scotland Yard in abject failure?" He looked sheepishly about him, suddenly aware they might be overheard. "Confess to the commissioner that the case was beyond me?" Bowman looked around for signs that anyone was listening.

"I do not think the case is beyond you," Graves said, pointedly. "Not when you have your wits about you."

Bowman thought long and hard. "I am sorry, Graves," he conceded at last. "I shall endeavour to comport myself in a more seemly fashion." It was clear from the sergeant's expression that he was doubtful. "What more can I do?" Bowman spread his arms wide.

"Suit the action to the word, sir," Graves said. "We owe it to Fletcher Cousins and the others." He let the words sink in before clapping the inspector on the shoulder. It seemed there was a chasm of silence between them. When Bowman spoke at last, it was with such a low whisper that Graves could barely hear him.

"Do you know when I killed my wife?"

Graves sat forwards, staring into Bowman's troubled eyes. "Of course, sir," he began, carefully. "I was there."

"No," Bowman interrupted, shaking his head. "Not in Hanbury Street. I killed my wife the moment I became a detective." He met the sergeant's gaze.

"I don't understand." Graves whispered, puzzled.

"If I had not joined the Metropolitan Police, I should never have been on Hanbury Street that day."

Sensing his distress, Graves attempted to calm his companion. "She might still have volunteered at the Women's Refuge," he soothed. "She might still have been there."

The inspector was grateful for the gesture, but even he could see his sergeant's heart wasn't it.

"Yes, Graves," Bowman lowered his eyes to the table as he explained. "But I would not have fired that shot."

Graves was speechless.

"That one single moment, my joining the Yard, led to her death at my hands." He looked up again, pleading. "What man could live with that?"

XIII

Confrontations

Lord Melville was in his element. As he marshalled the estate workers across the causeway from Larton Manor, he set his granite face to the low morning sun and leaned on his cane for support. His straw boater felt tighter than last year and he feared he could not bear to wear it all day, but he was pleased that he had, at least, managed to squeeze into his white cotton trousers. He had worn his favourite striped braces more for effect than for any practical purpose, matching, as they did, the necktie he had knotted around his collar. Pleased with the morning's work so far, he gazed across the road to the open land that stretched down to the river. Already he could see the division in progress. Those from the Rise kept themselves to the left of the field as it sloped down to the Thames, those from the Village busied themselves on the right. Occasional glances were thrown between them and even the odd shout but, aside from that, no communication was entered into. After lunch, they would be joined by the residents of the Dean, certain that the day's proceedings were solely for their benefit. A line of marquees had sprung up along the riverbank, and Lord Melville guided his men towards them with their trestle tables. Finally came the estate skiff. Sleek, smooth and polished to a shine, it took six men to carry it. With the tributary from the boathouse so depleted of water, Melville had made the decision to have Marigold carried across the grounds to the river, her oars laid carefully along the length of her hull. All being well, this year would mark the third in succession that the Larton Estate had won the race. From his vantage point on the causeway, he could see several carts and drays unloading their wares. Workers and stallholders milled about, sizing up the competition and adjusting their prices accordingly. The horses that were not employed to drag or carry stood munching lazily at the grass. Seeing the last of the stragglers across the road, Melville followed his boat to the riverside, acknowledging with pride the appreciative looks of the villagers. Melville was used to the doffing of caps and expected deference. He was rarely disappointed. Conversations ceased as he passed by and those involved would tug at their forelocks in greeting.

"Good morning, Lord Melville," offered a smart young man in starched collar and tie. "I see Marigold's back for more."

Melville nodded, graciously. "And I will be back for more of your excellent beer, Mr Cribbins."

Cribbins bent to lift a large keg from a nearby dray to his trestle table. It joined a line of others, all lying on their sides and waiting to be drained by appreciative customers. "I'll be sure to save your favourite draft," he replied, obsequiously.

Melville nodded condescendingly and moved on, twirling his cane in his hand as he walked.

"Here, Lord Melville?"

Melville looked up to see his men standing by the river. A line of little craft had been laid on the bank, each tilted on the grass at an ungainly angle.

"Set her down at the end of the row," he commanded, striding towards them in his eagerness to view the competition. He was pleased to see it was no competition at all. Five other boats had been arranged by the water's edge, some in a better state of repair than others. Melville allowed himself a smile as he appraised his rivals with an expert eye. Many had broken or missing rowlocks. One displayed small nail holes where the trim had come away. He was certain two of them would sink.

Satisfied that he was certain of victory yet again, Melville turned to see Maxwell Trevitt shouldering a large basket to a rickety table.

"So you've got the cherries in?" he asked as Trevitt placed the basket before him.

"Such as I can, Lord Melville," he seethed. "I was up at the crack of dawn with just the wife for company. We picked as many as we could. Another day and they'll go over."

Melville leaned in on his cane. He could tell Trevitt was maintaining his demeanour with some considerable effort. "Have you still not resolved your differences?"

"They will not budge," Trevitt seethed, puffing out his great barrel chest in indignation. "And I will not pay a penny more for their services." He looked around him, careful not to be overheard. "Reckon they've got it coming to them, anyhow."

Melville raised his eyebrows. "The gypsies?"

"Had Scotland Yard at my door last night," the farmer continued, his voice low. "I reckon he's onto them."

"With regard to what?"

"Cousins' death. I told the inspector there was bad blood between 'em. And how everyone in Larton knows you can't trust 'em. Reckon he swallowed it good and proper."

Melville's face was a mask, inscrutable. "Has he found any evidence to implicate them?"

Trevitt's eyes opened wide. "Who cares for evidence?" he scoffed. "There's not a man in Larton who wouldn't be happy to see the gypsies gone and Jared Stoker hanged." He cleared his throat noisily and spat onto the grass. "Beggin' your pardon," he added.

"Then who would pick your cherries, Maxwell Trevitt?"

"We're too late for this year, anyhow," Trevitt ran a chubby hand across his face then gestured to the meagre baskets before him. "I shall make do and mend for now." He cast his eyes around the field. He knew that, in order to survive, he would have to repair his reputation in the village. With the gypsies gone, he would need a new workforce. He would, in short, have to swallow his pride.

"Well," sighed Melville, "Larton is not known for its neighbourliness. I wish you well in your recruiting." Melville was sincere in his wish. If Trevitt could not send his harvest to market, then he would struggle to pay his rent to Larton Manor. Melville had big plans for the grounds this year and could not countenance a drop in revenue.

Trevitt dipped his head in a pretence of deference, before turning his attention to retrieving another basket from his hand cart.

All around, the preparations were in full swing. A great marquee was raised in position at the centre of the field, its canvas sides swinging gently in the warm morning breeze. The moment it was secured, a motley collection of villagers arrived, each with a chair and a case. In unison, they snapped them open to reveal a variety of musical instruments. An elderly man in a jaunty cravat cleaned his battered trombone with pride as the strains of a violin rose into the air. To the east side of the field, a line of shies and stands was marked out with string and wooden posts. Here, there would be games for the children. A small man swamped in a pair of dungarees was preparing the ground for hooplah and skittles. Lord Melville recognised him as the blacksmith and sauntered over to speak with him, his cane sweeping aside drifts of freshly cut grass as he walked. As he opened his mouth to congratulate the smith on his expert shoeing of one of his favourite horses, there came a shout from near the road.

The smith looked up from where he was engaged knocking a post into the ground and swore beneath his breath.

"They've got a nerve," he rumbled.

As Melville raised his eyes to the road he saw a ragtag gang of dissolutes enter the field. The effect was immediate. If the villagers had so far been keen to indicate their divisions from each other, now they came together as one. It seemed, despite their differences, that the people of Larton could agree upon one thing; their antipathy toward the travellers. Tools were dropped in unison and chores were abandoned unfinished. Stalls were left unmanned and carts unloaded as, almost to a man, the villagers moved to confront the gang, Maxwell Trevitt at their head. Rolling up his shirtsleeves as he walked, he thrust his great fleshy chin before him in readiness for a fight.

There were perhaps twenty of them, each of them walking at speed towards the river. Jared and Ida Stoker led them onto the field, marching in time to the sound of a squeezebox. They appeared to not have a care in the world, which irritated the villagers all the more and, in particular, Trevitt.

"There's nothing here for you, Stoker," the farmer hissed, his broken nose flushing with anger. "Get your filthy camp packed away and be gone."

"There's no man here can stop us," Stoker replied, his hands on his hips. His long hair lay over his shoulders.

"Nor no woman, neither," added Ida looking round. "Though

from the sight of them they'd put up a better fight."

The travellers behind her laughed.

"That one's wearing my scarf!" A young woman with a basket of flowers had stepped from the crowd to point at one of the men. "I hung that out only last week and it disappeared. I'd know it anywhere."

"Don't be daft," the man replied, fingering the scrap of bright material tied around his neck, "I've had the thing for years."

"I had tools taken from my forge these last few days," piped up the smith. "Reckon I know where they've gone, too."

"Same place as my stirrups!" called another. "They were cut from my horse in broad daylight."

"Happen we'd find them all up in Chalk Wood!"

"You're nothing but thieves and vagabonds," Trevitt spat. "And no doubt murderers, too."

The man with the missing stirrups raised his fists. "Get yourselves gone if you value your lives!" The shout was taken up by the other villagers. Those with tools still in their hands waved them in the air. "You'll find no welcome in Larton."

Jared Stoker chewed at a liquorice root he had taken from his pocket. "Happy enough for us to pick your cherries for a pittance, ain't you?" he leered. "Not so keen on us when we make our own terms."

"What time's the races?" asked Ida, airily. "Reckon we might put in a boat of our own." She nodded to a knot of trees by the river. "We could soon hollow out a trunk between us."

Trevitt took a step forward, burying a hairy fist in the palm of his hand by way of a warning. "We know what you did to Cousins and we'll see you swing for it."

There were more jeers from the crowd and several of the men spat upon the ground in anger. "If hanging was good enough for Cousins," called one to shouts of agreement, "it'll be good enough for you!"

"His wife blames you, Trevitt. So says William Oats." Stoker stripped a piece of the root with his teeth, sucking on its stringy flesh as he spoke. "P'raps Scotland Yard should ask you a question or two."

"My conscience is clear," rasped Trevitt. "I've got nought to hide."

Stoker raised his eyebrows at the remark. "I think you've got more to hide than many of us, Maxwell Trevitt."

Trevitt shifted uncomfortably where he stood, his fists momentarily dropping an inch.

"Gentlemen, please," Lord Melville intervened, his cane swinging before him. "Cannot the whole village come together for one day?" He turned to Stoker. "If you are here to help, you'll find employment enough. If not, there's no law to prevent you staying." He heard Trevitt harrumph behind him. "And we will not take the law into our own hands, will we, Mr Trevitt?"

It took a supreme effort of will for Maxwell Trevitt to give ground. Throwing up his hands in disgust at the turn of events, he backed away into the throng, muttering dark oaths beneath his breath. Slowly, the crowd dissipated and returned to their preparations for the regatta, many of them looking over their shoulders at the travellers in their midst.

As Ida Stoker threw her arms around her husband and kissed his cheek in delight, she noticed he was more guarded in his victory. "Small victories, my love," he breathed. "But we've yet to win the war."

The police station stood back from the road a little way from Larton Station. There was nothing particularly notable about the building with its soulless square windows and an unexceptional wooden door, save that it was clear from its diminutive size that the Larton Constabulary was a small force indeed. With a settled population of less than two thousand individuals, an allowance of just two officers had been granted to police the streets and keep the fragile peace between neighbours.

Constable Corrigan enjoyed his job to a point, but felt the challenge of dealing with the people of Larton and their many travails were second to the challenges of dealing with his sergeant, Aloysius Blunt. Blunt was a man in his sixties who had fallen into the service as a result of being the only man to apply for the position. He cared not a jot for policing, but rather treated his place in the Force as an excuse to do as little work as possible. And so it fell to Constable Corrigan to pound the streets in all weathers whilst Blunt manned the desk at the station. With few visitors, the sergeant would often abandon his post altogether, only to be found drinking in The King's Head or fishing off the bridge into the River Thames.

Never one to upset the applecart, Corrigan simply pocketed his one pound, three shillings and eleven pence every week and awaited the day when he might fill Blunt's boots himself and enjoy a life of similar ease. Judging from Blunt's wheezing chest and sweaty brow, that day might come at any time.

"I hope you are enjoying your sojourn to Larton, Inspector Bowman? You have certainly brought the weather with you."

Bowman regarded the man before him. Greville Whitlock had introduced himself as the coroner to Larton and the surrounding villages. Holding out a fleshy, slightly damp hand, he had gazed at Bowman through a pair of steel wire spectacles. He had an immense expanse of a bald head which reflected the light sufficient to make Bowman blink against the glare. Nests of wiry, white hair nestled above the man's ears and even, the inspector couldn't help but notice, in them. A luxuriant white moustache adorned his upper lip.

"I am not here to take the country air, Mr Whitlock," Bowman asserted, "but to investigate the death of Fletcher Cousins."

The coroner nodded, seriously. "But, of course. There is much gossip in the village, but I believe my findings are robust." As he spoke, Whitlock moved behind the desk that stood in the middle of the room. Aside from this, there was little other furniture. With himself, Graves, Whitlock and Constable Corrigan squeezed into the small office, Bowman noted wryly that there wasn't even enough chairs for them all. He pressed his fingers to his temples.

"Please, inspector," offered Whitlock with a kindly smile. "Won't you sit?"

"You believe Cousins committed suicide?" replied Bowman, ignoring him. He noticed there was no trace of the local accent to his voice.

"Indeed," replied Whitlock simply, lowering himself into the chair behind the desk. "And that is what I shall say in my report." Constable Corrigan stood by the window, his hands behind his back. He was in full constabulary uniform save his hat that he had hung on the stand by the door.

"Just what is the constabulary's position here?"

Corrigan turned into the room and sighed. He gave every indication of rather being anywhere else. "It fell to me to alert the coroner to Cousins' death and arrange for any evidence to be collected and witnesses to be questioned." Bowman noticed that the ever-dependable Graves was scratching at his notebook.

"Were there any witnesses?"

Corrigan shifted uncomfortably on his feet. "Not to the actual act, inspector, no."

"Any evidence?"

"Not beyond the rope, itself," Corrigan smirked.

Bowman's moustache twitched irritably on his upper lip. "I assume you spoke to Mrs Cousins, as my sergeant did?" Bowman gestured to Graves beside him.

There was a pause. "I did not see the need."

"And I understand he has a son." Bowman looked to his companion.

"Tom," Graves confirmed.

"Yes, Tom." Bowman turned to Corrigan again. "Was he questioned as part of your investigations?"

Corrigan nodded. He could see the way the interview was going. "He's slippery as a fish," he offered. "Can't say I've had the chance to catch him yet."

Bowman's temples were beginning to throb. He was aware of a film of cold sweat upon his forehead. "Constable Corrigan," he persisted, 'do you concur then with the coroner's findings?"

Corrigan nodded, simply. "Leaving aside the village gossips, inspector, I do. Yes."

Bowman wiped the sweat from his forehead with a sleeve. Noticing the gesture, Whitlock stood to implore the inspector to sit once more. Refusing the invitation again, Bowman turned to lean nonchalantly against the wall.

"I understand the finger of suspicion points to the gypsies in Chalk Wood." He was grateful to feel the cool of the brick through his clothes.

Greville Whitlock smiled sweetly as one may smile at a child, his double chin wobbling over his collar as he spoke. "It is my experience, inspector, that any number of ills may be laid at the gypsies' door. I dare say," he chuckled, "that if they were indeed guilty of all that was alleged of them, they would have little time for anything else." He shared a look with Constable Corrigan, who was at least kind enough to return the coroner's smile.

Sergeant Graves was flipping through the pages of his notebook. "Mrs Cousins told me her husband was deep in debt."

"That's right," Corrigan concurred. "Maxwell Trevitt is known as a hard taskmaster and seldom pays on time." Graves was at his notebook again, scratching at its pages with the stub of a pencil. "As a consequence, Cousins had borrowed money where he could not pay it back and even gambled at the Windsor races." Corrigan looked directly at Bowman in conclusion. "All common knowledge amongst the people of Larton."

"You see, inspector?" Whitlock offered, benignly. "A little local knowledge is worth many hours of interrogation."

Graves was nodding to his superior, gesturing to his notebook with his pencil. "All this squares with Mrs Cousins' statements, sir."

Whitlock's eyes were twinkling behind his glasses. "So it has taken two detectives come from Scotland Yard to confirm what we already knew!"

"Then what finally drove him to take his own life, constable?" Bowman asked with a forced politeness. "In your opinion?"

"Cousins was a proud man," Corrigan began, resting his weight upon the windowsill. "He left the gypsy life when he fell for Florrie Smallpiece here in Larton. It's worse than a crime for a man to marry outside the gypsy circle, inspector, almost a sin. Yet Cousins met a woman whom he wished to take as his wife. He left the gypsy life to marry her."

"When was this?" Sergeant Graves asked, his pencil poised.

"Their boy must be twelve or so," Corrigan puffed out his cheeks. "He was born the year after."

"Hence the bad blood between Cousins and the gypsies that Trevitt mentioned." Bowman's frown cut deep into his forehead.

The constable continued. "When Trevitt chose Cousins as his

go-between, he must have thought it a good idea. Like turning poacher to gamekeeper."

"In fact," Bowman said thoughtfully, "it put untold pressure upon him."

"And we know what can happen to a man under pressure," insinuated Greville Whitlock from behind the desk. "Don't we, inspector?"

The remark hit Bowman off guard. Swallowing hard, he scrutinised the coroner's face but saw nothing beyond a beatific smile. Perhaps the comment had been made in all innocence.

"I'm afraid Mr Cousins relieved the pressure with alcohol."

"What did the post mortem reveal?" The inspector recovered himself. "Anything beyond the signs of his drinking?"

The silence in the room was palpable. After sharing a glance with Corrigan, Greville Whitlock was bold enough to break it.

"Out here, inspector," he began with a weary note to his voice, "we are not blessed with the resources at your disposal."

"There was no post mortem?" Bowman's eyes were wide with disbelief.

Corrigan cleared his throat. "I did not think it necessary."

Bowman was taken aback at the remark. "You, Constable Corrigan?"

"As the coroner's officer here in Larton, I have the power to rule out the need for medical evidence in cases of accident and suicide." Corrigan was looking pleased with himself. "The local parish must bear the costs of all such investigations. It falls to me to weigh the need against the public purse. I did not think there was value in it."

"The misuse of alcohol is common enough, is it not, inspector?" Whitlock was smiling again. "I'm afraid I see it often enough to recognise it anywhere." Bowman looked to his feet, unable to hold the coroner's gaze. "In short," Whitlock continued, "I am satisfied that Fletcher Cousins took his own life."

Bowman had to acknowledge that all he had to suggest otherwise was Lord Melville's disquiet.

Clearly believing the conversation over, Whitlock rose from his chair and clapped his hands together. "I am glad to have been of service," he beamed, pulling at his waistcoat.

"There is, however," interjected Bowman with a glance to Graves, "the matter of the other deaths."

Whitlock was struggling to maintain his genial demeanour. "Other deaths?" he asked, slowing his step as he made for the door. "Inspector Bowman, I have been coroner here for a little over three years. I am afraid you will have to be a little more specific."

Bowman nodded to his sergeant that he should continue.

"Those of Trooper Sharples of Larton Dean," Graves said, flipping through the pages of his notebook, "and Erasmus Finch of Larton Village."

Whitlock drew his face up in an approximation of a smile. "What of them, sergeant?"

"You recorded them both as suicide."

"Indeed I did," Whitlock nodded, causing his jowls to wobble almost comically. "One, as I recall, from a bullet wound, the other from falling."

Bowman walked to the other side of the desk and planted his fists upon it for support, leaning his whole weight upon them. In truth, he was feeling most unsteady on his feet. Still, he thought, he must not sit. "You boast, Mr Whitlock, of your three years as a coroner - "

"A little over, in fact," Whitlock interrupted, twinkling. "It is important to be precise."

"Quite so," Bowman demurred. "And in your little-over-three-years in post, have you ever known three men from the same village take their lives in such close proximity to each other?" The inspector raised his eyebrows. "Both in time and geography?"

Whitlock crossed his arms across his plump chest. "In time, certainly," he sighed. "In geography, why not? Life here is hard, inspector," he continued, a pained expression upon his face. "You and I are learned men of the world. We might consider ourselves fortunate. We may enjoy the comforts afforded us by the Empire's beneficence." He cast a glance at Corrigan. "Larton is full of simple souls who are denied their share." Bowman thought he caught a look of irritation in the constable's face. "The Empire, I'm afraid, barely stretches to the shires. If you lived among these people, Inspector Bowman, I do not think you would find it at all unusual that there might be some in Larton for whom life is intolerable." There was that look again. "After all, we all have our troubles, do we not, inspector?"

Bowman turned to his sergeant with a meaningful look. It was clear that Maude, having witnessed the inspector's start to the day, had been free with her opinions again. Word spread fast in so small a place. Reasoning that attack was the best form of defence, he rounded on the constable.

"Constable Corrigan," he hissed. "Would you say that, in each of these three cases, your investigations have been thorough, complete and exhaustive?"

Corrigan stood square on to the inspector. "As much as our resources allow, yes."

The corners of Bowman's mouth twitched. "That is some caveat, constable."

Corrigan took a breath, clearly growing weary of the conversation and not ashamed to show it. "We are somewhat overlooked in Larton. We are simply not allocated the men you are used to at Scotland Yard."

Bowman could not help but rise to the bait. "One man may be equal to ten Scotland Yarders," he spat, his voice rising in volume. "If only he asks the right questions."

"Are you suggesting, Inspector Bowman," Whitlock asked in all innocence, "That my verdicts in these cases are unsafe?" He looked almost hurt by the insinuation. "Sharples was a troubled man. He had lived through much." Whitlock blinked at the inspector, the lenses of his spectacles catching the light from the small window.

Bowman turned to the diminutive coroner. "I had the fortune to talk to Captain Kreegan who also lives in the almshouses by the church in Larton Dean."

"Sharples' neighbour," said Corrigan, nonplussed. "What of him?"

"He was rather forthcoming with the details of the day he found Trooper Sharples." Bowman had folded his arms across his chest, smoothing his moustache absently as he spoke.

"As he was to me during my investigation of the case." Corrigan was sounding exasperated.

"If you'll forgive me, inspector," Whitlock interjected. "You do not seem to be drawing towards any particular point."

"Enlighten me, Constable Corrigan," Bowman ploughed on, ignoring the coroner's plea. "How did you arrive at the conclusion that Sharples took his own life when, upon hearing the exact same evidence from Captain Kreegan, it was clear to me that he must have been murdered?"

Even Sergeant Graves was surprised at the announcement. He rested his pencil carefully upon his notebook and closed the pages around it.

Whitlock sought to break the moment. Walking back around the desk, he took his seat again, leaning back and making steeples with his fingers as he spoke.

"Do go on, inspector. I am certain we could all benefit from your wisdom."

Bowman swallowed. The small breakfast Graves had insisted he eat at The King's Head was lying heavy upon his stomach. "Kreegan told me how he heard a shot from Sharple's house before the sound of breaking glass."

"Quite so," agreed Whitlock with a measured tone. "It seems he broke the glass of a small box as he fell against it. He used it for the safe keeping of certain mementos from his army years, his service revolver included."

"Ah yes, his service revolver," Bowman exclaimed. "The very gun you say he used to end his life."

"We do not just say it, inspector," Whitlock smiled. "All the evidence points to it."

Bowman nodded. "Where is the gun now?"

Whitlock shifted his weight, causing the chair to creak beneath him. "It has been returned to the Royal Horse Guards in Windsor. It is government property after all. I am sure it will see service again."

"So quick?" Bowman raised his eyebrows.

"I saw no reason to keep it."

"I assume that tests were run before its requisitioning? To see if the bullet that did away with Sharples may have been fired from its chamber?"

"There was no need," Corrigan interrupted. "It's as clear as day he was killed by a bullet from his own gun, loosed by his own finger upon the trigger."

"There was no sign of forced entry, inspector," Whitlock offered. "No sign of burglary. In short, no reason why foul play should be suspected."

Bowman slipped his hands into his pockets as he thought. "And yet the case was locked."

Corrigan shrugged. "What of it?"

The inspector rounded upon him. "Would you have me believe, Constable Corrigan, that Trooper Sharples removed his gun, locked the lid to his box, shot himself, then fell forwards onto the glass lid."

Corrigan threw his arms wide in a gesture of futility. "Inspector Bowman," he sighed, "you will know that there is an event in the village today. An event at which I am expected to be present in my capacity as the local constable."

"Yet surely the force of the bullet would have resulted in him falling backwards?" It was a simple enough assertion. Bowman watched the two men carefully.

"Perhaps he did," conceded Corrigan, simply.

"But I saw blood on the opposite wall to the sideboard where the box was placed. He must have been facing the sideboard and the box as he pulled the trigger."

Whitlock looked to the constable as he stood by the window, his mouth hanging open in confusion.

"If that is indeed the case," Bowman concluded, a look of victory upon his face, "Just what caused the sound of breaking glass that brought Captain Kreegan to Sharples' door?"

XIV

Regatta

"You're convinced it was murder, then?" The two detectives had eschewed the opportunity of hailing a cab from the station. Instead, they joined the steady stream of people walking to the regatta. The Larton Donkey disgorged itself of day-trippers intent on enjoying the day's convivialities by the river. Bowman noticed smarter carriages rattling past from the Dean, their passengers reclining in their finery as they stared with disdain through the open windows. Ladies held their handkerchiefs to their noses in protest at the dust kicked up from the horses'' hooves. The horses were bigger and smarter than any that Bowman had yet seen in Larton, including those in service at Larton Manor. It seemed that every carriage was grander than the last, and Bowman noticed a few stragglers from the Rise cast their eyes up in envy as they rattled past. Everywhere, mused the inspector as he walked the dusty road with his companion, there seemed to be a sharp line drawn between those that have and those that have not. He had not expected to see that line drawn so sharp in the country. Here there were crops in the fields and fruit on the trees, a glut of food that could feed the village three times over. Yet, twice a day, the produce from the farms and orchards was loaded onto carts and drays to be sent away. Most of the profit would then be spent in rent, all of it destined for Lord Melville and the Larton Estate, and so many of the villagers were held in thrall to a system where they worked the hardest for the smallest gain. Only those who had escaped into the respectable professions or, such as those in the Dean, had benefited from a wise investment had found the means to plough another furrow.

"Yes, Graves," Bowman replied as they approached the causeway between the Rise and the Village. "I believe Sharples was murdered. There is a detail in the case that I find most puzzling." He squinted into the sun, fighting a heavy throbbing at his temples.

"The glass breaking after the shot," Graves nodded. "If he fell backwards and not onto the case at all, how to account for the glass breaking after he had shot himself."

The two men paused to lean over the bridge on the causeway. They stared into the shallow, murky water of the small tributary beneath, each deep in thought. Dragonflies danced amongst the bulrushes with butterflies and bees. A hungry heron stood still as a statue, its beady eye alert to every ripple in the water. Every now and then, a burp of bubbles would break on the water's surface, indicative of life beneath or the movement of mud on the riverbed.

"What's our next move, sir?" Graves shook his blond curls in the heat.

"It seems the whole of Larton will be gathered for the regatta today, Graves," Bowman replied. "It's the perfect opportunity to dig a little deeper. I would like to learn more of Erasmus Finch's death, too. It would not surprise me at all if the two deaths were connected."

"But not that of Fletcher Cousins?"

Bowman shook his head. "I am convinced Fletcher Cousins killed himself."

"If there is a pattern to the deaths," the sergeant concurred, "then Cousins is an aberration, anyway. He died on a Tuesday." Graves' blue eyes twinkled in the sun. He was at his best when in the midst of a mystery, Bowman had noticed. He seemed to treat each case as a puzzle such as one might give to a child, as nothing more than a diversion. To Bowman they were confirmation of just how low the human spirit could stoop in the pursuit of self-interest, self-advancement or self-protection. In his experience, murder was as pure an expression of the self as he could imagine. In that one act, a person's spirit was laid bare in all its primitive, primal brutality, shorn of the trappings of the civilised world.

"As you say, Graves, if the pattern is to be repeated, there may be a death today."

"But what's so special about the second Saturday of each month?" Graves let go a stone he had found on the road, and watched it fall to the water with a plop.

Bowman smoothed his moustache between a thumb and forefinger. "Perhaps we might better ask what happened in the days preceding. We must learn more of Erasmus Finch and his fall from the church tower."

Graves whistled air between his teeth and shrugged. "But, how? Seems like most of the village is like a closed book to us."

"Then today might prove the perfect opportunity." Bowman leaned back from the balustrade, suddenly conscious of the warmth radiating from the bricks as they baked in the sun. "Put yourself in their shoes, Graves. Two detectives from Scotland Yard arrive within their midst to pry and snoop. We don't look like them or even sound like them. No wonder they're suspicious. We're the outsiders here, Graves." Bowman gestured across the road to where the regatta was in full swing. He could hear the band playing something approximating to a military march. What they lacked in natural talent, he mused, they certainly made up for in enthusiasm. "Today of all days," he continued, "they might well present themselves more pliable to investigation. We must take whatever opportunity we may find to gain their trust. Only then, I believe, will we know what happened to Trooper Sharples and Mr Finch."

Turning back to the road, neither Bowman nor Graves noticed the tousled headed child with a freckled face who, hiding beneath the bridge with his dog, had heard every word. As the detectives ambled slowly away in the heat, the young boy hid his makeshift tent from view with some rushes from the river. Grabbing his hound by the scruff of his neck, he made his way carefully from his camp so as not to be seen and turned his feet towards Chalk Wood.

The open stretch of land that separated Larton Rise from the Village was regarded as a no-man's-land. Part of the Larton Commons, it was maintained by the Freemen of the Borough for the use of all and grazed by sheep belonging to the Larton Manor estate. In a village so beset with petty rivalries and ancient complaints, it was the one parcel of land not contested by the locals. The Queen of the May was proclaimed here every year, the goose fair made its home here in the autumn and, today, the Larton Regatta spilled from the riverbank across the field to the causeway. An area totalling some forty acres was given over to stalls selling beer from local breweries, fruit from local orchards and even livestock from local farms. A pen of pigs had been set by the entrance to the field, their squeals and grunts acting as a welcome to the revellers. Chickens scratched at the ground by a fruit stall, often darting this way and that to avoid the heavy boots and walking canes that weaved amongst the throng. It seemed the whole village had turned out for the regatta. Even on the slope leading from the causeway, blankets had been laid for picnics. Ladies in their finest dresses sheltered from the heat of the sun beneath parasols and umbrellas whilst the men stood and chatted in groups, pipes clamped tight between their teeth. Even on such a day, it was clear there were divisions between the villagers. Discrete knots of people clung together, nudging and nodding at other groups across the field. Children ran between their legs, even the poorest of them having made concessions to the spirit of the day. Ragged ties were knotted around their frayed collars, battered hats were perched precariously on their heads. They darted between the stalls to try and filch an apple or two. Many of the revellers stood in the shade of one of a number of large marquees along the riverbank. The grandest of them all, festooned with bunting and flags of all nations, was reserved for the finer people of Larton Dean. They sat, remote and aloof, upon a raised stage. The intention was to give them as fine a view as possible of the ensuing races, but it also served to remind the villagers of their place in proceedings. They had even been spared the walk to the river, their marquee opening to a small track that gave access from the road to their coaches. Thus, they had only to manage a few steps to their sheltered position above the riverbank, from where they might survey the hoi polloi baking in the sun. Their children looked on with equal measures of disdain and envy at their poorer contemporaries below. One of the rougher children had even broken through the fence to the pigpen and, much to the farmer's consternation, was now riding the largest pig about the pen as if it were a charger and he a knight of the realm. His parents stood nearby, clearly drunk at even this early hour, laughing at the spectacle and cheering the lad on.

As Bowman stepped gingerly over a couple rolling amorously on the grass, he joined a queue at a stall selling fresh lemonade. The stallkeeper regarded the inspector with suspicious eyes as he poured his drink from a large, earthenware jug.

"You're the Scotland Yarder?" he leered from beneath a cloth cap. Bowman couldn't help but notice the man's teeth. They protruded at alarming angles, each a different colour to its neighbour.

"I am," Bowman confirmed as he downed his drink. His thirst was so violent and his head so thick that he did not care that he could barely taste the lemons. "Are you local?"

"As local as they come," the man sneered. "Three generations of my family have run the general provisions store on the high street, just opposite The King's Head."

Bowman nodded. Alarmingly, the last of his drink had contained a portion of dusty grit. "Did you know Erasmus Finch?" he asked, running his tongue around his teeth.

"As well as any man could." The man attempted a knowing smile. "But I'd rather talk of his widow." He ran his tongue over his lips as he nodded across the field. Turning to follow his gaze, Bowman saw a rather comely young woman dressed in a black crinoline dress and resting an open umbrella on her shoulder. She stared absently before her, a small basket in the crook of her arm piled high with walnuts. The inspector noticed she seemed entirely alone. Not one person stopped to inquire after her health. In fact, the villagers skirted around her, keen to give the widow a wide berth.

"Who knows what'll become of her now," the stallholder grinned. "Reckon she'll be open to offers soon enough." Bowman turned in time to see the man giving him an exaggerated, lascivious wink. Bowman was alarmed at quite how unabashed the intimation had been. Looking around him, he saw several other men standing about the stall, each catching the man's eye and returning the gesture with a low, knowing laugh. One leaned over to flick the man's cap from his head.

"Don't think you'd stand a chance with your wife watching, Phelps," he laughed.

The now hatless man appealed to the inspector. "Is looking at a comely woman now a hanging offence, inspector?"

Bowman rolled his eyes as he turned away, reaching for his mouth to wipe the grit from his lips with the back of a sleeve. The men around him laughed all the more.

Crossing the field to join his sergeant, Bowman fancied the woman in black had noticed him. She seemed to follow him with her sad eyes as he walked, though he was embarrassed to find she forwent the opportunity to return his smile.

"There you are, sir," Graves exclaimed, munching on an apple.

"Keeping the doctor away, Graves?" Bowman quipped drily, looking about him at the throng.

Graves grinned. "It's working so far, sir." Finishing his apple, he threw the core to the grass and wiped his hands on his trousers.

"Just beware," Bowman continued, his voice low and conspiratorial. "It's the second Saturday of the month. If the pattern is to be repeated, there might well be another death today."

Graves' eyebrows rose. "Here, sir?" Looking around the bustling field, he found it doubtful such a thing could be attempted in so public a place.

Bowman's frown cut deep. "I would say it was the perfect time and place, Graves. The whole of the village is here including, perhaps, the murderer. It would not surprise me at all to learn that they had struck already."

"Where?" Graves looked about him, suddenly alarmed.

Bowman turned to him. His head, at last, had ceased its relentless throbbing. "There is no better hiding place than in a crowd," he cautioned.

Graves took in the scene around him with fresh eyes. Looking closer, he saw a fight had broken out on a grassy bank. Two men threw their fists at one another while a third tried to intervene. Over by the band, he saw a young woman slap a suitor about the face. Eager to escape his advances, she turned and ran to an older, rather severe-looking couple that Graves took to be her parents. The father glared at the young man from beneath a straw boater. Behind them a knot of travellers, Jared Stoker among them, gathered, talking amongst themselves. Every now and then, they would cast dark looks at certain of the villagers. One or two of the revellers rose to the bait, squaring up to them with raised fists before moving on. Over by a clump of trees, Graves noticed a figure lying face down on the grass, unmoving and unnoticed. The crowd moved around him without so much as a glance. Graves' heart quickened. Just as he was about to move towards the man, a gang of youths approached the prone figure, prodding him with a foot. At last, he roused himself, reaching up to take the tankard of ale offered him by his friends. Graves shook his head.

"You're up!" The shout came from the riverbank. There, the boats were being lifted from the grass by their crews; a motley collection of labourers, shopkeepers and villagers in various states of dress. Many of the men had stripped to the waist in anticipation of a dunking, their wives standing to applaud them as they lowered their boats into the water.

"They've roped me in, sir," Graves explained, responding with a cheerful wave. "I'm to row a boat with the shopkeepers."

Bowman looked over to the riverbank. There were six or seven boats in all, each now bobbing about on the river. Oars were passed from the bank and laid in their hulls as the crews stepped carefully aboard. The inspector could see that one man was already chest deep in the water, gaily splashing at his crew members as they took their seats. He was a large man with a bald head and fleshy shoulders. "Haul him in!" called a wiry fellow with a pipe from the shore. At his command, two men leant from the boat to drag their fleshy comrade over the rowlocks to his place. Wholly out of the water now, he could be seen in all his splendour. A great white belly wobbled as he rolled in the hull. "Put him at the back," the man continued, "The extra weight'll keep yer prow up!"

"Or sink 'em!" laughed a man from another, sleeker boat by the bank. Bowman recognised him as Phelps the stallholder who had served him his gritty lemonade.

"That's my boat," Graves offered, excitedly.

"Well done, Graves," Bowman nodded, impressed. "Whether

they'll know you for a champion or a fool I can't yet tell, but they'll know you well enough by the race's end. Then, perhaps we'll make some progress."

Graves waved again towards the crew and loped towards the riverbank, his long legs stepping over those already seated on the grass to enjoy the spectacle. He was pleased to see that Maude from The King's Head had joined the throng. He caught her eye as he stretched a leg over the side of the boat and took his place on the starboard side.

Looking along the line of boats, Bowman saw that they each held a crew of five. He recognised Prescott the driver and the estate gardener from Lord Melville's estate in the smartest boat of all. It was sleeker than the rest and polished to a shine. The word 'Marigold' was painted in a long, flowing script along the prow. Next to it, a wider boat sat low in the water, crewed by a gang of burly lads Bowman took to be farm workers. They had the skin of those who spend their days in the open elements. They seemed to shine in the sun as much as any polished wood. To huge cheers, they were already having to bale out the boat of the water that had seeped in between the rickety planks. Cupping their hands, they fought to keep afloat.

"It'd be a fine thing if you made the starting line!" the man with the pipe laughed, and the crowd cheered all the more.

Standing amongst it all was Lord Melville, leaning on his cane and looking pleased with proceedings. Bowman was about to approach him, when his eye was caught by the woman behind the table on Trevitt's fruit stall. Standing in the shade of an umbrella, she seemed barely to be enjoying the day at all. As all around her dissolved into hilarity, she stood with her eyes cast down at the grass, hardly daring to meet anyone's eye. Trevitt's wife.

"Mrs Trevitt," Bowman began as he approached. He noticed she flinched as he spoke.

"Forgive me," she whispered, her voice lacking force. "How can I help you, sir?" She gestured at the table before her. Bowman could see she was low of stock. A few blemished cherries rolled in the bottom of a basket.

"I am Detective Inspector Bowman," the inspector continued.

"Is your husband not at his stall?"

The woman shook her head.

"Is he rowing, then?" Bowman cast his eyes back to the water where the boats were lining up to start their race.

"He's taken the cart back to the farm. We're low on fruit." She looked away, almost apologetically. In fact, thought Bowman, everything about her was a gesture of apology. Her feet turned inwards as she stood, shifting her weight restlessly from side to side. As she wrung her hands together in agitation, Bowman noticed her nails looked bitten and cracked. She regarded him from under her brows as she spoke, seemingly grateful for the curtain of hair that fell across her face.

"Mrs Trevitt," Bowman began, his moustache twitching, "I wanted to thank you for last evening's dinner."

The woman nodded, absently. Bowman could not help but notice that her cheek was bruised. Pausing to take a breath, he wondered how best to proceed. "Did you not consider joining us at the table?"

Mrs Trevitt met the inspector's gaze. She had the look of a scared animal. "It is not my place, sir," she whispered, clearly afraid of being overheard.

Bowman knew enough to tread carefully. "I have been married, Mrs Trevitt," his own use of the past tense stuck in his throat. "I know that not every marriage can be as happy as mine."

The woman before him looked unsure how to respond. Her eyes darted about her as if in fear.

"What is your place on the farm, Mrs Trevitt?" The bustle of the regatta proceeded apace as Bowman leaned over the table.

"My place is to be Maxwell Trevitt's wife," she stammered. "That is enough."

Bowman felt his neck burning beneath his collar. "Would that include working on the farm?"

"There is always something to be done, inspector." Her voice was stronger now. "Life is hard here, and the work harder still."

Bowman nodded. "Would that account for the bruises upon your wrists?" The woman's eyes widened at his impudence. "And upon your cheek?"

"Inspector Bowman," Mrs Trevitt hissed, "if you have been married, you will know that what passes between a husband and his wife is their business."

"Forgive me - " Bowman began, swallowing hard.

"You have caused trouble enough already," the woman spat as she bent to pick up her basket. "You would do well to keep your London ways to yourself."

"There are places you can go," Bowman offered, boldly. His mind flicked to the Women's Refuge in Hanbury Street. Surely there must be such a thing in the nearest town.

"You would have me in the workhouse?" Bowman was aware of the volume in her voice. Suddenly, she turned her face to the river. "What do you see on yonder bank, Inspector Bowman?" she asked.

Confused, Bowman turned to follow her gaze. Beyond the river lay a meadow in full bloom. "A field?" he offered, tentatively.

"I see spotted orchids, harebells and field poppies." She turned, slightly. "And there, beneath the sycamore; cornflowers and fiddleneck. You should know never to keep your horse there, inspector, on account of the ragwort that grows by the hedge. It is deadly."

Bowman frowned. "Mrs Trevitt," he stuttered, "I do not understand."

"Precisely." Mrs Trevitt drew looks from those around her as she continued. "I know my place, Inspector Bowman, and that is here in Larton, with my husband." Her eyes were suddenly stern. "Where is yours?"

With that, she gathered her wares about her and walked away without so much as a glance over her shoulder.

Looking about him, Bowman saw several people staring at him accusingly. It had been his intention to gain the villagers' trust today. He could only hope Sergeant Graves was having more luck.

A sudden, sharp, shriek from a whistle drew his attention to the river. All eyes were now on the line-up of mismatched boats arranged across its width. Bobbing on the water, they jostled for space on the starting line indicated by two young lads on opposite banks. Each held a flag in their hand, ready to raise when the boats were in line. The crowd at the bank was now ten deep, and Bowman noticed much pushing and barging to gain advantage. Shouts of encouragement rose from the throng, and brawls broke out amongst supporters of competing crews. Even here, the inspector noticed, the villagers found something to fight about.

Lord Melville had climbed a rostrum near the smart marquee by the starting line and now stood facing the river, a whistle in his hand. Bowman pushed forward to the riverbank. Beside him, a tall man bent to lift a small girl to his shoulders. She squealed with delight as she flew through the air, then cheered as she saw the boats before her. Far below, her friends laughed and paddled in the water. From here, Bowman could see Sergeant Graves in the second craft along, glancing around at the competition. He thought his boat looked a little low in the water. Catching the inspector's eye, Graves offered him a nod and a wink. Bowman nodded back and glanced further up the river. There, he could see the bridge that marked the finishing line.

Painted a garish blue, the iron structure had been opened with much fanfare just a few years before. Finally replacing the rickety ferry and punts the villagers had previously had to use, the bridge had at last provided the only crossing across the Thames for several miles. Having engaged the services of Brunel himself for its design, the newly formed Larton Bridge Company now found itself having to charge heavy tolls for its use, so much so that many of the local farmers could no longer afford to take their goods to market across the river. Bowman could see a few spectators strung out across its length, leaning over the balustrade as far as the tollhouse on the opposite bank. His heart in his mouth, the inspector suddenly remembered the significance of the day. If his suspicions were correct, there would be another death by the evening.

An expectant silence fell. All eyes were on Lord Melville who stood, alert to the flags at either side of the river. They had both been raised, a sign that the boats were in line. The crews sat bent over their oars, their bodies tense. Each man was focussed on the course ahead, their heads leaning into the wind. Even the children paddling at the riverbank had ceased their splashing. The crowd drew a collective breath and Bowman could not help being caught up in the moment. He looked between Melville and Graves' boat, hoping his sergeant would get the better start.

The whistle, when it came, was long and loud. The effect was immediate and extraordinary. Whatever decorum had been on display was now abandoned. A great cheer erupted from the riverbank and Bowman saw several people pushed into the water. Hats were thrown into the air and, alarmingly, Bowman saw handfuls of fruit being thrown at the boats to hamper the competition. The richer residents of Larton Dean abandoned their chairs under the shade of their marquee and pressed forward, shaking their fists before them and waving their glasses and bottles in the air. The band played Rule Britannia, badly.

The river was suddenly a cacophony of activity. The crews grunted as they leaned into their oars, gritting their teeth as they strained against the water. They shouted in equal measures of encouragement and abuse to their colleagues as they set their faces to the race. Soon, the water was a swirl as oars dipped and rose against the swell.

Melville's 'Marigold' pulled ahead straight away, gaining half a length with ease in the opening moments of the race. Prescott had taken it upon himself to call time for his fellow crewmembers, ensuring an even stroke and a formidable forward motion. Two other boats, those crewed by rival farmhands, had failed to start, their oars tangling viciously at the whistle. It took precious seconds to disengage. In the meantime, one team had lost their nerve and their timing. They veered off to the furthest bank, much to the evident chagrin of their leader who sat at the rear, his red face seemingly fit to burst in his rage. He took to his feet in a vain attempt to take command, pointing fruitlessly in the direction of the bridge as if the gesture alone would solve everything. The rival boat, in the meantime, sought to take advantage of the confusion. As the crews of the leading boats looked back at the commotion, so they slowed. The farmhands found their stroke and pressed onwards, coming to within a length of the shopkeeper's boat before they pulled away. Graves was in his element. Laughing gaily, he put all his weight to the oar, feeling the heft of the water beneath his blade. They pulled forward with every stroke. His shoulders were burning with the exertion, his legs ached as he strained against his seat, but still he found the strength to throw his head back and laugh. And it was at that moment that disaster struck.

Bowman fancied he heard the sound from the riverbank. Even amidst the noise from the crowd, it was unmistakable; the sickening crack of wood on bone. As he fought to see through the melee, it was clear that something had gone dreadfully awry. The shopkeepers' boat was slowing in the water, the oarsmen lifting their blades from the water in alarm. A long whistle blew and everything stopped. The inspector's heart was in his mouth. He searched for Sergeant Graves. There, where he should have been, was an empty seat. Bowman's stomach lurched.

"Graves!" he called. Heads turned towards him. He stepped closer to the riverbank and saw a shape in the water. The twist of a shirt mingled with a mass of curly, blond hair.

"Graves!" he called again, wondering why no one else was rushing to his aid. Suddenly more afraid for his companion than he had ever been, Bowman threw off his jacket and waded into the water. "Graves!" he called again. Knee deep into the river now, Bowman threw himself with abandon into the water. He barely noticed his boots weighing him down. Breasting the swell and gasping with the cold, he closed on the shape in the river. It seemed for all the world like so much flotsam. Swallowing water, Bowman reached out and grabbed a hold of Graves' shirt, pulling his prone body towards him. "Graves," he gasped, "can you hear me?" Pinching water from his eyes, Bowman gazed down at the sergeant's face. A smudge of blood ran from his hairline, across his brow and down a cheek. His jaw hung slack. Ominously, his eyes were closed. Cradling Graves' head in the crook of his elbow, Bowman struck out for the riverbank, suddenly aware he was alone in his endeavours. As he neared the shore, he found a foothold in the mud and stood, heaving Graves from the water. As Bowman stood with the sergeant in his arms, lifeless and inert, he shook the water from his hair and looked about him. Amongst the press of people crowded on the riverbank to watch, not a single one had come to render assistance. Instead, they stood in silence, as if detached from proceedings. Some folded their arms across their chest, displaying no intention to help. Upon each face, Bowman saw expressions of indifference. From their attitude and bearing, the inspector sensed a quiet satisfaction that the two detectives from Scotland Yard had received their just deserts. Lord Melville himself stood upon his rostrum with a look on his face that seemed somewhere between disapproval and disappointment.

Later, Prescott would insist it was an accident. During the confusion at the starter's whistle, he would say, the Marigold had drifted from its line to the bridge and rammed the shopkeeper's craft. The jolt had been enough to unseat Sergeant Graves who had leaned against the boat's side for support. Lifting an oar to push the boats apart, Prescott had inadvertently made contact with the sergeant's head. And so he had pitched backwards, unconscious before he'd even hit the water. All this he would relate to the crowd around him in The King's Head that night. For now, however, he stood in his boat, silent and brooding.

"Please," Bowman rasped, his throat dry from his exertions, "someone call a doctor!" He lowered Graves carefully to the grass, turning him on his side to release the water from his lungs. He heaved a sigh of relief as Graves coughed up a quantity of the river, his breathing settling into a rasping wheeze.

"I hope I may be of assistance, inspector?"

Looking up into the sun, Bowman squinted to see a familiar, elderly gentleman sporting a luxuriant, white moustache and steel wire spectacles.

"Mr Whitlock," the inspector breathed. "We need to get him to his bed and to dress this wound." Looking down at his own dishevelled clothes, Bowman noticed he had Graves' blood upon his hands. Just as he bent to lift the sergeant from the grass, there came another cry.

"Look!" It was the girl upon her father's shoulders. "A fire!" The crowd turned as one to see where she was pointing. On the horizon some two miles off, a plume of smoke rose from the trees.

"The gypsies' camp!" called a man from the musicians" marquee. As the crowd bumped against each other for a better view, a group broke ranks from the throng. Walking with long strides at first, they soon broke into a run, calling others of their kind from the field to join them. At their head, a youthful looking man was at full pelt, his long hair whipping at his face as he ran. Leaving the regatta behind him, Jared Stoker scaled the rising ground to the causeway, his voice rising into a note of panic.

Maxwell Trevitt met the travellers on the road from Larton Rise. Pushing a barrow of cherries before him, he paused periodically to wipe the sweat from his hands. The sun was at its hottest now and he cursed the regatta for having been held on such a day. Still, he would sell some of his harvest, at least. The streets around him were almost empty. Just about the whole of Larton had gathered by the riverside. Soon, he knew, the jollities would be forgotten and Larton would return to a village where every man existed in a state of enmity with his neighbour. It had been ever thus, he mused as he grabbed the barrow again, and no doubt it always would be. As he crossed the railway line at Larton Station, he heard the sound of boots on dust. Looking ahead, he saw Jared Stoker running at speed towards him, his face flushed. Behind him came his cohort, calling and shouting between them.

"Bold as you like," hissed Stoker as he approached. "How can you be so brazen?"

Trevitt slowed his stride. "Get out the way, Stoker," he brayed. "There's enough filth on the road as it is." His hand went involuntarily to his cheek as he felt something whistle past his ear. Looking down at his fingers, he saw blood. Another stone caught him on the shoulder and he looked up to see three or four men taking aim again. They were clearly agitated by something.

"If you've had a hand in that, Maxwell Trevitt," Ida Stoker screamed, her cheeks streaked with tears, "there's nothing you have that will be safe." Her legs almost buckled beneath her as she raised a trembling hand. Trevitt turned his head to follow her gaze. There, where the trees met the sky, hung a dirty smudge of smoke. He was about to protest his surprise, when he felt a blow to the back of his head. It was enough to make his vision swim. The bright light from the sun seemed harsher still. Swaying on his feet, he turned into the path of another fist, this time aimed squarely at his jaw. His eyes seemed to shake in their orbits at the force of the blow. Soon, he was surrounded by Stoker and his men. He barely had time to raise his hands before they set upon him, their blows falling about his head and upper body. Spitting broken teeth from his mouth, Trevitt doubled up and raised his arms about his head to protect himself. A jab to the kidneys sent him to the ground.

"Jared, leave 'im!" Ida was keening. "We've got to get to the camp!"

Just as Trevitt felt he was going to black out, he heard a whistle blowing, long and loud. Tasting dust in his mouth, he looked up to see Constable Corrigan wading into the fray. One by one, he pulled the remaining men off Trevitt and slung them across the road. Staggering to regain their balance, they looked to their leader.

"Let him be," Stoker commanded, his breath coming fast. "We need to get to Chalk Wood."

"You would do well to pack whatever you've got left and go," called Corrigan after them as the gypsies continued on their way. Pulling Trevitt to his feet, the constable hooked an elbow beneath his arms, dragging him across the dusty road to the police station. "All right, Trevitt," he soothed. "Soon have you cleaned up." With a mighty effort, Trevitt found the strength to walk unaided. He wiped the blood from his face with a tattered sleeve.

"Those bastards will suffer," he panted. "I'll raise the whole village against them!"

With that, he straightened himself up to his full height, shook himself loose from Corrigan's grip and made his way back to his barrow. Muttering darkly under his breath, he gripped the handles with his broken hands and, with a curse, continued on his way.

The fire burned all night. Stoker and his men had been relieved to find it had been set at the tree where Cousins had been found and not in their camp at all. Working in unison, the travellers had cleared the undergrowth around their tents and caravans to prevent the blaze from spreading. They had lopped at branches and even felled the smaller trees. Starved of fuel, the fire eventually burned itself out in the early hours of the morning. Charred tree trunks smoked gently in the early light, lending a misty air to the woods around the camp. It was notable that no one from the village came to their aid although, once or twice throughout the night, Stoker had the impression they were being watched. As the gang had toiled to bring the fire to heel, he had noticed, from the corner of his eye, a figure in the woods. Lifting his head from his work to peer deeper into the trees, he had seen the figure fleetingly before it disappeared, melting into the undergrowth and the confusion about him.

XV

Consequences

Following the accident, Inspector Bowman brought Graves back to his room at The King's Head on a barrow. He almost felt like apologising for the indignity. The coroner ran to his house, promising to return with a medical bag while Bowman and Maude manhandled Graves up the stairs. He was struck again by the lack of assistance afforded by the villagers. The young sergeant swung between a disturbed sleep and a confused, delirious state that could barely be described as wakefulness. His head rolled from side to side. His low, keening moans cut Bowman to the quick. Maude fetched fresh, hot water from the kitchens in a large earthenware jug. She cleaned Graves' wound as best she could while Bowman retreated to his room to change into a dry shirt and trousers. Upon his return, he found Whitlock applying a bandage to Graves' head. Bowman stripped his companion of his wet clothes. More than once, he caught Maude pretending to avert her gaze.

"He is concussed," Whitlock opined. "As you might expect after such a blow." Bowman noticed again that he exhibited no sign of the local accent. No doubt he had moved to Larton in pursuit of a quieter career. Bowman felt almost sorry for him. He watched as Whitlock administered a dose of Cerralgine. "Food for the brain," he declared as he spooned the noxious liquid between Graves' lips. Bowman took the opportunity to look his companion over.

He was a sorry sight, indeed. His curls were contained beneath an already-stained bandage, fastened with a pin. His skin looked paler than Bowman had ever seen, his lips blue and bloodless. He shivered uncontrollably as he lay back on his pillow, but whether he was conscious of the action or no, Bowman could not guess. Those eyes that had but recently been so full of life and mischief, now seemed to have no light at all. Graves stared straight ahead, blank and unseeing, evidently unconscious to all proceedings.

"I will leave you with a quantity of cocaine drops to be administered every four hours," Greville Whitlock concluded, rising from the bedside to snap his bag shut beside him. Maude nodded, solemnly.

"I will stay with him," she whispered.

"Perhaps that is just as well," the coroner nodded. "The next night and day might well be crucial."

Bowman nodded, sadly."Might we have some fresh, hot water, Maude?" The inspector gestured to the ceramic bowl of water at the washstand. Aside from the pictures on the wall and the rug on the floor, Graves' room had much the same layout as his own.

"Of course." The young woman bobbed her head and collected the bowl, trying hard to avert her gaze from the water it held. It was tinted red from the cleaning of Graves' wound and thick with clots of mud and blood.

Bowman closed the door after her with a soft click and sighed. "Are you Larton's only doctor?" He could not help but regard the sergeant on his bed as he spoke. He seemed to be moving in and out of consciousness; sometimes still, sometimes fitful and restless. A sheen of sweat clung to his forehead. His sheets were stained.

"Larton has a doctor, Inspector Bowman, but you would never have found him so quickly at the regatta." The coroner smiled gently, patting his case with a hand as he spoke. "You are lucky I have kept the tools of my trade."

Bowman nodded. "What brought you to Larton, Mr Whitlock?"

Whitlock shrugged on his coat. "My late wife. She spent much of her childhood in a nearby town and fancied she would rather spend her later years near home." Straightening his collar, he was suddenly wistful. "They were fewer in number than we had hoped."

Bowman flicked his eyes to the coroner. "I am sorry to hear that," he said.

Whitlock took a breath. "I was able to bring her comfort in her final hours, inspector. What husband could do more?"

Bowman sat on Graves' bed. His mind was suddenly back on

Hanbury Street. Anna's death had been so swift and Bowman so distraught that he had not thought to offer her comfort as she died. With a pang of guilt, he remembered how it had been Graves who had rushed to her side. It had been Graves who had commandeered a carriage to take her body to hospital, Graves who had taken charge. Bowman chewed his lip. He had never thought of the moments following her death before. Perhaps he had wanted to deny them, or his lack of action. He had cowered by the roadside, his heart in his throat at the dreadful realisation of what he had done. How could he have faced her, even in her final moments? His memories were a blank. He had fallen through the ground, retreated from the world to a space of his own mind's devising, and he had stayed there for seven months. Perhaps he was still there now. He could not bear now to look at Graves, just as he had been unable to look at her. The figure on the bed reproached him. In that moment, Bowman felt a profound lack of worth. His mouth dried. With a start, he realised the coroner was speaking.

"We are fortunate men, are we not inspector, in that in our professional lives, we bring comfort to others?" Whitlock was cleaning his spectacles on the lining of his coat. "As coroner, I bring certainty where there is doubt. That is the good I do." Whitlock replaced his spectacles upon his nose and leaned over the inspector. "What good have you done here, Inspector Bowman?"

Bowman blinked. He wasn't sure how he should reply.

"In the short time since your arrival," Whitlock continued, quietly, "Larton has practically fallen apart." His voice was steady and uneven, betraying no emotion. "The gypsies' camp is ablaze and Mr Trevitt has been set upon."

Bowman felt his face flush and his neck burn. "You cannot lay all that at my door."

Whitlock nodded. "Was it your idea that Sergeant Graves should take part in the regatta?" he asked, simply. His face was all concern, his eyebrows knitted together in an expression of sympathy.

"It was his own idea," Bowman sighed. "Although born of my desire to gain the villagers' trust." He felt a tremor in his right hand as he spoke. He gripped it hard, digging his nails into the palm. Would it never be still? Looking back up at the coroner, he saw that he had noticed the movement. He held his gaze, afraid to look away.

"Ah," Whitlock said, sadly. "Then perhaps you bear a responsibility for his condition, too." He clutched his doctor's bag to his chest as he made for the door.

Bowman heard the challenge in the coroner's voice, and stood to meet it. "I am here to investigate the deaths of three men, Mr Whitlock." He clutched at the bedstead, suddenly unsteady on his feet.

Whitlock paused with his fingers on the handle, then turned into the room. "We are proud men are we not, inspector?" Bowman frowned. "It is a hard thing to admit when we are wrong." Whitlock's kindly face was creased into a mask of concern.

"I must be allowed to investigate the matters before me."

The coroner looked pointedly at the feverish man on the bed. Graves was shivering with cold in spite of the evening heat. "At any cost?"

Bowman felt his gorge rise at the remark. "Sergeant Graves would have it no other way," he said, still not daring to look at his companion.

Whitlock's eyebrows rose on his forehead. "What a shame he is not able to confirm that himself." Flinging the door open, the coroner stepped onto the landing beyond, pausing only to deliver a final thought before he left. "Larton is a village like no other, inspector. You have kicked at a hornets' nest. You should not be surprised if someone gets stung." With a final, sad look to Sergeant Graves, Whitlock shut the door behind him, leaving Inspector Bowman to swallow nervously and consider the implication of the coroner's words.

Bowman, as he expected, did not sleep. Unable to contemplate the thought of eating, he had foregone his dinner and, after seeing that Sergeant Graves was comfortable for the night, elected to return to his room. He had left the sergeant in the care of Maude, confident that her obvious feelings for him would ensure her undivided attention. Now Bowman lay on his bed, stock-still. His room was directly below Sergeant Graves' and every now and then he would hear the sergeant groan or mumble incoherently. Once, he even caught the plaintive strains of a lullaby drifting through the ceiling. Maude had evidently found a way to soothe her troubled patient as she mopped his brow. The song reminded Bowman of his life before the accident on Hanbury Street. It reminded him of simpler times. He could not help but think of how his fortunes had changed in so brief a time. In a little over a year, every certainty had dissolved, everything he had thought solid and permanent had proven illusory. He could not help but think of the destruction in his wake.

Bowman lifted his hands before his eyes. The fingers on his right hand twitched involuntarily. He felt a cold sweat on his neck. His breath came short and quick. As he lurched forward, he felt he was floating up through the ceiling, through the roof and away. The world turned beneath him, without him, in spite of him. Far below, a young girl was hanging on a makeshift scaffold by St. Saviour's Dock. Anthony Graves was standing in a gathering crowd of onlookers, his face contorted with horror. He knew her. Kitty Baldwin had been hanged as a warning from the Kaiser.

The scene dissolved around him and he flew further. Now he looked down, impossibly, into Hardacre's den. Below him, in the gloom, stood Sergeant Williams, Inspector Treacher, Graves and, there by the ragged curtain that led to Hardacre's cell, the inspector himself. All were held in the middle of some action, like a tableau in a play. Time was frozen. In the doorway stood Jabez Kane, his scarred face leering in the dark. Before him, he held Constable Evan with a knife to his throat. Bowman heard a high-pitched scream like the whistle of some huge locomotive and, slowly, the scene played out before him. Kane's knife swept across Evan's neck, the resultant slick of blood spurting into the room and onto the floor. As the life drained from him, Bowman was sure the young constable looked directly at him, his eyes burning with a dreadful accusation.

Finally, as he knew he would be, he was at Hanbury Street. There below him, he saw an image of himself, coat tails flapping in the wind, gun in hand. The shot was loosed and Bowman knew a train of events had been set in motion.

The image retreated as Bowman fell down to the ground. The earth pressed in around him, against his shoulders, his legs and face. He clawed at the sod in desperation. The realisation came as the weight of the earth pressed against his chest, squeezing the breath from his lungs. Bowman wasn't just in the ground. He was in his grave.

He was brought to his senses by a knocking at the door. Snapping his eyes open, he realised he was sitting in the chair by the fireplace. The morning light streamed through the open curtains. Bowman pressed a hand to his chest to still his thumping heart. The knocking came again. Collecting his wits, he found the strength to respond.

"Come!" he rasped, instinctively, and the door swung open on its hinges. There, framed in the doorway, was the not inconsiderable bulk of Detective Inspector Ignatius Hicks.

XVI

Chapter And Verse

"Ah, Bowman," boomed Hicks from the door. "There you are." The bluff inspector clamped the bit of his pipe between his teeth. It wasn't long before a noxious cloud of smoke had drifted into the room, all but obscuring the light from the window. Despite the early heat, Hicks was dressed in a long astrakhan coat that hung down to his portly calves. A rich, burgundy waistcoat strained across the expanse of his chest, the buttons groaning in protest against his girth. The collar of his shirt was open. His only other concession to the temperature was the absence of a cravat at his neck. Ludicrously, he had not thought to remove the battered top hat that teetered on his head. It knocked dangerously against the top of the doorframe as he stood, his hands on his wide hips. His great beard bristled with agitation as he spoke.

"Where can a man find a decent breakfast in these parts?"

Bowman pushed himself up from the chair in alarm. "You have been sent for?" he stuttered, unable to conceive of any other reason why Hicks should have joined the fray.

"Much against my better judgement, believe me." Hicks breezed into the room, catching his hat in his hands by the brim in one deft movement. "I understand you're a man down." Heaving his weight against the sash window, he threw it open to admit some air.

Bowman wrung his hands. "Sergeant Graves is - " he hesitated. "Indisposed."

Hicks turned into the room. "So I hear." He glared at his fellow inspector. "Scotland Yard received a wire late last night from Lord Melville. I was despatched in the early hours to provide assistance."

And, mused Bowman wryly, no doubt to report back on his own condition. With a lurch, he realised what a picture he must present. His shirt tails hung loose about his waist, his sleeves were rolled up to the elbow. His hair hung lank upon his head and his chin was rough with the beginnings of a beard. He cleared his throat before he spoke.

"Then you know the details of the case?" Bowman shifted uncomfortably where he stood.

Hicks nodded. "The commissioner is most concerned to hear that you have placed one of his officers in harm's way in the course of your investigations."

Bowman resented the implication. "I can think of no police investigation that did not come without its attendant risks."

Hicks appeared satisfied with his response.

"Perhaps you will find some breakfast downstairs," Bowman offered, attempting a more casual air. "If you will exercise a little patience, I shall present myself at the table in good time."

"Ah!" Hicks rubbed his enormous belly. "Then I shall do just that." He seemed to salivate at the thought. "But where might I find Sergeant Graves?"

"He is in the room directly above us," Bowman explained. "And I am sure he will be as delighted to see you as I am."

Hicks gave no indication of hearing the disdain in Bowman's voice. Instead, he drew on his pipe to release a final haze of blue smoke, gathered his coat about him and made for the door with great galumphing strides. In just a few moments, Bowman heard the inspector's boots on the ceiling above.

The smell of kippers almost turned Bowman's stomach as he alighted the stairs from the landing. There, at a table by the window, sat Inspector Hicks. If he knew that most of his breakfast had lodged in his beard as he ate, he did not seem unduly bothered. He dug into the two fish on his plate with an almost religious fervour, his forehead creased in concentration, his mouth hanging open to receive his fork. The fish looked entire, Bowman noticed, heads, tails and all. Between mouthfuls, Hicks would wipe his mouth upon his sleeve so that, already, Bowman could see his cuffs were marked with a greasy sheen.

"He looks in a bad way," Hicks announced as he saw Bowman take his last step into the room.

"He is," the gaunt inspector replied, softly.

"Accident, was it?" Hicks was tearing great lumps from a hunk of bread as he spoke.

"I do not believe so."

"Oh?" Hicks paused between mouthfuls, his bushy eyebrows rising on his forehead. He motioned that Bowman should sit with him for breakfast, pushing the opposite chair away from underneath the table with a dusty boot.

"It's a question of timing, Inspector Hicks," Bowman said as he eased himself into the chair. Pulling himself in, he placed his elbows on the table and made steeples with his fingers as he explained. "Three men have died here in the last eight weeks. The results of the inquests suggested self-murder, but the latest, that of Fletcher Cousins, is an anomaly. There is a peculiar detail that unites the other two cases." Looking up from his hands, Bowman saw Hicks shovelling great forkfuls of fleshy fish into his mouth as he listened. Reaching up with his pudgy fingers, he probed his wet mouth for errant bones, wiping the resultant mess on the lapels of his coat.

"Go on," Hicks commanded through a mouthful of poached kipper.

"Both men died on the second Saturday of the month. A Trooper Sharples supposedly blew his brains out on the Fourteenth of May, one Erasmus Finch threw himself from the church tower on the Eleventh of June."

"And yesterday was the second Saturday of July." Hicks nodded slowly as he reached for a tankard of ale. "That is certainly a peculiar detail."

"Furthermore," Bowman continued, warming to his theme, "there are certain inaccuracies in the case of Trooper Sharples." Hicks withdrew the tankard from his lips, leaving a beery froth on his beard. Bowman ploughed on. "Sharples kept his old service revolver in a locked, glass-topped wooden case. A neighbour reports hearing the sound of breaking glass *after* the shot was fired. The coroner found he had fallen against the glass but it is clear to me the man fell backwards, away from the case."

"Then what caused the sound of breaking glass?"

Bowman paused, waiting for his thoughts to arrange

themselves sufficiently that he might speak them aloud. "I believe," he began, "that Sharples was shot by another gun, entirely." Hicks leaned back in his chair. Bowman fancied he heard the spindles on the backrest creaking with alarm. "Sharples' gun was never tested but sent with undue haste back to Windsor. We cannot know if the bullet that killed Sharples came from his own service revolver."

"And the breaking glass?" Hicks repeated.

Bowman leaned in. "Having shot Jedediah Sharples, the murderer smashed the glass of the case, removed the gun and placed it next to the body. That would account for the glass being broken after the shot was fired, and for the case still being locked upon examination." The inspector's moustache twitched upon his upper lip. "Someone tried very hard to make it appear that Sharples had taken his own life with his own gun. It is clear to me that the man was murdered."

Hicks stared blankly back. "To what end?"

Bowman wasn't entirely certain Hicks believed him. "I do not yet know," he confessed. Rising from his seat, he paced the floor to the window, his hands behind his back as he gazed into the street beyond. There was a steady stream of villagers along the road, all heading in the same direction. Bowman recognised some faces from the regatta. They were dressed in smarter attire this morning. Even the children were dressed in their neatest clothes. "There was no evidence of a break-in at Sharples' house, so I suggest he knew his assailant and let him in willingly."

"Then it could have been anyone in the village," Hicks scoffed. He impaled the second fish to the plate with his knife as if in fear it would fight back. Bowman let the thought sink in. Any one of those people outside could have killed Trooper Sharples. Did they think they had got away with it? "If not suicide," Hicks continued, "what was the motive for murder?"

"There was no evidence of burglary," Bowman shrugged. "If Sharples wasn't killed for something he had," he mused, almost to himself, "perhaps he was killed for something he knew."

Hicks belched. "Where is your evidence?"

Bowman shook his head. "Aside from Sharples' neighbour, a

Captain Kreegan, Larton is a closed book. I am regarded with suspicion and my conduct questioned by everyone."

Hicks noticed a note of self-pity in Bowman's voice. "Are you able to pursue your enquiries sufficiently?" He looked his companion up and down. Bowman's clothes hung upon him as if they were a size too big. His skin was grey and his eyes bloodshot. In short, he did not look his best.

Bowman sighed. "Perhaps the answer lies with Erasmus Finch, the second man to die. I intend to call upon his widow this morning."

"You'll be going to church first, of course." Maude was stepping off the stairs into the doorway, a bowl of water in her hands and a towel slung over her shoulder. "I'm sure the good Lord will forgive me if I stay here with Anthony." Hicks raised his eyebrows at the use of the sergeant's Christian name. Bowman turned back to the window. Of course, it was Sunday. That would explain the steady flow of passersby in the street. They were heading to All Saints Church for the morning service. Maude blushed as she continued. "Will you be wanting breakfast before you go, inspector?"

"I can recommend the poached kippers," offered Hicks. "Though they're not a patch on the devilled eggs at the The Silver Cross." The portly inspector stabbed at a fish head on his plate. The very thought turned Bowman's stomach.

"I have no appetite for breakfast," he smiled, weakly. A worried look crossed Maude's pretty face as she left. Bowman picked at his fingers.

"So," began Hicks as he pushed his chair back from the table, "shall we to church?"

Inspector Bowman walked the short distance from The King's Head with his head down, not daring to make eye contact with the villagers around him. Despite this, he was recognised by several and felt himself subject to the usual looks and nudges that had become common currency in recent months. Lifting his head to cross the road, he recognised Phelps the shopkeeper walking with a much younger lady and what seemed to be at least half a dozen children. They each exhibited the same array of alarmingly haphazard teeth that left Bowman in no doubt but that they belonged to Phelps. The shopkeeper lifted his hat in a gesture of greeting, but Bowman could tell from the man's eyes that it was a mockery. He cast his eyes back down to the road and walked on. Inspector Hicks sauntered breezily at his side, picking bits of kipper from his teeth in between drawing on his habitual pipe. He was not afraid to offer anyone a cheerful greeting as he strode to the church, but it was seldom returned. For the most part, he was met with looks of disapproval or disbelief. Bowman was not sure at all that he was doing much in the way of winning over the villagers.

All Saints Church stood a hundred yards from the river Thames by Larton Bridge, its high flint walls glinting in the sun. From its tower, the bells rang out to call Larton Village to prayer. It was a scene played out at each of the churches in the three parts of the village. A potential force for unity, the three churches ensured that Larton, in fact, remained divided even in worship. All Saints served the Village, St Anne's served the Rise and St Luke's, the Dean. Sermons were used to engender rivalry and the lustiness of the worshippers" singing held up as a mark of just how pious, or hypocritical, each congregation was.

As Bowman and Hicks rounded the corner into the pretty churchyard, they were greeted by a throng of people, all pressing at the door to get in. He noticed not a single word was shared between them. Even here, the villagers regarded each other with suspicious eyes, as if every gesture or look had some underlying motive that was not entirely to be trusted. Children were gathered close under protective arms and hands were thrust sullenly into pockets. Bowman let his eyes wander to the church tower and allowed himself a shiver at the thought that a man had, but a few weeks previously, seen fit to end his life by throwing himself from it. It stood, without a steeple, some sixty feet high and was crowned with a flagpole and weather vain.

"Inspector Bowman!" Bowman recognised the voice. Turning from the church, he saw Lord Melville limping towards him. "I see you have reinforcements," he wheezed, pointing to Hicks with his cane. There was no insinuation in his voice, thought

Bowman, even though Hicks had been sent as a direct response to Melville's wire the night before.

"This is Detective Inspector Hicks," Bowman said, trying to affect a casual air.

"The pleasure is all mine," Hicks beamed as he drew on his pipe, "Your Lordship." Bowman did not think he had ever heard him sound so obsequious.

Looking around him, Melville affected a conspiratorial tone. "You have made quite the name for yourself, Inspector Bowman," he breathed. "I must admit to finding your methods quite impenetrable."

Bowman thought he heard Hicks guffaw at the remark. Turning to face him, he saw the rotund inspector drawing innocently on his pipe.

"Larton is proving impenetrable," Bowman insisted. "But I am making progress."

"In what regard?" Melville fixed him with a penetrating gaze. Bowman remembered the despairing look on Melville's face at the regatta as he had recovered Graves from the river.

"With regard to Fletcher Cousins. I am certain he did indeed take his own life."

Melville nodded. "I see. And the other cases? Those of Sharples and Finch?"

"My investigations are ongoing." Bowman was convinced he could almost feel Hicks rolling his eyes beside him.

"Well, I am sure Inspector Hicks will be of great help."

Bowman was about to smile when he realised there was no hint of irony about Melville's assertion. "I am sure he will," he concurred.

Melville leant over his stick. "You will be interested to hear, no doubt, that Maxwell Trevitt has convened a village meeting on his farm after church."

"Trevitt?" asked Hicks, just a little too loudly.

"He is the farmer on whose land Cousins was found hanged," Bowman explained, patiently.

"And, local gossip would have it, is responsible for the fire in the gypsy camp last night." Melville shook his head.

"Has such a meeting happened before?"

"Never," Melville shrugged. "But the village has had its interest piqued. I have no doubt that there will be a great many in attendance."

"Then what are the reasons behind the meeting?" Hicks tried his very best to give the impression of being deep in thought.

"Some say he is to deliver a public confession, others a denial."

"Then it is as well that we should be there," Bowman nodded to Hicks.

"Undoubtedly," Hicks agreed, puffing on his pipe. With that, Lord Melville tipped his hat and returned to his wife and children on the path.

The two inspectors joined the throng at the entrance and soon passed under the plain portico above the church door to find themselves standing in the stone nave. The air, chilled by the thick stonework, caught in Bowman's throat and he instinctively pulled his shirt collar tighter around his neck. Looking up, he saw the interior of the roof was criss-crossed with a lattice of wooden rafters. To his left and right, beyond original Norman arches, later side extensions allowed for smaller chapels and anterooms. On the south wall, tombs stood in recesses in the stonework, ornate likenesses carved into their sides. As his eyes adjusted to the gloom, Bowman saw the walls were punctuated at intervals with coats of arms, carvings and busts to Larton's more celebrated luminaries. As they made their way to an empty pew, Bowman saw that both he and Hicks were afforded a wide berth by the villagers. Despite the size of the congregation and the lack of space, it soon became apparent that they were to sit alone. Hicks looked around to see that certain of the congregation would clearly prefer to stand at the back of the church rather than join the two detectives in their pew. Glancing back to Bowman, he shot him a look of accusation.

"Just what have you done, Bowman?"

Bowman let the question go, preferring instead to point out those he knew to his portly companion. Among them, he noticed Prescott the driver and the gardener he had seen at Larton Manor. Lord Melville cast a reproachful eye in Bowman's direction as he passed to his place among the pews. The inspector did his best to appear as though he had not noticed, though he feared the blush that rose upon his cheek gave him away. He pointed out the diminutive footman who had met them at the manor's door and several of the drinkers he had seen in the bar at The King's Head on his first night, among them Jenks, the man who had given Maude such trouble. Hicks nodded absently. As he cast his eyes across the congregation, Bowman caught sight of Greville Whitlock. He stood at the back of the church in conversation with the vicar, stretching his shining head up to the rector's ear. Seeing the inspector, he raised a hand in greeting, his eyes twinkling amiably. Bowman settled back in his seat, determined to avoid the sly looks from the villagers, the accusatory glances from his companion and the judgement of the figure on the cross above the altar.

All Saints was presided over by the Reverend Proudfoot. From his vicarage to the church, he had only to walk a short length of path but, often, even this was a challenge. Proudfoot was known for his love of drink and would often declaim from the pulpit while clearly in his cups. He was a tall, angular man of late middle age with wild looking eyes and a shock of hair to match. A pot belly was accentuated by his cassock so that he looked for all the world as if he was, miracle of miracles, with child. The subject of many a joke by the parishioners, he was, nonetheless, a fearful speaker and commanded attention with ease. His basso profundo reverberated to the great oak beams that traversed the roof of the church and seemed to make the very pews beneath them quake with fear. In the throes of his sermonising, his bony hands would reach before him as if into the afterlife itself and his eyes would roll to the heavens as though he alone had access to their secrets.

The organ music that had been playing quietly as the congregation filed in suddenly ceased. There was a moment of pregnant expectancy and suddenly a great fanfare rose from the pipes behind them. Recognising the signal, the faithful rose as one to their feet, clearing their throats and straightening their clothes about themselves. Furtive glances were cast up the aisle to where a modest procession had begun its progress through the church. The Reverend Proudfoot was accompanied by a curate, and each was dressed in the black and white robes of their calling. The curate carried a golden crucifix before him, wearing an expression somewhere between solemnity and haughtiness that seemed to come naturally. Proudfoot trod carefully behind him, his ruddy face and bulbous nose already flushed from the little wine he had allowed himself in the vestry. Behind him walked half a dozen young boys dressed in the white vestments of the choir. Their faces shone in the dim light and they giggled as they caught each other's eye. Their hair was parted in the middle of their heads and combed tidily down to their ears. It was clearly something of a joke between them that they should be presented so smartly once a week, and Bowman hazarded a guess that if he were to meet them outside the church on an ordinary day, he should not recognise them. Each held a hymnbook in their hands and scanned the congregation for their family and friends.

The organ played 'Guide Me O Thou Great Jehovah' as the little party progressed through the church, diverging at the altar to find their places; the choir to the western side of the chancel and the curate and priest to the end of the nave by the north transept. There stood a large, raised lectern reached by six or seven wooden steps. It stood before a pillar on which hung an oak board displaying the numbers of the hymns to be sung that morning. As the music stopped, there came the sound of shuffling feet and rustling clothes as the congregation sat once more. A silence descended. All eyes fell upon Proudfoot as he reached the steps to the lectern. There was much interest as to how he would manage his ascent considering his condition. Reaching out his bony hands from beneath the folds of his robes, he clutched at the short banister that had been fixed to one side. Heaving himself slowly up, he stopped at each step to steady himself, swaying slightly as he stood like a sapling in a breeze. Bowman was sure he heard a giggle from one of the pews. Looking at his companion, he saw Inspector Hicks was taking the proceedings with the utmost seriousness, his great beard resting on his chest as he contemplated the hymnbook in his hand.

At last, Proudfoot was in his eyrie and the congregation fell to a fearful hush beneath his castigating eye. Gripping the lectern with both hands, Reverend Proudfoot leaned his weight against the wooden structure, scanning the congregation with an imperious gaze. Bowman fancied his eye fell upon him. Proudfoot paused with just a hint of a smile playing about his wet, fleshy lips.

"In the parables, Jesus says the Kingdom of God will be given to a people that will produce its fruit." Proudfoot let the words settle upon the upturned faces below. "There was a landowner who planted a vineyard, put a hedge around it and built a tower. Then he leased it to tenants and went on a journey." The reverend's voice was rich and textured. It carried with it a natural authority. It was, in short, a voice that demanded to be listened to. "When vintage time drew near," he continued, "the landowner sent his servants to the tenants to obtain his produce." Proudfoot made a fist of his hand. "But the tenants seized the servants. One they beat, another they killed, and a third they stoned." He brought his fist down on the wooden lectern as if to illustrate the force of the beatings. "The landowner sent other servants, more numerous than the first, but they treated them in the same way." Proudfoot sucked in air between his teeth. "Finally, he sent his son to them, thinking, 'They will respect my son.' But when the tenants saw the son, they said to one another, 'This is the heir. Come, let us kill him and acquire his inheritance.'" Proudfoot paused, aware of the drama in his tale. The very air in the church seemed to crackle with expectation. "They seized him," he declaimed as he reached for a crescendo, "threw him out of the vineyard, and killed him."

The congregation sat perfectly still in their pews, awaiting the denouement.

"A parable is a lesson, an opportunity to learn of God's wisdom." Proudfoot leaned towards the congregation and lowered his voice as if revealing a truth heretofore unknown for the benefit of their ears only. "In the parable of the tenants, it is written that those who come among us are our enemies. They seek to overturn our ways, to disrupt the lives we lead. God punishes those who would interfere."

Proudfoot's eyes again came to rest on Bowman, and the inspector sensed several of the villagers turn to glare in his direction.

"I say to them, the Kingdom of God will be taken away from you and given to a people that will produce its fruit."

Now all heads were turned to face the two detectives. They sat alone on their pew, suddenly uncomfortable in the full force of the villagers' gaze. The implication in Proudfoot's sermon was clear. Suddenly, Bowman was afraid.

"We will now sing hymn number five hundred and fifty two," Proudfoot concluded. "Judge Eternal, Throned In Splendour."

As the congregation rose as one to their feet, the organ struck up the opening bars of the hymn. Clearly oblivious to the implicit threat in the vicar's sermon, Inspector Ignatius Hicks joined them, throwing his head back to lead in the singing with such gusto that many in the congregation turned their heads in surprise and those nearest him covered their ears for fear of being rendered deaf.

The service over, the Reverend Proudfoot stood at the door with a collection box. Worshippers were confronted with the rattle of the box and the faintest scent of alcohol as they filed back out through the door. Very few made any donation at all, though Bowman saw Lord Melville making great play of depositing a guinea through the slot cut into the lid. Once through the doors, the children ran among the gravestones until reprimanded by their parents. Bowman kept his eyes to the path as he exited, leaving Inspector Hicks to throw a coin into the box for them both.

"I do hope your sergeant is recovering." The inspector looked up to see Greville Whitlock standing with Constable Corrigan, sheltering from the sun beneath the shade of a large yew tree.

"He is," Bowman replied. "Your ministrations have proven to be most efficacious."

"And this is his replacement?" Constable Corrigan looked Inspector Hicks up and down as he approached.

"This is Greville Whitlock, Inspector Hicks," Bowman

announced to his bluff companion. Curiously, Bowman noticed Whitlock look behind him.

"Then you will be assisting Detective Inspector Bowman?" Corrigan asked of Hicks. Out of his police uniform, he seemed a much smaller man.

Bowman looked around at the departing crowds. As they made their way between the graves, many of them paused to look back at the lean inspector with the moustache, even having the audacity to go so far as to point and snigger in his direct eye line. When he spoke at last, it was with a voice distinctly lacking in confidence.

"Sergeant Graves is recovering well enough, but I am reaching a crucial point in my investigations." He was aware of Whitlock's eyes boring into him. "Inspector Hicks is just the man to help bring them to a conclusion."

"He believes the soldier was murdered," Hicks interjected without prompting. "Though the evidence is scanty, to say the least." Bowman could hardly believe the nerve of the man. Hicks stood, his hands on his hips, puffing at his pipe. Whitlock did his best to suppress a smile.

"I am to turn my attention to the death of Erasmus Finch today," Bowman explained.

"Ah, yes," breathed Whitlock. "A tragic case, indeed." He glanced up to the tower as he spoke. "What could possess a man to throw himself from a church tower?"

"What, indeed?" Hicks scoffed.

"That is what I intend to find out." Bowman was eager for the conversation to be over, and eager to be rid of Hicks.

"But what is there to investigate?" Whitlock asked innocently, his wide moustache parting to reveal a kindly smile. "It cannot have been anything but self-murder, as I found in my report. You think it possible he was dragged up there and thrown off?"

"It is my place to consider all eventualities, Mr Whitlock," Bowman replied, suddenly distracted. "The better to arrive at a conclusion. Would you excuse me?"

Darting up the path, Bowman left the men to their speculations. Inspector Hicks rolled his eyes at his companion's retreating back. "Inspector Bowman is somewhat *erratic* in his methods." Drawing deep on his pipe, Hicks shook his head. He clearly thought to have a method at all was dangerously avant garde.

Bowman was grateful for the diversion. As Whitlock proclaimed his incredulity at Bowman's findings, the inspector had noticed a familiar face amongst the crowd, weaving their way through the cemetery gate and out to the road beyond. Phelps, the shopkeeper, stomped away from the church, clearly losing patience with the gaggle of children that ran alongside him. A young woman in a long summer dress with a high neckline walked a pace or two behind, trying to rein in the children as best she could. The rolled up parasol she carried over her shoulder proved to be the perfect implement to keep them in line.

"Mr Phelps," panted Bowman as he caught up with them at last. Phelps turned to him in surprise.

"Mary," he leered, his teeth protruding at an alarming angle, "this is the inspector I was telling you about." The young woman looked the inspector up and down, plainly unimpressed with what she saw. She gave a surly nod.

"Be quick, whatever you've got to say," she grumbled to her husband. "We've got to see what Trevitt has to say."

Phelps rolled his eyes. "What did you think of the sermon, inspector?" he leered. Bowman chose to ignore the question and the note of amusement in the man's voice.

"Mr Phelps, I wish to talk to Erasmus Finch's widow. Do you know where I might find her?"

"He knows where to find her," Mrs Phelps interjected, brandishing her parasol at her husband. "Every man in the village knows where to find her." She jabbed Phelps in the shoulder as she spoke.

"Leave me be, woman!" Phelps squealed, rubbing at the wound with nicotine-stained fingers. He turned again to the inspector. "How is your young sergeant?" Again, there was a note of amusement behind the words.

"Recovering," replied Bowman, simply. His eyes flicked involuntarily across the road to The King's Head and the window that he knew gave into Graves' room.

"I'm glad to hear it," Phelps attempted a friendly smile. "Just shows what can happen when you pry into matters that don't concern you."

"An address, please," Bowman breathed. He looked around them as he spoke. Once again he noticed people actively avoiding him, even going so far as to cross the road so as not to be approached. Phelps was shifting his weight from foot to foot, clearly feeling uncomfortable at being seen to be in cahoots with a Scotland Yarder.

"He knows it well enough," bellowed his wife. "He's made enough deliveries to her door, and overstayed his welcome, too." She gave him another prod with her parasol.

Phelps was now the butt of the joke, a position with which he was clearly painfully familiar. Bowman heard sniggers around him.

"She lives in yon cottages," the shopkeeper said quickly, eager to bring the conversation to an end. "Number Three."

"And tell the witch to get stuffed from me," Mrs Phelps pointed her parasol at Bowman, causing the inspector to step back in the road to avoid her.

"Watch yer step, filth," seethed an old man in a cloth cap and torn jacket. As the Phelps family continued along the path to the shop, one of their children turned from the line to poke out his tongue at the inspector, a look of disdainful insolence on his face.

Turning to the cottages Phelps had mentioned, Bowman saw Inspector Hicks striding from the churchyard.

"Hicks," Bowman began as he approached, "I have a matter to attend to." He smoothed his moustache between his finger and thumb as he spoke. "Perhaps it would be best if you went to Trevitt's meeting alone. I am too well known."

"You have certainly made quite the impression, Bowman, I will grant you that," Hicks boomed.

"Question him with regard to the blaze in Chalk Wood. He has never hidden his antipathy towards the gypsies there." Bowman slapped at a fly on his neck. "Meet me at The King's Head when you are done. I wish to check on Graves before we proceed any further."

"I wouldn't worry," Hicks said, airily. "I'm sure the lass is giving him her full attention." He gave Bowman a salacious wink that, given the circumstances, the inspector found most distasteful. He grabbed at Hicks' sleeve as the portly inspector moved away.

"Trust no one, Hicks," Bowman cautioned, his eyes narrowing as he looked up and down the street. Hicks regarded him with wary eyes and nodded slowly. The words were barely out of his mouth before Bowman realised that perhaps the person he should trust least of all was Hicks. He had no doubt the inspector had been sent as much to keep an eye on him as conclude the investigation. A cold sweat pricked suddenly at his back. Was Hicks intent on sabotage? It would certainly suit him if Bowman were to fail. He could imagine the bluff inspector even now, standing before the commissioner to take full credit for the closing of the case. Lord Melville would undoubtedly commend him to his old friend. A promotion would inevitably ensue. Bowman grit his teeth. He had often found Hicks a hindrance in his investigations, but had never considered that he would prove a wilful obstruction. He might well be in league with the people of Larton, Bowman thought with a lurch. He looked around at the villagers as they filed past, each on their way to Trevitt's mysterious meeting. Perhaps they were to discuss the obtrusive inspector and what should be done about him. Was Graves just the start? Was Hicks working with them? Perhaps matters went to the very top and even the commissioner was implicated. Bowman had often felt a thorn in the Yard's side. It would serve many people if he was discredited, not least the portly inspector before him.

"Bowman!"

Bowman blinked.

"My arm," Hicks said, simply. "Would you let me have it back?"

With a jolt, Bowman realised he still had a hold of the man's sleeve. He was gripping the material so hard that the muscles in his fingers had cramped.

"I am sorry," Bowman panted, letting go of Hicks' arm. He

licked his lips.

"Are you quite well?" Bowman knew the question was loaded. Hicks raised his eyebrows in the expectation of an answer.

"It is very hot," Bowman offered.

"It is that," Hicks replied, not at all convinced. He raised his eyes to the bright blue sky. There was not a hint of a cloud to be seen. "And I dare say it'll get worse before it gets better."

Bowman nodded as he turned away to cross the road. That, he mused to himself ruefully, was the wisest thing Hicks had ever said.

XVII

Mob Rule

The word had spread through Larton like a fire from tree to tree. As the morning services were concluded in each of Larton's churches, so the congregations turned their feet to Trevitt's farm in Larton Dean. The shopkeepers and professional men of the Village joined the workers and field labourers of the Rise on a progress to the high ground in the distance. Only the well-to-do of Larton Dean declined to join them. Aloof as ever behind their wrought iron gates and tall yew hedges, they hid themselves away as they always did, content to let the life of the village continue around them, determined not to be involved.

The cherry trees seemed to groan with the weight of their load. Their boughs, heavy with fruit, drooped to the ground. Wasps buzzed from branch to branch, drunk on the plump, overripe cherries. Left unpicked, they had fallen to waste. Just a few days had seen them turn to a soft, inedible mulch, fit only for the insects and birds.

The ground was hard and unyielding beneath their feet as the villagers headed to the large barn that stood on the perimeter of Trevitt's farm. Those who had not spoken with one another for decades deigned to exchange eye contact. There were looks of surprise at the sheer numbers who had given up their Sunday at Trevitt's invitation. Suspicion had given way to curiosity. Swept up in the movement of people through the village, no one had wanted to be left behind. It was an irony not lost on many of them that Maxwell Trevitt had managed to unite the village. It remained to be seen to what end.

William Oats stood by the entrance to the barn, leaning on the handle of a fork. Under Trevitt's instructions, he had cleared the ground and erected a small stage at one end of the building; a simple structure comprising some old boxes lashed together with rope. Ordinarily, the barn would be bursting with produce. Box after box would be stacked to the roof, each containing the spoils of a hard day's picking; cassir cherries. Known for their rich purple hue and sweet taste, it was said they were enjoyed by no less a person than the Tsar of Russia. It was, Trevitt was wont to remark, a most imperial fruit. It could fetch an imperial price, too. Packed and loaded onto carts at the farm, box after box would be transferred onto the Larton Donkey for the journey into London's markets. Covent Garden, Berwick Street, Victoria Park and Shepherds Bush were loyal customers, seemingly insatiable in their appetite for the dark purple jewel that hung from Trevitt's cherry trees. Sold by the box or the bag, they were the unmistakable sign that summer had arrived; displayed to great effect in the grocer's window, or sold by the roadside from barrows with pretty awnings.

Oats stood aside to watch the barn fill with curious villagers. He recognised just about every face from the blacksmith to the grocer and from the barber to the landlord. One face, however, eluded him. Just as the last of the stragglers rounded the hill to the orchard, they were joined by a mountain of a man in a long coat. He had an impressive beard that spread across his chest from his chin and a battered top hat was perched on his head. His arms swung in wide arcs as he walked, as if the action would propel him faster on his way, and a plume of smoke curled from the bowl of a pipe that he held tight in his teeth. Oats had never seen the man before, and he noticed that he walked alone and unremarked into the barn behind the throng, taking a position along the back wall from where he could better observe proceedings.

The crush of people in the barn warmed the air quickly and soon the villagers were wilting in the heat. The few women present fanned themselves with their hands, the men mopped at their brows with their sleeves. Just as they were sure they were at the receiving end of some grand joke, Maxwell Trevitt appeared. Limping onto the makeshift stage, he eyed the crowd for a moment, the bruises on his face shining in the gloom. A cut beneath his eye had spread across his already broken nose, and he periodically pressed his hands to his ribs to alleviate the pain.

"For five generations," he began at last, his voice thick with emotion, "the Trevitts have grown cherries in Larton." He spread his arms wide. "Everything you see around you has sprung from the fruit that grows on my trees."

"Shame you haven't shared it with the rest of us!"

Trevitt peered into the crowd, trying to find the heckler. His eyes rested on a young man with long hair and a longer face.

"Albert Pickering," Trevitt began, "if ever you should leave the village and find yourself at Covent Garden, you will find the name of Trevitt and the village of Larton is held in high esteem."

"What good is that to us?" Pickering spat. "We'd rather have food in our bellies than be held in high esteem."

"He's too busy hiring gypsies!"

"So they can steal our things from underneath our noses!"

There was a murmur of agreement from the crowd and even a spontaneous burst of applause from a man in the corner.

"They bring nothing but trouble," the man interjected. "But Trevitt doesn't care for that, so long as he gets his cherries picked!"

There were more shouts of agreement. Trevitt sensed he was losing his audience.

"I've learnt my lesson," he shouted from his makeshift podium, "and I've learned it hard." He rubbed at his cracked ribs with a hand as the crowd fell into a suspicious silence. Taking a painful breath, he adopted a conciliatory tone. "Perhaps it is time to come together," he continud. "To come together as a village for the good of the village."

"He says that now the gypsies won't work for him," called a voice from the crowd. "And he'll no doubt pay us a pittance, too."

"I shall pay you a fair rate, just as I paid them," Trevitt pleaded. In truth, he had no such intention. "I have a matter of days before this year's crop spoils." He held his hands before him in a gesture of supplication. "Help me bring it in and you'll share in the profits." Anyone who knew Trevitt well would know how those words stuck in his throat, and how hard he was already thinking of ways to disentangle himself from his promise at a later date. He cared not for the consequences, only of getting the fruit from the trees to market. In truth, he was desperate. His treatment at the hands of Stoker's men had only confirmed that their relationship had been shattered. There was no prospect of the gypsies ever working for him again, and that left him with a dilemma. Who would bring in the harvest? Swallowing his pride for the time being, he had decided upon a strategy. He looked around him at the faces in the barn. From their expressions it looked like it might just be working.

"And if we don't, will you burn us out of house and home as well?"

Trevitt turned to the man in the corner. "I did not set that fire in Chalk Wood," he asserted, then lowered his voice to a whisper. "Though in truth, I wish I had."

Suddenly, there was agreement. "They've had it coming!" called Albert Pickering. "I would've carried the torch for you if I'd known." Trevitt noticed several nods of agreement. One man even clapped Pickering on the back for the remark. And, in that moment, Trevitt saw his course.

"Then perhaps we should make an end of the matter," he said, testing the waters. "Once and for all."

"I'd like to see them pay for everything they've stolen!" The remark was greeted with a round of applause from the assembled crowd.

"And for keeping our womenfolk in fear of their lives!" This was greeted with a cheer.

"They live like animals," Albert Pickering hissed, his eyes blazing. "Perhaps they should be beaten like animals."

"Let's drive them from the village!"

Trevitt looked on, amazed. He had never expected it to be so easy. Like putting a match to dry grass, he had ignited something in the villagers' hearts. What was more, he realised, was that he was enjoying it.

"Then what are you waiting for?" he boomed. "There are tools enough in the barn. Grab what you can and let's teach 'em a lesson!"

The most enormous cheer erupted from the throng as they each turned to the walls. There hung scythes, rakes and shovels; all they needed to show the travellers of Chalk Wood that

Larton had had enough. Men, women and even children grabbed at the tools, swinging them before them as if trying them for size. Weapons in their hands, they spilled from the barn with a single intent; to find the gypsies of Chalk Wood and mete out their revenge.

William Oats stood by the door, distinctly unimpressed by the spectacle. Resolving to have no part in proceedings, he was about to turn his feet towards home, when his eye was caught by the large man with the beard and long coat. The only man without a weapon, Oats noticed him standing alone by the back wall, giving every indication of being at a complete loss as to what he was best to do.

XVIII

A Widow Speaks

Newman's Cottages stood back from the road behind a dilapidated fence. Their front gardens had been all but abandoned in the onslaught of the summer sun. The soil lay in unbroken lumps where it had been turned, the earth baked as hard as the shards of flint that littered the ground. Here and there, hardier plants clung to fence posts or languished by the path. Cheerful poppies stood tall by the gate, and Bowman noticed a patch of onions growing beneath a window. Number Three stood in the middle of the row, presenting a sad face to the world. The woodwork around the windows was brittle and cracked, flecks of paint peeling away to float like coloured dust to the neglected ground below. A small porch stood out from the facade, its roof a patchwork of hastily arranged tiles. Not all were of the same size, with the result that several holes were visible in the porch roof. A wooden trellis bent away from beneath an upstairs window, the dry skeleton of a climbing plant gripping to it for support, even in death.

Even as he approached, Bowman was aware of being watched. Through the reflection of the road behind him, he could see a face peering from the corner of the downstairs window. Large eyes blinked at him, and Bowman was put in mind of what it is to face a scared animal in the woods around his Hampstead home. The inspector knocked at the door. Glancing through the small pane of cracked glass set into the wood, he could see the claustrophobic porch beyond and an open door to a small parlour. A vase of dried flowers sat upon a sideboard. From where Bowman stood on the doorstep, they looked like white roses. Soon enough, he heard movement within; the furtive, shuffling sounds of someone preparing for company where they had been expecting none. Suddenly, a face loomed from the dark of the porch towards the small window in the door.

Taken by surprise, Bowman stepped back. In truth, his

conversation with Inspector Hicks was still ringing in his ears. He pressed a hand against his chest to calm the thumping of his heart.

The door was forced open a matter of inches, just enough to allow Prudence Finch a full view of the man before her. She seemed to cling to the door for support, Bowman noticed, like the dried stick clinging to the broken trellis beside him. It was clear she had no intention of breaking the silence first.

"Mrs Finch?" Bowman spoke up at last. "I am Detective Inspector Bowman of Scotland Yard."

There was no hint of feeling in the woman's face as she replied. "I know who you are." She looked up and down the street. "I dare say there's no one in Larton who doesn't."

She turned to look at him, expectantly. Bowman at once felt under scrutiny. He swung his hat from his head and smoothed his hair with a hand. Catching his reflection in the door, he was suddenly aware of how thin he had become. "May I speak with you?" he asked, softly.

"With regard to what?" Though possessive of the local burr, her voice was clear, her face difficult to read. It was an odd question, thought Bowman.

"The death of your husband, Erasmus Finch." He felt foolish at once.

"I am a woman alone, Inspector Bowman, and widowed, too. How would such a thing look to the village?"

Bowman felt he was being tested. "I should expect, if it were any business of theirs at all, it would look like the widow of a dead man was cooperating with an investigation into her husband's death."

There was another silence as his response was weighed and considered. Bowman heard the screaming of swifts above him. He was aware of the sweat on his back.

"Have you not brought enough trouble to the village already, inspector? Erasmus is dead. What good can you do?" Mrs Finch moved to close the door abruptly in the inspector's face.

"I am here on the express instructions of Lord Melville and the commissioner of Scotland Yard."

Mrs Finch opened the door again, a little wider this time.

Bowman could see she was a slight figure, still in her Sunday dress from church. Her hair was pinned up on her head, framing an oval face with dark, almond shaped eyes. The faintest of lines had begun to appear around her mouth, but she was still clearly a young woman with all the attendant energy of one who has yet to meet her middle years.

"Ah, yes," she breathed. There was a touch of cynicism to her voice. "Lord Melville, who cares so much for Larton that he holds us all to the wall."

"How so?" Bowman leaned in, genuinely interested to hear her response. There was something about Lord Melville that he did not care for and he had felt it reflected at the regatta the day before. He had noticed much tugging of forelocks and doffing of caps in his Lordship's presence, but they had been accompanied by sneers and sideways glances the moment his back had been turned.

With a final look up and down the street, Prudence Finch was plainly satisfied their exchange had passed unnoticed. "You had better come in," she said. "Before you are seen."

"How long have you lived in Larton?"

The cottage looked even smaller on the inside. A single room greeted him from the porch, with one door leading out to a small lean-to kitchen and another to a flight of stairs which looped up and round to the upper floor. A single picture of a country landscape hung on the wall above the small fireplace. There was very little furniture besides the sideboard and two chairs that had clearly seen better days. Bowman could see an attempt had been made to disguise their decrepitude with the addition of a pair of threadbare blankets. Beneath them, he noticed straw stuffing bursting out of the seams, the headrests worn and discoloured.

"Will all your questions be of such a private nature, inspector?"

Bowman looked up, guiltily. "Begging your pardon, Mrs Finch." He lowered his voice. "The death of your husband might well shed light on at least one other in the village."

The woman before him seemed to weigh her options before

moving into the kitchen and gesturing the inspector sit with him at a rickety table. There was such limited space in the room that Bowman considered refusing the offer. He decided, however, that such a response might appear unduly rude, sensing he was going to have to work much harder to gain Mrs Finch's trust. Pulling a chair from the table, he cast his eyes about him. The small lean-to was little more than some ill-fitting panes of glass fixed into a rotting wooden frame. The inspector was certain it would provide little shelter during the more inclement months of the year. As it was, the sunlight streamed into the room, giving sustenance to the few potted herbs that were arranged on shelves near a small cooking range. A heavy porcelain basin was placed against the wall, though Bowman saw no evidence of running water. Looking through the glass to the scrappy gardens beyond, he saw there were no fences to separate the plots. Some small beds of vegetables lay scorched and neglected.

"I am afraid," he continued, "it is imperative that I know the details of your husband's life in Larton if I am to make any sense of it at all."

Mrs Finch looked down at her lap. "I had thought to be out of my Sunday best by now." She reached up to remove the pin from her hair.

"I will be as brief as I can," Bowman assured her.

Mrs Finch rubbed her hands together nervously as she spoke in a gesture that Bowman found immediately beguiling. "I have lived in Larton for some six years, since I married Erasmus."

"Then you are not from Larton originally?"

"Erasmus was born in Larton Rise but we met across the river in Wootton Green. My family have farmed there for generations, though not with any great success." She stared out and across the garden as she spoke, revelling in her private memories. "I was the Queen of the May." The corners of her mouth turned up at the memory, and she drew herself up in her chair with pride. "I was quite the catch in those days."

Bowman did not doubt it. Now her hair was loose about her face, he could see the odd wisp of grey. Beyond that, Mrs Finch had clearly retained whatever looks had first attracted Erasmus

Finch.

"Then Erasmus brought you here?" Bowman noticed a strand of hair caught between her lips.

"The lot of a farmer's daughter is not a happy one, and her prospects are slim. Erasmus offered me the hope of advancement."

Bowman cast his mind back to the Berkshire Chronicle's reports of Erasmus' death. "The newspapers say he worked for the railway."

"And that is so. He was a clerk at Reading Station." Again, she puffed herself up with pride at the thought. "He had an office with his name at the door."

"And so you married?" Bowman placed an elbow on the table and rested his chin on his hand. He felt strangely at ease listening to the details of someone else's life. It was, he realised, a distraction from having to consider his own.

"Eventually," Prudence Finch was saying, "but not so quick as to be unseemly." She folded her arms in front of her, defensively. "Then I moved in with Erasmus at his parents" house in Larton Rise, just near the station. I took work at Larton Manor but I was not liked at work or at home. His parents were - " she paused. "Difficult."

"Why?" Bowman was engrossed.

"Because I was not from Larton," Mrs Finch said, simply. "In the eyes of the villagers here, there is no greater crime." A rueful smile played about her lips. "They can hardly bring themselves to be civil to each other, let alone those from across the river."

Bowman thought back to the countless sly looks and suspicious glances he had encountered in just two days. "The people of Larton do seem somewhat insular," he concurred. "I can imagine you encountered a certain resistance."

"Quite simply, I have always been a stranger in Larton. I am considered different, *other*." Prudence Finch shifted on her chair. "The feeling was only compounded by the two of us making the biggest mistake of all."

Bowman raised his eyebrows. "Oh?"

"Moving from the Rise to Larton Village."

Bowman nodded in understanding. "I can imagine," he

sighed. From what he had learned of the people of Larton, that would have been a mistake indeed.

"It was generally held that we had risen above our station," Mrs Finch shrugged. "Erasmus had sought to better our condition, that is all, but we were not accepted into the Village."

Bowman smoothed his moustache. "Larton is a strange place, indeed," he mused.

Prudence allowed herself a wry smile at Bowman's observation. "You have a gift for understatement, inspector," she teased. "To be born in any of the three constituent parts of Larton is to die in them. There is a fierce sense of identity here, and woe befall any who would seek to challenge it."

Bowman blinked sweat from his eyes. He was finding it hotter here beneath the glass than even outside. Raising a hand to shield his eyes from the sun, he chose his words carefully as he continued.

"So your husband would undoubtedly have made many enemies on account of his ambitions."

"Doubly so," Mrs Finch agreed, forcefully. "The people of the Rise shunned him for his pretensions to a better life in the Village, while to those in the Village we would always be outsiders." She paused, looking down at her hands in her lap. "Even Erasmus" parents shunned us." She swallowed. "They had nothing to do with us from that day to this, even after Erasmus" death."

Bowman could tell he was approaching difficult territory. He shifted his weight in his chair, leaning further over the table so as to watch Mrs Finch all the more carefully. She blinked furiously, clearly fighting back the tears at the memory.

"And your employment at Larton Manor?" the inspector probed, gently.

Mrs Finch shrugged again, as if the whole affair was beyond her. "I did not fit in there," she said, simply. "The staff implicated me in a minor scandal, the supposed theft of some jewellery. The driver, Prescott, was chief among them."

Bowman did not doubt it. There was something about Lord Melville's driver that he did not trust. "I was summarily dismissed," Mrs Finch continued. "I was innocent, of course but, for an additional punishment, Lord Melville saw fit to raise the rent on our cottage." She looked around her, sadly.

"You are a tenant to Larton Manor?"

"I should say most of the village is, inspector. We are all in thrall to the Larton Estate and, as such, all subject to Lord Melville's whims."

The frown on Bowman's forehead deepened. "You believe that is why your husband took his life?"

Mrs Finch nodded. "With no employment for me and the rent increased, I'm afraid Erasmus found it too much to bear. He took it upon himself to end his life." She rose abruptly from her chair to stand and face the garden through the glass. "And I will never forgive him for it." Through the heaving of her shoulders, Bowman could tell she was crying. Pulling a handkerchief from a sleeve, Mrs Finch dabbed at her face, clearly determined not to be seen in so vulnerable a condition.

"Perhaps he saw no other way," Bowman soothed, rising clumsily from his chair. Feeling his head swim at the sudden movement, he leaned against the table to get his breath. His mouth was dry. It was notable that Mrs Finch had not seen fit to offer him a drink upon his arrival. Perhaps that was as well, he thought. She would not, in any case, have offered him the sort of drink he craved.

"There is always another way," he heard the woman at the window sniff. "There has to be." Finally, she turned to face him, her eyes red. "God has granted us life, inspector. It is up to us to live it to the full."

"That is not always the easiest course to take," Bowman heard himself say.

"Life is never easy," Mrs Finch scoffed. "But Erasmus' cowardice has made mine worse. With no husband and no employment to be had for me in Larton, I can no longer pay my rent to Larton Manor." Bowman heard a tremor in her voice. "It is surely a matter of a few days before I am thrown to the mercy of my family in Wootton Green."

Bowman was taken by surprise at Mrs Finch's choice of words. "You think your husband a coward?" he stammered. He had not considered Erasmus' suicide, if suicide it was, in those terms.

The woman nodded her head. "He had not the courage within him to face his difficulties, difficulties we could surely have overcome together."

"Perhaps," Bowman allowed. "But he cannot have been in his right mind."

Prudence's gaze had fallen to Bowman's hands on the table. "I see you are a married man, inspector." Bowman's eyes flicked to the ring on his left hand. A simple, gold band, he could not bring himself to remove it. Mrs Finch was moving closer now, her eyes appealing to him. "Surely you can understand?" Bowman could not avoid her gaze. "A marriage is a union is it not?" she continued. "It makes us doubly strong. But Erasmus has gone, and I am diminished." Bowman felt the depths of her despair. "I am halved."

"You cannot blame him for wanting peace." Bowman's words sounded distant to his ears, as if he were overhearing a conversation from another room.

"Surely to live is all?" There was a note of desperation in Mrs Finch's voice. "He was not even permitted a full Christian burial." This was almost too much for her, and Bowman saw her try to stem the tears again. Breathing deeply, she calmed herself enough to continue. "Do you think, inspector, he is damned?"

Bowman could not find the words. How could a god grant free will to his creations, then damn a man for seeking respite from the trials of life? And yet he knew the Church's teachings were against it. It was only recently that those who had committed self-murder had been permitted burial in holy ground.

"Mrs Finch," he said at last, "what did you notice about your husband's behaviour in the weeks leading up to his death?" Bowman loosened his collar with a finger. "Was there a specific incident that may have weakened his resolve?"

Mrs Finch sat again, her head tilted in thought. "Some weeks before," she began, slowly, "he was suddenly possessed of a levity quite unlike him. He gave me to believe that our condition would soon improve, that he had found a way through our difficulties."

"Did he say what it was?"

"He did not." Mrs Finch wrung her hands as she spoke. "But his jubilation proved short lived."

"Indeed?" Bowman was concentrating hard.

Prudence Finch took a breath. "One evening, he returned from an evening at The King's Head to find an envelope beneath the door. Upon Erasmus opening it, there was a sudden and distinct change in his demeanour. He became at once withdrawn and melancholy."

"Could you more precisely tell me when he found the envelope?"

"I can," Mrs Finch nodded. "It was towards the middle of May, the very day before the old soldier was found dead in the Dean."

"Trooper Sharples," Bowman whispered.

"And Erasmus was dead just four weeks later."

A pause hung in the air long enough to admit the screeching of passing swifts.

"How was your husband's behaviour following the discovery of the envelope?"

"Erratic," Mrs Finch allowed. "He would disappear for hours at a time, returning in an agitated state."

"Where did he go?"

Prudence spread her hands wide in a gesture of futility. "I do not know."

Bowman's moustache was twitching at his upper lip. He cleared his throat. "Did he not share with you the contents of the envelope?"

"He did not, inspector," Mrs Finch's eyes narrowed in thought. "But there was something peculiar about it."

Bowman lifted his eyes to meet her gaze. "The lettering or a postmark?"

"It had been delivered by hand," Mrs Finch continued, slowly. "But there was a design upon the envelope such as I have not seen before. It was... most strange."

Bowman was leaning even further forward on his elbows. "Mrs Finch," he breathed, urgently, "could you reproduce the design for me?"

With a dip of her head, Mrs Finch rose again from her chair and walked back into the parlour. Bowman was left alone for a moment; just enough to attempt to calm his breathing. There was a familiar throbbing at his temples. Leaning forward, he pressed the heels of his hands against his eyes. He felt empty to the pit of his stomach. He could not remember how long it had been since his last meal. Days, perhaps. He doubted he could have kept it down, at any rate. His stomach felt clenched as if in anticipation of some dreadful event. There was a knot in his belly. Breathing slowly now, he leaned back in his chair with a sigh, just in time to see Mrs Finch return with a pen and a bottle of ink. She laid a clean, fresh envelope upon the table before sitting to begin her work, her tongue poking beguilingly between her lips in an expression of concentration.

Bowman stood to peer over her shoulder at her handiwork. Dipping the nib of her pen in the inkbottle, she first drew the prongs of some implement, joined by a hinge at the top and angled like the hands of a clock pointing down. Pausing for thought, she replenished her pen and drew a right angle beneath it, its two arms pointing up the page from its vertex. In the space between the two designs she fashioned a crude shape resembling a tree or, thought Bowman, a sheaf of corn. Suddenly, his breath came fast. Sweat pricked at his forehead and his lips dried.

"Are you sick, inspector?" Mrs Finch enquired, concerned.

Bowman's head was swimming. He was certain he had seen that design before.

XIX

Fuel To The Flames

Detective Inspector Ignatius Hicks was struggling. He had found the walk from Larton Village to Trevitt's barn in the Dean hard enough. Now, he found himself tramping uphill to Chalk Wood, every step harder than the last. Soon, he was left straggling behind the villagers. He had watched as they streamed from the barn, each with a tool or improvised weapon in their hands. For a moment he was torn. Should he attempt to stop them or walk back to the police station in the Rise for help? He soon dismissed the former, being vastly outnumbered by the throng of villagers intent on making their point. Trevitt had whipped them up to such a frenzy that they were all on his side. Even those who had been against him at the beginning had evidently seen fit to set aside their differences in the pursuit of a common enemy. They had strode from the barn as a mob, each with a determined look upon their face. Some wielded pitchforks and shovels, others had gathered lengths of wood or discarded tools from the barn floor. Hicks felt nervous of confronting them in such a state. He also dismissed walking down the hill to the Rise in order to enlist support. In the time it might take for him to walk the distance, the war in the woods might be won or lost. His best option, he thought as he lumbered up the hill, was to accompany the villagers to the travellers' camp in the hope of interceding at the point of their meeting. He would then make his presence and his purpose known, relying on his expert skills of negotiation to reach a peace between the two factions. He had not considered the walk.

Puffing out his cheeks with exhaustion, Inspector Hicks swung the hat from his head, fanning his face with the brim. He wiped the sweat from his forehead with the hem of his coat and reached into a deep pocket for his tobacco. Tapping his pipe against the stump of a tree, he loaded it with fresh fuel and struck a match against the heel of his shoe. He drew deeply on the smoke as the match flared in the bowl, the resultant smog rising into the canopy like a will-o"-the-wisp. Hicks squinted through the smoke at the villagers as they receded into the distance. Just a minute to recover his breath, the plump inspector reasoned, and he would join them. Leaning on the tree stump for support, he let his eyes scan the fields and trees about him. Looking down the hill, he was presented with an open vista stretching to Larton Rise and the Village beyond. The land rose the other side of the valley into a wooded escarpment, the ribbon of the River Thames threading its way through a patchwork of fields at its base. Ricks of hay were stacked at intervals and, even on a Sunday, Hicks saw those villagers who had not deigned to join the march on Chalk Wood scything at the long grass. Turning to his left, his eyes fell upon a dilapidated farmer's cottage he took to be Trevitt's farmhouse. Even from this distance, he could see it was in need of attention. A chimney pitched dangerously to one side upon the roof and several of the walls leaned at a crazy angle. The whole effect, mused Hicks as he caught his breath, was of a building that had given up the struggle to remain upright. Just as he determined to gird himself and follow the villagers, Hicks' attention was caught by a movement in a woodpile by the cottage wall. He was sure he saw a wisp of smoke curling from the wood. Cursing under his breath that he might never be granted a moment's rest, the inspector gathered his coat around him and lumbered off with such speed as he could muster.

Soon, he was approaching a small out-building by the cottage. A makeshift door hung from its hinges at an alarming angle, allowing access to a small, ragged form that, even now, darted inside for more fuel. Quickening his step, Hicks negotiated his way through the debris in the farmer's yard to the cottage wall. Stamping at the fire with his foot, he extinguished the flames before they caught a hold, reaching down to remove a smouldering log and flinging it clear of the pile. Then, positioning himself by the outbuilding's ramshackle door, he tried hard to steady his breathing so as not to be heard. Just as he readied himself to enter, he heard a low, rumbling growl behind him. Turning, he was confronted by a large lurcher with a sharp nose and beady eyes. Its upper lip curled away from its teeth as a guttural snarl resounded deep in its chest. It stood stock still, its muscles tensed in anticipation.

"Duke! What's the matter with you, boy?" Hicks heard the voice from within the building. It was the high-pitched call of a youth. As if to confirm his suspicions, a young boy with freckles and tousled hair suddenly appeared at the door, an armful of logs held close to his chest.

"Duke!" He called again. "Quit yer hollerin'!"

He barely had time to look up before he felt a hand pinching at his ear. Dropping his load in alarm, the young lad squealed with pain.

"Hey! What yer doin'?" he yelled. "Let go of me!"

"Stand your friend down and I'll think about it," Hicks responded, pinching harder.

"He won't hurt you," the boy insisted, squirming with discomfort. "He's all bark and no bite, the useless good for nuffin'."

"Is this Trevitt's house?" Hicks thundered.

"Might be," the young lad spat, defiantly.

Hicks twisted harder at the boy's ear. "And just what do you think you were up to?"

In response, the lad kicked at Hicks' shins. The inspector allowed himself a chuckle as he held his young assailant at arm's length. He was so small that, even at such a short distance, his arms and legs flailed helplessly in the air, failing to make any contact whatsoever.

"He's a murderer," the boy screamed, his face flushed.

"Well, let's see what he's got to say about that, shall we?" Hicks marched the boy away from the farmhouse, his dog whipping between them uselessly as if the whole incident was one big game.

"And let's see what he thinks to you setting fires against his house."

The villagers had ascended the hill to Chalk Wood. Had they been of a mind, they might have paused to admire the view that encompassed the whole of Larton; Dean, Rise and Village. The land rolled away beneath them to a bright blue horizon, the perfect hunting ground for the wheeling kites that circled on the warm air, their keen eyes on the fields below. As it was, the irate mob barely faltered as it made its way along the track into the clump of trees at the brow. Of one mind, they marched almost in time, the occasional shout and whistle echoing into the trees above them. The smell of burnt wood assailed their nostrils, the conflagration of the night before clearly still smouldering ahead of them. As they reached the turning through the undergrowth that led to the travellers" camp, Trevitt raised his hand to bring the crowd to a standstill. Strangely, the woods were quiet. Aside from the heavy breathing of the villagers and the scurrying of squirrels in the branches above them, there was not a sound to be heard. Trevitt scowled. He had expected to have been met by now. He was certain Stoker would have employed a lookout following the fire and the incident outside the police station. Crouching low, he made his way into the traveller's camp, his followers at his heels. Wielding his pitchfork ahead of him like a scythe, he quietly cleared his way of nettles and stepped stealthily into the clearing. The stark, chalk walls of the old quarry towered above him, studded with rocky outcrops and clumps of grass. The plaintive song of a blackbird pierced the still air.

"They've gone!" Trevitt heard someone shout behind him.

"Then good riddance to 'em!" called another.

Looking about him, the farmer saw all the evidence of a camp in hasty retreat. The grass and bracken lay flattened where the tents had stood. The ground, dry as it was, was marked with all the signs of hasty activity. Great ruts had been gouged into the dirt where the caravans had been pulled away. Over by the escarpment wall, Trevitt saw a pile of discarded waste. Looking down to the ground, he noticed a thin stick of liquorice root protruding from the earth, its end chewed and misshapen. With a ghastly smile disfiguring his wide face, he took enormous pleasure in grinding it into the ground beneath his boot.

"We're rid of the filth!" he shouted as he turned, holding his fork high.

A great cheer erupted from the throng in front of him. Several of them spilled into the quarry to confirm the matter with their own eyes.

"Happen they'll think twice before they return," called a woman with an improvised cosh. She spat on the ground in disdain.

Trevitt nodded, satisfied. "We have no need of them!" he rounded. "There's work for you all if you want it. There's cherries in those trees need picking!"

A silence fell upon the crowd. The man nearest to Trevitt leaned on his spade.

"That's all very well," he said slowly. "But I reckon you need us more than we need you." The crowd around him nodded as one. "We'll need to talk terms afore we agree to anything."

Trevitt looked into the throng. Every man and woman before him stared back in defiance. The silence was broken by a call from the back of the crowd.

"Maxwell Trevitt!"

The villagers turned as one to be greeted by the sight of a large, bearded man dressed in a long, ankle length coat and top hat clutching a young boy by the ear. A large lurcher gambolled at their side, sniffing the air excitedly.

"Who's that?" Hicks heard a woman ask. "And what's he doin' with young Tom Cousins?"

"I saw that man with the Scotland Yarder at church this morning." William Oats stepped out of the crowd, wiping the sweat from his forehead with the back of his hand. "And he was at the meeting in the barn."

"You have some questions to answer, Maxwell Trevitt," Hicks thundered, his great beard bristling before him.

"What you doin' with my Tom?"

The crowd turned again to see a middle-aged woman struggling through the undergrowth, a small baby clutched against her breast. Florrie Cousins pushed her way through the throng and squared up to Detective Inspector Hicks. "Who are you?"

The bluff inspector drew himself up to his full height. "I am Detective Inspector Ignatius Hicks," he announced, biting down on the bit of his pipe. If he had hoped to inspire awe amongst the villagers, he failed. His words were greeted with little more than a snigger from the man leaning on his spade. "And I found this lad setting a fire at Trevitt's farmhouse," he concluded. Hicks pushed the boy into the clearing before him. Dog and mother rushed towards the lad, the former licking him excitedly about the face, the other pinching her features into a look of reproach.

"What on earth have you been up to, Tom?" she scolded, lifting the boy to his feet and brushing the dirt from his clothes. The baby in her arms let forth a cry at the sudden movement.

"Setting a fire, eh?" Trevitt scowled. "That boy's fit for nothing but locking up, inspector."

"I'll be the judge of that," Hicks returned, grandly.

"You murdered my father!" Tom ran at the farmer, his fists raised before him.

"Get this animal off me," Trevitt called to Florrie Cousins. "I had nought to do with Fletcher Cousins' death."

"You drove him to it!" Florrie was stomping towards Trevitt, her chin jutting before her in her rage. "And now you've condemned us to the workhouse." Heedless of the small child in her arms, her voice rose in volume as her passions overwhelmed her.

"Seems to me there's only one thing that might drive a man to take his own life, and that's having a wife like you at home!" Trevitt grinned at his own joke, a wide smile spreading beneath his broken nose. Having heard enough, Tom Cousins made a fist and drove it into Trevitt's groin, stepping back as the farmer doubled up in pain. A fair number in the crowd laughed out loud at the scene playing out before them. One even shouted encouragement to the young boy with the freckles and unruly hair.

"That's a boy, Tom, don't hold back!"

"This man withheld my husband's pay because the gypsies would not work!" Florrie was appealing to the crowd, "He cannot be trusted!"

"And what of the gypsies, Trevitt?" Hicks raised his voice above the melee. "Did you raise the fire that threatened their camp?"

Trevitt was still catching his breath, his hands held

protectively between his legs. "Ask the lad," he gasped, his eyes rolling back in his head with the pain. "He seems to have a liking for setting fires."

"Tom?" Florrie Cousins took her son by the shoulders. "Did you set the fire near the gypsy camp?"

There was a silence. The crowd seemed to lean in as one as Tom's gaze fell to the undergrowth beneath his feet.

"Tom?" Hicks moved a step closer, his arms folded across his great chest.

"I couldn't bear the thought of him hanging there," Tom said at last. "I want the whole thing gone. Forest, camp, farm and all!" As tears sprung from his eyes, he buried his head in his mother's breast. Heavy sobs escaped him as his shoulders shook, uncontrollably.

"It's alright, Tom," his mother soothed, stroking his hair, "No one was hurt."

Shaking their heads, the villagers began to disperse. Some threw their tools down on the forest floor, clearly disappointed at the anti-climax. Trudging despondently away, several of them muttered sourly under their breath, throwing suspicious looks at the detective inspector in their midst.

"A shame Scotland Yard gave them warning," Hicks heard one of them say as they skulked back through the woods towards the Rise. "If it weren't for them we could have shown Stoker what's what."

Inspector Hicks strode forward to clap his hand on Tom's shoulder. "It seems you've caused a lot of bother, young Tom," he said. "But you saved the gypsies a beating, too." He turned his attention to the woman at Tom's side. Rocking from side to side to comfort her baby, she presented a picture of motherhood that was quite lost on Inspector Hicks. "And next time you suspect someone of criminal activity, Mrs Cousins," he began, stroking his great beard, "might I suggest you look to your own family first?"

With that, Hicks turned his great bulk away to start his journey back down the hill, flailing his arms about him in a vain effort to clear the overhanging twigs in his path.

XX

A Picture Of Health

"An envelope?"

Inspector Bowman was relieved to find Graves sitting up in his bed. As he tucked into a bowl of soup, there was something of his usual demeanour about him. Although his curls hung limp on his head and his skin was sallow, there was a light in his eyes that Bowman recognised. A clean bandage encircled his head, tied delicately at the back and fastened with a pin. Maude had plainly been excelling in her duties.

"With a design on the front like that I saw in Sharples' cottage." Bowman stroked his moustache. "The box which contained his revolver bore such a design. Two geometric shapes, one above the other."

Bowman had pulled the only other chair up to Graves' bed. A window had been opened to admit such air as there was and, with it, the sounds of the street. Occasionally, a carriage rattled past on some errand, or a child would shout to another across the road. The peaceful scene seemed a world away from the frenetic events of the day before. If it had not been for the wan figure before him, Bowman could easily have believed that they had not happened at all.

"What do you think was in it, sir?" Graves scraped the bottom of the bowl with his spoon, eager to enjoy his soup to the very last drop.

"That, Graves, I do not know." Bowman leaned back in his chair, stretching his legs before him and clasping his hands behind his head. "But Finch's demeanour changed almost the moment he read it."

"Was it a threat, then?"

Bowman chewed his lip. "Or an instruction, perhaps?"

Graves wiped soup from his lips with the back of his hand and placed the bowl on the floor beneath him. "To do what?"

Deep in thought, Bowman sprang to his feet and walked to the window. "I have turned that thought over in my mind again and again," he sighed. "And there is only one answer I can think of."

Graves blinked in anticipation as Bowman turned back into the room.

"To kill Trooper Sharples."

Graves let the inspector's words sink in. "You think he was commanded to do so?"

Bowman was pacing now, his hands deep in his trouser pockets. "We must assume that Sharples knew his assailant, or why else would he have let him in?"

Graves nodded. "That would seem reasonable enough," he agreed. "Would Finch have been capable of such a thing?"

Bowman stopped in his tracks. "If he was desperate enough." He took a breath to collect his thoughts. "Mrs Finch told me how Erasmus had overreached himself when he moved with his wife to the Village. The rent was much higher and they were reliant on a second income from Mrs Finch's employment at Larton Manor." He spread his hands before him. "When she was dismissed from her work on a trumped up charge and Lord Melville raised the rent even higher by way of punishment, Erasmus Finch was at a loss."

"So you think Finch killed Sharples for financial gain?"

"I believe he was offered financial relief in exchange for Sharples' death."

"But why?" Graves lifted himself higher against his pillows until he was sitting bolt upright, keen to follow Bowman's train of thought. "Who would have made him such an offer?"

After a pause, Bowman loped heavily across the room to sit on the bed beside his sergeant. Although he was relieved to see Graves somewhat recovered from his ordeal, he could not shake a feeling of guilt at his companion's condition. It was a feeling he had grown quite used to.

"Sergeant Graves," he began, quietly, "what do you know of the Freemasons?"

Graves raised his eyebrows in surprise. "I know that they're a secret society. I've heard talk of strange ceremonies and such like, but no real details. Lodges, they call 'em. They're rather difficult to get to the bottom of." He rubbed at his eyes with a hand. "Some say they're intent on infiltrating our most esteemed institutions, Scotland Yard among them."

"Then you know as much as I," Bowman nodded. "They make use of certain designs as part of their ceremonies, chief among them, that of the square and compass. It may be seen on various buildings in London if you care to look."

"And you're saying such a society exists here?" Graves eyes were wide.

Bowman leaned in, conspiratorially. "They exist everywhere, Graves." There was something about the look on Bowman's face that gave Graves pause. He noticed a wild look about the inspector's eyes, his gaunt features set in an expression of intense desperation. As he held his hands before him imploringly, Graves saw a familiar tremor had returned to Bowman's fingers. He looked away sadly as the inspector rose from the bed, placing his hand back in a pocket to conceal the trembling.

"But who would want Sharples dead? You said yourself he had only been in Larton for a few months."

Bowman stood at the mantelpiece, his foot kicking absently against the metal grate. "Sharples moved here from Windsor, his army days long done. After years of destitution, hanging on to such personal belongings as he could, he was offered an almshouse in Larton Dean. Let's suppose he was a Freemason, as evidenced by the design I saw on his display box. What, do you suppose, would be his first course of action upon arriving here?"

"To seek out a local lodge?"

"Precisely. He attended a local meeting, the same night that Erasmus Finch received his envelope. The following day he was dead."

"So Finch received the envelope after the meeting?"

"His widow said he returned from an evening at The King's Head to find it beneath his door." Bowman turned dramatically. "I suspect he had actually been at the Lodge meeting, too."

"Finch was a Freemason?" Graves whistled through his teeth at the implications.

Bowman nodded. "And so bound to carry out the instructions in that envelope. To kill Sharples."

"But the papers say he was shot by his own hand," Graves said in exasperation. "And by his own gun. If that is not so, then what is the truth of the matter?"

Bowman turned to face his companion square on. "I suspect the answer to that, Sergeant Graves, lies beyond the confines of Larton."

His thoughts were interrupted by a sudden commotion at the door.

"Get off me!"

Bowman shared a look with Graves, both recognising the shrill voice from the landing. The door was flung open on its hinges and Maude spilled into the room, carrying a fresh jug of water in both hands. She squirmed and writhed as she stood, scowling at the great beast who even now pinched her about the waist.

"Hicks!" Sergeant Graves exclaimed in surprise.

Hicks cleared his throat, suddenly aware of his fellow detectives. "Sergeant Graves," he bellowed in a voice far too loud for the room, "I trust you are recovering sufficiently?"

"I am well enough to put up a fight to protect a lady's honour, Inspector Hicks," Graves scowled from his sickbed.

"What news?" Bowman asked impatiently, advancing on the portly inspector.

"In short, Bowman," Hicks began, clearly relishing being the centre of attention, "the gypsies were gone before the villagers could set about them."

"So that was the purpose of Trevitt's meeting?" Bowman asked in disbelief.

"He raised their hackles good and proper, but the gypsies had moved on before they had their chance."

"And the fire?"

"All the work of Fletcher Cousins' lad." Hicks drew his pipe from a pocket. "He admitted as much."

"Poor boy," sighed Graves. "He lost his childhood when he lost his father. I saw him at the Cousins' house when I interviewed Florrie."

"That's no excuse to burn the wood down." Hicks struck a match against the mantelpiece and puffed at his pipe, filling the room with a noxious fug in a matter of moments.

"Grief is a funny thing, Inspector Hicks," Graves mused. "It can lead to many strange behaviours." Suddenly embarrassed at his remarks, he cast a furtive glance to Bowman. The inspector looked away, swallowing hard.

"Then he was the figure I saw in the woods," Bowman said quickly. "Watching Trevitt and I at the tree where his father died."

"His widow was keen to blame the farmer for his death," Hicks blustered.

"Maxwell Trevitt is hardly a man of spotless character," Bowman's mind flashed back to the bruises he had seen on Mrs Trevitt's arms. "But he is no murderer. It is a sad fact that Fletcher Cousins felt driven to take his own life."

"How he could leave his wife and two children to fend for themselves is quite beyond me," Hicks announced, puffing fitfully at his pipe.

"None of us knows the true state of another man's mind," Bowman cautioned. He walked again to the window. "In the midst of all this drama," he sighed, "from yesterday's regatta to the march on the gypsy camp, it seems the villagers have quite forgotten the deaths in their midst. Perhaps that's exactly what the murderer would wish."

"Larton seems just the place for such a man to hide," Graves offered from his sickbed. "A village so at odds with itself that Sharples and Finch can die almost without comment and be forgotten so quickly."

"Not by us, Sergeant Graves." Bowman's frown cut deep into his forehead as he thought.

"But where do the answers lie, Bowman?" Hicks shrugged.

There was a pause as Bowman turned from the window. "Not in Larton," he mused aloud.

"Then, where?" Hicks scoffed.

"Erasmus Finch was sent to kill a man who had only been resident in Larton for some three months or so. Perhaps the answers lie further back." Suddenly galvanised, Bowman retrieved his hat and jacket from the foot of Graves' bed. "Inspector Hicks, I would ask you to call upon Mrs Prudence

Finch of Newman's Cottages."

"She would have had her fill of Scotland Yard by the end of the day," Graves smirked.

"Perhaps," Bowman smiled, pleased at his sergeant's return to form. "But if Sharples was shot with Finch's gun and not his own, then that weapon must have been concealed somewhere." He turned to Hicks. "Find it."

"And where will you go?" Hicks drew back the folds of his coat and placed his hands in his pockets.

"To the place where the story begins," Bowman called over his shoulder as he moved to the door in haste. "To Windsor Barracks."

XXI

Enlightenment

The Sunday train to Windsor was a stopping service that necessitated a change at Slough. Bowman was relieved to have a carriage to himself throughout most of the journey, the exception being the appearance of an old woman at Burnham who dropped shells to the floor from the seat opposite as she demolished a bag of walnuts. Bowman fought hard to avoid her eye. The fields and woodland rolled past as the inspector gave himself up to the gentle roll of the carriage. There were few people at work on a Sunday, but Bowman saw couples and families out for country walks and riders on horseback traversing the lanes. A gang of youths had made camp by the railway line, whooping and laughing as the train whistled its approach.

Soon enough, Windsor loomed large on the horizon. The train curled round to head straight for the castle in so direct a fashion, Bowman was sure he would disembark within its precincts. As it was, the great beast hissed and spat its way to a halt at a platform some hundred yards from the castle, but near enough that Bowman could see the Royal Standard hanging limp in the still air. Her Majesty was at home. As he stepped from the carriage into the heat of the evening, Bowman wondered for a moment if she might have any idea at all that he had averted a tragedy on board the royal yacht only a matter of weeks before.

As he made his way from the station towards Thames Street, the inspector's progress was impeded by an old man in an invalid chair. A three wheeled affair, it had a chassis of battered and split wickerwork, its single front wheel attached to a long metal handle that served as a tiller. The figure in its seat looked scarcely any more robust. A frail, old man with a lined face, he gazed up at Bowman through bloodshot eyes. A shapeless coat, a world too wide, was thrown across his shoulders. Even in the heat, a faded blanket lay across his lap, but this could not disguise the loss of a lower limb.

"Charity, sir?" the old man pleaded with an outstretched hand.

Bowman slowed his pace and reached into a pocket. "I am here for Combermere Barracks." He sorted through some change in the palm of his hand as he spoke, trying hard to hide his distaste at the smell that rose from the pitiful figure before him.

"I know it well enough," the old man rasped. "I gave Her Majesty the best years of my life, now I sit beneath her window to remind her." He gestured with a trembling hand over his shoulder to the castle. The walls rose high from the road like a cliff edge, sheer and impregnable.

"Were you stationed here?"

"Twelve years with the Blues on a shilling a day," the old man replied, a note of bitterness in his voice.

"The Blues?"

"The Royal Horse Guards," the old man explained. "A shilling a day spent on kit and provisions left me with nothing." He tapped the stump of his leg with a cane. "Lost m' leg at Balaclava," he grimaced. "Discharged in Fifty Five, been here ever since."

Bowman was taken aback. Then the man had been in this condition for almost forty years. He had done far better, he mused wryly, to survive four decades in this decrepit state than he had the Battle of Balaclava. In short, he was lucky indeed to be alive at all.

Bowman leaned as far forward as he dared to drop his change into the palm of the old man's hand. The smell was almost overpowering. "Is there no help to be found?"

"Ask Her Majesty," the old man replied, dryly. "I'm sure she could spare a jewel or two."

Bowman nodded. "Where might I find the barracks?"

"Follow the road round away from the river." The old soldier peered at the coins in his hand. Seemingly satisfied at the amount, he sat back in his chair with a sardonic grin. "Tell them Trooper Fenton wants his leg back."

Bowman tipped his hat and rounded the corner onto Thames Street, glad of the sweeter air. The cobbled street was devoid of the usual weekday bustle, but even so there were sightseers aplenty. A family sat on the grass slope beneath the battlements, basking in the shade afforded them by the grey walls above. Well-dressed couples promenaded slowly from the Great Park, picnic baskets in hand, parasols whirling gaily over their shoulders. Children stood playfully to attention before the statue of Queen Victoria that stood at the castle entrance. Erected just five years before, the likeness was a testament to the sculptor's artistry. The self-styled Empress of India stood, imperious in bronze, atop a plinth of polished red granite. She was dressed in the formal regalia suited to her exalted position, a sword in one hand, the orb of state in another. Looking down from her lofty height, she seemed to hold herself apart from the mortals of Windsor. Perhaps, mused Bowman, this was how her subjects preferred their queen; resolute, eternal and a world apart from the frail old woman that dwelt within the castle precincts.

Turning his feet from the statue, Bowman continued past the Guild Hall and a haphazard parade of pretty shops, all closed, on his way to Combermere Barracks. Named for Field Marshall Lord Combermere, they lay a mile to the southwest of the castle and occupied an area of some twenty acres. Home to the Royal Horse Guards for almost a hundred years, the sprawling barracks included a riding school, opened just a decade before. Soon, the red brick wall marking its circumference reared before him, and Bowman made for the impressive gatehouse.

Presenting himself before a man in full military uniform, Bowman reached to retrieve his papers from his jacket pocket. He noticed the three stripes emblazoned across the soldier's upper arm.

"Detective Inspector George Bowman," he announced. "Of Scotland Yard."

The sergeant was an officious looking man with a lean face and what could only be described as mocking eyes. Lifting his head from a ledger on his desk, he looked Bowman up and down before reluctantly giving his attention to the identification papers before him.

"And just what brings you here, Detective Inspector Bowman," he began in a clipped, nasal voice, "that cannot be laid at the hands of the military police?"

Bowman cleared his throat, already irritated at the man's manner. "I am investigating certain matters in the village of Larton." The man returned him a blank, bored look. "To aid my enquiries further, I wish to have access to the muster rolls of the Royal Horse Guards."

The sergeant raised his eyebrows. "On a Sunday?"

Bowman regarded the man before him. He had about him the air of one who had found his station in life, far from the front line and its attendant dangers, and had settled there with relief.

"The law never rests," Bowman breathed.

The sergeant stared back, daring the inspector to break his gaze while folding the papers slowly with his delicate fingers. With just the hint of a smile playing about his thin lips, he waited for Bowman to snatch the papers back before pushing his chair from the desk. As he rose, Bowman saw that he was tall and ramrod straight. He wore a pair of riding jodhpurs tucked into polished, knee-high boots and a smart, black tunic decorated with gold braid.

The sergeant led Bowman out and around a bustling parade ground, busy with mounted soldiers. Aside from their military regalia, they were each armed with a curved sabre clipped to their side and a tall helmet with a red plume. At a command from a senior officer, the men presented their arms from on top of their chargers. Several of the horses snorted their displeasure at being pressed to perform on such a warm evening, before being led in formation through the main gate on some engagement about the town.

"That's Fourth Company," the sergeant announced as he walked stiffly across the parade ground. "Back from Africa where the Boers are causing trouble. Mark my words," he barked, "we've not heard the last of them."

Bowman, as tall as he was, fought to keep pace with the man ahead of him.

"We're a proud regiment, inspector," the sergeant intoned, "with a long history. I hope your enquiries are of a specific nature. Our records go back a long way."

"There is a soldier I wish to know more of, that is all."

The sergeant shook his head, clearly irritated at the seeming mundanity of the matter. "These records exist for our own purposes, inspector, not for public perusal." He led the inspector round a corner to a quieter part of the barracks. Long, low buildings stretched away in uniform rows between a square of stable blocks. Bowman saw groups of soldiers marching in unison, turning to salute their senior officers as they passed. Impeccably dressed in their tunics and jodhpurs, they were an impressive sight. Bowman could not help but compare the fresh-faced soldiers before him with the shadow of a man he had met at Windsor Station. How many of those before him, he wondered, were doomed to such an end? A life on the front line was harsh to be sure, but it seemed to him that life after service might be harder still. The sergeant was standing before a squat building resembling a small chapel. He held the door open impatiently, gesturing that Bowman should enter.

"This is the library and archive," he said absently. "If your man was ever part of the Royal Horse Guards, you'll find him here."

It was like stepping into another world, far from the bustle of the parade ground. Bowman was immediately struck by the silence in the vast room. He was suddenly aware of the blood rushing in his ears. The room was open and airy, but the dark wood panelling gave it a strangely claustrophobic feel. Light streamed through the large, stained glass window set in the furthest wall, but was soon smothered by the gloom. Dust motes rose and fell as the air shifted about shelves and bookcases, each of them groaning with books, papers and albums. Bowman turned to face a mezzanine, a third the length of the ground floor, home to yet more records and ledgers. There was a damp, leathery smell about the place. The sound of the door closing behind him resonated to the ceiling and Bowman turned to see the sergeant waiting expectantly as if for instructions.

"You must at least tell me the man's name," he sighed, testily.

"Jedediah Sharples," Bowman replied. "Trooper Jedediah Sharples, invalided out the army some time around Eighteen Eighty Four."

The sergeant pursed his lips in thought. "Just after the

campaigns at El Teb." He lowered his voice to a whisper. "There were dreadful losses for us there." He seemed to relish the very idea.

Turning abruptly, the soldier made for the ladder that rose to the mezzanine. The dust disturbed by his feet hung in the air behind him as he climbed. Bowman, having noticed the man had walked to a regular internal rhythm across the parade ground, saw that he even climbed the ladder in time to some unheard military drumbeat.

"The Royal Horse Guards were raised in Sixteen Fifty on the orders of Oliver Cromwell," he was declaiming into the room as he climbed. Bowman thought that very fact explained much. "Upon the restoration of King Charles II, we became the Earl of Oxford's regiment." The sergeant stepped off the top of the ladder, reaching out to the balustrade that ran the length of the mezzanine floor for support. He stood for a moment, scanning the shelves before him.

"Why 'The Blues'?" Bowman asked.

"An assumed name taken from the colour of the regiment's coat at the time. The coat has changed," the sergeant added. "But the name remains." He turned to gaze down at Bowman from the balustrade. "And there's no man that's served with the Blues that doesn't carry pride and gratitude in his heart."

Bowman thought of Trooper Fenton in the station concourse. The inspector was sure he harboured many feelings in his heart towards the Blues, but he doubted gratitude was among them.

The sergeant had retrieved the required volume from a low shelf to his left, and carried it down the ladder with a practised care. "We served in the French Revolutionary Wars and in the Peninsular War." He walked to a desk near a low window, gesturing with his head that Bowman should join him. "We fought with distinction at the Battle of Waterloo."

"You are quite the historian," Bowman relented. The man before him had taken on a whole new persona. Where he had been stiff and formal, he now seemed at ease, his eyes alight with a fervent enthusiasm.

"I am a soldier sir," he snapped. "And any soldier lives and breathes for his regiment." He caught Bowman's eye. "And yes, dies for it too, if the occasion demands it." Bowman thought the man might burst with pride.

The sergeant slammed the book down on the tabletop, dislodging a cloud of dust as he did so. Bowman noticed the regimental badge embossed in the leather, the motto beneath proclaiming, 'Honi soit qui mal y pense'; Evil be to him who evil thinks.

"Muster rolls," he announced. "First and Second Battles of El Teb, Eighteen Hundred and Eighty Four."

Bowman looked around him with fresh eyes. "Is every campaign recorded here?"

"Every man who has ever served, fought or died in service with the Blues is to be found amongst these shelves," the soldier responded, haughtily. "Every campaign of every battle is catalogued, many of them represented on the walls around you."

Bowman peered around the room. In the gloom, he had not noticed the pictures on the wall. One entire length of the building was given over to formal prints of The Royal Horse Guards. They stood in stiff, formal poses, some astride their horses, some on foot, in divisions and companies. "Daguerreotypes," Bowman whistled, impressed.

"The regiment has been fortunate enough to retain the services of a photographer for the best part of twenty years." There was something in the manner he adopted as he spoke that gave the inspector to understand that the sergeant himself was responsible for the pictures on the wall.

The sergeant leaned over the table to lift the cover on the volume before him.

"This is part of the record of the campaigns at El Teb, including troop movements, provisions and personnel. You should find your man listed here." He stabbed at the page with a finger then stood back, clearly convinced he had done enough. Bowman shuffled closer to the table, leaning on the table to survey the book before him. The sergeant had opened it on a page showing a list of names in alphabetical order.

"These are all the men who fought with the Blues at El Teb?"

"Half the regiment were engaged in action, some two hundred

men. They are listed before you." The history lesson over, the sergeant had adopted the same, bored tone Bowman had noticed at the gate.

The inspector traced his finger down a column on the left hand side of the page displaying the surnames of those involved in the campaign.

"Sandford, Scanlon," he intoned to himself. "Sharples!" He followed the row with his finger. "Jedediah, Trooper." He saw entries for the man's date of birth, hometown and service number. Then, a single word; 'injured'.

"Here's our man," Bowman confirmed, his brow furrowed in thought. "What becomes of an injured soldier?"

The sergeant cleared his throat, suddenly awkward. "He would be treated in the field for his injuries and then, if he could not fight, sent home."

"Back here?"

The sergeant shrugged, "If his injuries were sufficient to prevent a return to duty, and he was of no further use to the Army, he would be discharged."

Bowman's moustache twitched. He balked at the idea that a man could be considered no longer of use. There, in the final column of the page, he could indeed make out the abbreviation, '*dis.*" Whoever had held that pen hadn't even done the trooper the courtesy of spelling out the word in full.

"Trooper Sharples ended his days in an almshouse some ten miles from here," Bowman whispered.

The sergeant nodded. "Then he was fortunate, indeed."

Bowman flicked absently through the pages as he thought. Trooper Jedediah Sharples had suddenly been given flesh in his mind. Injured during a battle on foreign sand, it seemed to the inspector that Sharples had been forsaken by his regiment and, by extension, his country. He had enjoyed just three months in the almshouses at Larton Dean. Bowman did not consider him at all fortunate, as the sergeant had maintained.

As Bowman's eyes fell again to the pages before him, he noticed an entry in a final column that perplexed him. "*Des.*," he read aloud, "What is meant by that?"

The sergeant shifted uncomfortably where he stood.

"Deserted," he said, as matter-of-factly as he could.

"Is such a thing common?"

The sergeant chose to take the question as a personal affront. "Certainly not!" he barked, a little too loudly. Noticing his own voice echoing back to him from the rafters, he took a moment to compose himself. "El Teb was brutal, but there was only one incident of desertion."

Bowman looked back along the row on the page where he had stopped. "Talbot, Joseph," he read aloud. "Corporal Of Horse."

"That's the man," the sergeant spat, barely able to disguise his disdain.

"What is known of the circumstances?"

The sergeant approached the table again, snapping the book shut in front of him. "Warfare is a complicated matter, inspector," he said curtly, "One must remember that the success of a war may be built on incidents of failure."

"Was El Teb such an incident?"

"It was," the sergeant marched back to the ladder with the book. "And Corporal Talbot is well known for his part in it." On the mezzanine once more, the sergeant returned the volume to its place on the shelf. "A raid at El Teb by the Mahdists took the British expeditionary forces by surprise. They were a thousand strong."

"How can that be laid at Talbot's door?"

"Corporal Talbot failed his men in the heat of battle." The sergeant stepped off the ladder, his face distorted into an expression of contempt. "He mistakenly led them to open ground rather than the safety of the mountains." He grit his teeth. "Such an action was bad enough. Rather than face the consequences with his superiors as a gentleman would have done, the rascal turned his heels and fled." The sergeant's face was flushed with emotion. "He deserted."

"Was he caught?"

The sergeant paused, barely able to speak the word. "Never," he said, at last. "Fifty seven men lost their lives as a direct consequence of his actions, and scores more were injured."

"Including Trooper Sharples," Bowman nodded. "Had he been caught, what would have been Talbot's punishment?"

"With such a catastrophic loss of men," the sergeant offered, brusquely, "there could be only one punishment. He would have been put to death by firing squad, and that would have been too good for him." The sergeant was making fists with his hands as he spoke, barely able to contain his rage.

Bowman turned to the wall behind him. A sea of faces gazed back from their places in the picture frames, each company or division and the personnel it contained identified by a small, metal plaque beneath. His habitual frown cut deep into his forehead.

"Is Trooper Sharples to be seen in these photographs?"

"Of course," the sergeant replied haughtily, pulling himself up to his full height. "Took the picture myself in Eighty Three."

The soldier led Bowman two-thirds down the room and pointed to a picture some eight feet from the ground. "The Blues of Eighty Three," he announced solemnly. "This is Sharples' company," he took a breath. "And Talbot's, too."

Bowman craned his neck to view the picture in the poor light offered by the stained glass window. It held maybe twenty men in total, just a fraction of those who had fought at El Teb. With a shudder, the inspector wondered just how many had returned. With reference to the small plaque beneath, Bowman was able to pinpoint Trooper Sharples with ease. Standing proudly in his uniform, he held the reins of the horse beside him. Sharples was possessed of a long, aquiline face and a pair of prodigious mutton chop side-whiskers. He looked lean and strong, the very epitome of the British soldier. Whoever would have thought, mused Bowman, that within ten years of this photograph being taken, Trooper Sharples would be found dead not on the battlefield, but on the floor of an almshouse in Larton Dean?

Glancing down again, Bowman searched for the name 'Talbot' on the inscription. It seemed he was the officer on the horse beside Sharples. Looking back at the picture, Bowman caught his breath. There, sitting proudly astride his charger, his curved scimitar held aloft beside him, sat a very familiar figure indeed.

Quite unexpectedly, Bowman found Prescott waiting for him

on the platform at Larton. As the train heaved into the station, the inspector noticed Prescott's polished landau standing in the forecourt. The two black mares stood pawing at the ground in their impatience while the driver leaned nonchalantly against the rear wheels, his lean features angled to the train as it arrived. He stood almost to attention as Bowman rounded the corner from the platform.

"Inspector Bowman," Prescott began, his rural drawl seeming all the stronger after Bowman's time at the barracks, "Lord Melville asks that you visit him at Larton Manor." Prescott opened the door to his carriage as he spoke. "He said to say he has some information that might prove useful in your investigations."

Bowman broke his stride to consider the proposition. Stepping gingerly to the carriage, he lifted his boot to the footplate. It was at that moment, just as he heaved himself aboard, that he felt the cosh on his head, a splitting pain across his skull and the rapid approach of a profound darkness as he slipped into unconsciousness.

Detective Inspector Ignatius Hicks had allowed himself a little lunch before commencing his enquiries at Newman's Cottages. Leaving Sergeant Graves to sleep, he had prevailed upon Maude for a bowl of steaming soup and a pie from the oven. His appetite sated, Hicks hoisted his bulk from the chair and stepped from The King's Head to the street beyond. It was eerily quiet. The searing heat, he guessed, was keeping people indoors to enjoy their day of rest. Within minutes he was sweating. His heavy coat clung to his back and his neck was wet beneath his beard. Approaching the cottages, he rested at the gate to catch his breath. There was no sign of anyone being at home. With a little luck, he thought to himself, he would be back at The King's Head within minutes to enjoy an ale or two and the company of the barmaid.

Peering through the window, Hicks could see right through the small parlour to the lean-to kitchen and the garden beyond. There, he saw a flurry of activity through the glass. Mrs Finch was at work upon her plot. Looking about him, Hicks took the path around the front of the cottages to the gardens that lay to the rear.

The terrace of low buildings sat amongst a small area of scrubland that had been fenced in for a large, shared garden. Beds of dry earth were arranged with brittle flowers, bending in the heat for lack of water. As he trod along the grass verge that separated the beds, Hicks saw a demure looking young woman, still clearly in her Sunday dress. Improbably, she was squatting on her haunches, digging a small hole in the dirt with a trowel. Beside her lay a small tin box, such as might contain biscuits or confectionary.

The young lady looked up in alarm as Hicks' sheer girth blocked the sun from her work and she was plunged into sudden shade.

"I do not wish to alarm you," Hicks said as gently as he could. "I am Inspector Hicks from Scotland Yard."

The inspector noticed the young woman managed to look both confused and guilty at the same time. "I have spoken to your colleague just earlier this afternoon," she stammered. Her eyes flicked involuntarily to the tin box at her side.

"Mrs Finch?" Hicks asked, innocently, "might I ask why you are working in your garden in your Sunday best?"

Slowly, the woman stood, shaking the dust from her skirts. Mrs Finch let her trowel fall to the dirt and bent to retrieve the box. Even Hicks, not usually so sensitive to the fairer sex, noticed her bottom lip beginning to quiver.

"Inspector Hicks," she began, faintly, a tear springing to her eye. "I am afraid Erasmus did a terrible thing."

She passed the tin with trembling hands, and Hicks lifted the lid on its rusty hinges. There, laid upon a quantity of newspaper, was a gentleman's revolver.

XXII

A Baptism

Bowman felt like he was drowning. Gagging, he swung his head violently to one side. Attempting to raise his hands to his mouth, he discovered they were tied to the arms of the chair on which he sat. His feet were secured to each other.

"Don't worry, inspector," came a familiar voice, "I have administered a mild sedative, that is all." There was even a note of concern. "For the pain."

Bowman fought against the numbing of his senses. He recalled the knock to his head as he had boarded Melville's coach. "Prescott?" he breathed, trying to focus his eyes on the room about him.

"Yes," came the voice again. "He is proving a very useful initiate. He was even diligent enough to follow you to Windsor." Bowman could see Melville's driver standing in the shadows of an alcove, leaning nonchalantly against the wall. He looked for all the world as if he was waiting for a train at Larton Station. He played with a match between his teeth. "He is not plagued by self doubt as Erasmus Finch was," the voice continued. "He proved to be most bothersome."

"Where am I?" Bowman croaked.

"You should consider yourself honoured, inspector. Only those dedicated to the Craft are permitted entry here." Bowman looked around the room in which he was held. A vaulted ceiling loomed down at him from the darkness. Here and there, strange symbols were etched onto the walls, one of which he most certainly recognised; the square and compass. Three other ornate chairs were placed at the cardinal points of the compass. The air was cool, leading the inspector to believe he must be underground. In all, it had the feel of a Holy place.

"You are even seated in the east. The Grand Master's place."

"Where am I?" Bowman repeated with force. Despite the sedative, his vision was beginning to clear. As he focussed on the alcove before him, he could see a figure, resolving itself in the gloom. As it stepped from the shadows, the diminutive figure allowed himself a genial smile, his steel wire spectacles glinting in the candlelight.

"Welcome," he said with a leer, "to the Larton Lodge of the Masonic Brotherhood."

Bowman writhed in his seat. "Greville Whitlock," he hissed.

Whitlock smiled, quite benignly. "It is a strange thing, Inspector Bowman. I have gone by that name for almost a decade, and yet still it takes me by surprise." He gave a chuckle.

Bowman thought back to his meeting with Whitlock outside the church that morning. For a moment, as he had introduced Inspector Hicks, the coroner had seemed distracted as the inspector mentioned his name.

"I have a theory, inspector," Whitlock was intoning, "that identity is malleable. In short, we are who we choose to be."

Bowman felt his head reeling. "Just as you chose to abandon your fellow soldiers at El Teb?"

The coroner threw back his head, his bald pate reflecting the light of the candles. "You are quite mistaken," he laughed. "That was Corporal Joseph Talbot."

"You are one and the same."

"Not so!" There was a sudden steel to Whitlock's voice. "Joseph Talbot died on the sands at El Teb, just as Greville Whitlock was born. I am reinvented."

"As a murderer."

There was a pause as Whitlock turned away. "That is most unfortunate," he whispered. Bowman was struck at the wide variances in the man's demeanour. It worried him. "I was the victim of a dreadful happenstance, that is all."

"You are a wanted man." The inspector started to pull at his bindings, flexing the muscles in his wrists to loosen the ties. Suddenly, Whitlock turned. Had he noticed?

"No, inspector." A wide grin spread across his face. "I am a respected pillar of the community. Isn't it delicious?"

"Why Larton?" Bowman blinked. Either as a result of the drugs he had been administered, or the twine that bound his feet, he found he couldn't feel his legs.

Whitlock was pacing the length of the room, like some caged

beast. "I had spent years in fear of discovery, but here I could hide in plain sight. My late wife brought me here in her final years. It seemed perfect. In Larton, I found a village in a constant state of conflict. The villagers are too busy looking over their shoulders to look too closely at me, an educated man risen to the position of coroner. I am beyond reproach." He paused at another of the four chairs in the room. "You would be surprised how far a little medical knowledge and some forged documents may take a man. In three short years, I was able to inveigle my way into every corner of the village. While their petty squabbles continued, I could thrive, the still waters beneath the swell. The Larton Lodge provided me with the perfect refuge. I could be protected."

A sudden dread ran cold through Bowman's spine. "Why are you telling me all this so freely?"

Greville Whitlock took his time with his response. Walking slowly to where Bowman sat, helpless, he leaned in close to the inspector's ear; so close, Bowman could feel the coroner's hot breath upon his neck. "Because tonight, inspector," he could tell Whitlock was smiling, "you are going to take your own life."

The moment seemed to hang in the air. Despite the sedative, Bowman's heart began to race. "The Lodge was dormant when I arrived," Whitlock continued, suddenly conversational. "I schooled myself in the Craft and placed myself at its head. From deserter to Grand Master. You see, inspector? We can be who we choose to be."

Bowman flicked his eyes to Prescott. If he was surprised or alarmed by anything Whitlock was saying, he chose not to show it. Instead, he continued to chew on his matchstick in the manner of one wholly bored with proceedings.

Bowman realised only time could save him. With time, he could loosen his bonds and stand a chance. "Then Trooper Sharples came to Larton," he elucidated, remembering the design on the trooper's display box. "A Freemason himself, he sought out the local Lodge. He recognised you from the campaign at El Teb."

Whitlock nodded, almost sadly. "I was certain he would report me to the authorities," he sighed. "He could not live, but

I could not be seen to act."

Bowman could feel the twine around his right wrist was loosening. Whether it would ever be loose enough to slip his hand through or, indeed, what he would do then, he could not tell. "So you sent Finch to make an end of the matter."

The coroner puffed out his cheeks in a gesture of despair. "He was a recent initiate in need of testing," he shrugged. "He was found wanting."

Bowman heard a chuckle from Prescott in his alcove, then turned back to face Whitlock. His vision was blurring again now.

"What did you promise him?

Whitlock spread his hands wide as if the answer was obvious. "What any man truly craves. Advancement."

"And financial gain?" Bowman had managed to move his hand so that his knuckles were almost passing through the binding.

"Not so!" There was that note, again, Bowman noticed. For a murderer, Greville Whitlock possessed an unerringly thin skin. The coroner calmed himself before continuing. "But Finch became a liability. To assuage his guilt, he demanded payment where I had promised none. Even though he threatened to expose me, I refused."

Bowman nodded to himself. Mrs Finch had mentioned her husband had disappeared frequently following Sharples" death. He had clearly been imploring Whitlock for payment.

"Finally, at our next meeting, I cut him loose, barred him from the Brotherhood. It seems he could not live with my decision or his conscience."

Bowman's hand was almost through the twine. He started to work upon his other wrist now, turning his forearm slowly this way and that in an effort to loosen the ties. "He jumped from the church tower the very next day."

"A grand irony, inspector," Whitlock announced, "That two of the three deaths you were called to investigate *were* the result of self-murder. Just as I recorded in my coroner's report."

"But, Sharples." For a moment, Bowman met Whitlock's eye and ceased his struggling for fear of being caught.

"Yes," Whitlock breathed, suddenly distant. "Sharples. He has proved to be my undoing."

Bowman leaned in slightly where he sat, eager to keep Whitlock talking. "Perhaps that is his revenge for your desertion at El Teb."

Suddenly, Whitlock was all fury. He lurched forward, grabbing the arms to Bowman's chair with such force the inspector was sure he was about to break them off. "I was not at El Teb!" the coroner roared, spittle flying from his mouth. His outwardly affable demeanour had slipped entirely and Bowman thought, in that moment, he was seeing the truth of the man. Whitlock seemed suddenly aware that he had lost control. Standing again, he straightened his spectacles and continued. "Joseph Talbot fought in those sands," he said, carefully. "He spent three months in the heat, evading capture. He underwent such horrors as can never be understood by those who choose a civilian life." Bowman felt he was implicated in the remark. "Joseph Talbot was a broken man, in spirit and body. If he was captured he would be put to death." Whitlock lowered himself onto the ornate chair opposite Bowman as he spoke. "Finally, he found passage at Trinkitat on the Red Sea coast, begging for food and charity." The inspector thought of Trooper Fenton at Windsor Station. "To evade death or the life of a fugitive, one option remained. He had left Combermere Barracks as Joseph Talbot. He must leave the desert as Greville Whitlock."

Bowman was aghast. Was it possible that a man may subdivide his very nature to become something new? Can he leave the past behind to rise, Phoenix-like from the ashes of his experiences?

"I thrived. I even married, though that did not last. Imagine reinventing yourself anew, inspector." Whitlock was drawing near again, his eyes blazing behind his steel wire spectacles. "Sloughing off your old skin like a snake to emerge a new man." He raised a knowing eyebrow. "Do you not find that attractive?"

Bowman stretched against his bindings. He knew it was no use, now. The feeling of paralysis was spreading from his legs and up his body. "What do you intend?" A note of panic was rising in his voice.

Whitlock looked upon him as a kindly uncle might look upon a child. "You have provided me with your perfect end, inspector, and I thank you for it."

Bowman blinked, confused.

"The whole of Larton knows you for a troubled man. Your collapse at The King's Head is quite the talk of the village." Whitlock leaned in again, staring deep into Bowman's eyes. "Given your condition, do you think it would surprise anyone if you were found to have taken your own life?"

Bowman writhed where he sat, straining his feet against the twine that bound them. He could barely move his chest to breathe.

"Oh, I wouldn't concern yourself," the coroner soothed. "The drug won't kill you. It is a calmative only. And, of course, I shall find no evidence of it in my report." Bowman breathed hard. "What would one more suicide mean in Larton?" Whitlock continued, his head cocked to one side. He seemed to observe Bowman with detachment, as one might view an experiment or a test case. "It would barely be remarked upon. I sense you would even welcome it, inspector." Again, he leaned in close to Bowman's ear. "Perhaps it would be a blessing."

Bowman suddenly felt Whitlock slip a gag around his head. He struggled against it, trying in vain to spit it from his mouth, the coarse material leaving a foul, metallic taste. Attempting a scream, he was suddenly aware of another sound in the air, distant and dreamlike. As Whitlock tied the gag around his head, Bowman was sure he could hear singing.

"Prescott!" Whitlock barked, and the driver sprang forward to loose the inspector's bonds. Bowman's legs and arms felt heavy as lead. Try as he might, he could not marshal them. Panic rising within him, he felt himself lifted from his chair by the two men. As one, they shuffled across the floor with their leaden cargo. With mounting horror, Bowman realised he was entirely in their thrall and quite unable to move.

The strains of Praise My Soul, The King Of Heaven drifted on the still air. Blinking into the light, Bowman suddenly knew exactly where he was. The two men had grunted and sweated their way up the stone steps with their heavy load. It took Prescott some time to release the locks and bolts before the door could open, but now they emerged from the abandoned crypt into the churchyard at All Saints Church.

"I wouldn't worry, inspector," Whitlock panted. "If Proudfoot knows of the Lodge beneath his feet, he doesn't care. He's too intent on hurling fire and brimstone upon his parishioners or seeking a Paradise of his own in the bottom of a bottle."

Bowman's heart lurched. With the village at evening service, there would be no one to call to, no passersby to raise the alarm. Biting at his gag, his voice stuck in his throat. He could make no sound, and move no muscle.

Keeping low by a boundary hedge, Prescott and Whitlock manhandled their burden through a gap in the undergrowth. Suddenly, they were standing on a slipway by the river, the blue wrought iron bridge soaring above them. Beneath it, the Thames raced past on its journey to London and the sea. Even here where it was at its prettiest, Bowman could sense a malign presence rolling and twisting within those currents. Whitlock had let go of his feet now, and Prescott dragged him by the arms down the slope towards the water. Bowman saw the coroner reach for a handkerchief to wipe the sweat from his brow. Whitlock stood with his hands on his hips as Prescott splashed into the water. Soon, Bowman felt the Thames lapping at his ankles. Prescott was stronger than Bowman could ever have imagined. In one swift movement, the driver removed the gag from Bowman's mouth, turned him face down and plunged him into the river. Bowman felt Prescott's fist on his back, holding him beneath the water. He felt the river floor against his cheek and the rush of water in his ears. Suddenly, he was heaved out again. Prescott had him with both hands, gripping at the clothes on his back as he waded into deeper water with his load. Bowman gasped for breath, looking desperately around him for any hope of deliverance. And then he was under again. The shock of the cold water caused an involuntary breath, and Bowman felt his lungs fill with stinking water. He thrashed with his arms as best he could, reaching out to grapple Prescott by the legs. The driver kicked at him with his heavy boots. One foot made contact with Bowman's chin, and he felt his jaw crack. At first, he fought against the water, gasping for breath and thrashing his legs against its pull. He turned and writhed beneath Prescott's iron grasp but then, in spite of himself, he stopped.

He gave in to the water. In his delirium, he welcomed it. And then he saw her.

It was as if the water was fathoms deep and there she stood, beckoning him. Her dress twisted about her in the water, her chin turned towards him. An outstretched hand gave Bowman to understand there would be no pain in his death, and he gave himself up to it.

And that's when he saw the bullet. It fizzed and popped in front of him, leaving a glittering trail in its wake. As he stared at it, uncomprehending, Bowman saw the faintest twist of blood dissolving in the water about it. Suddenly, Prescott was lying in the river next to him, his face contorted into a mask of pain. Bowman felt himself being dragged from the water. Away from her. He wanted to cry out, to reach for her. His heart leapt into his mouth as he realised he was losing her all over again.

The river receding behind him now, Bowman thrashed violently in Graves' hands. The young sergeant tried his best to soothe him, fighting against the pain in his own head.

"I've got you, sir!" he screamed. "I've got you!"

Bowman's eyes rolled in his head. He coughed river water. As the world whirled around him, he saw Inspector Hicks standing with a revolver in his hand. Greville Whitlock stood before him, his hands upon his head while there, in the river, Prescott swayed unsteadily, doubled over, clutching at a wound to his shoulder.

"Sergeant Graves saw Prescott's coach from his room at The King's Head," Hicks was booming. "Reckoned it odd that Lord Melville would take a coach so short a distance to go to church."

"Turns out it wasn't Lord Melville at all," Graves soothed as he let Bowman sink to the ground. Bowman was looking about him with unseeing eyes, his chest rising and falling with a ghastly rhythm. Spluttering painfully, he began to shake. "Anna!" he cried, the tremors increasing. His eyes bulged from their sockets as he fought to breathe. "Let me go!" he screamed.

"Sir!" called Graves, his eyes wide. "It's me! I've got you!" The young sergeant tried to hold the inspector's arms by his side. A flailing hand caught him by surprise and Bowman scratched at his cheek in a fury. "Let me go!" he roared in a voice Graves had never heard him use before. "Let me die!"

Graves cast a look to Inspector Hicks and swallowed hard. Motioning with his gun, Hicks gestured that Prescott should step from the water to join him. The bluff inspector could not help but be enthralled by the spectacle before him. Inspector Bowman thrashed and sobbed on the filthy ground, taking great, gulping breaths that shuddered through his entire body.

"Get Melville," Graves commanded. "And send a boy to the police station."

The revolver stretched out before him, Hicks led Prescott and Whitlock from the slipway. As they rounded the corner onto the street, Graves saw the coroner look back to the water, a ghastly smile spreading slowly across his face.

XXIII

Coda

Sergeant Graves could barely look. For his own safety, Detective Inspector George Bowman had been strapped to a low bunk in the back of the dray, leather thongs pulled tight across his chest, his waist and feet. Bowman grit his teeth as he writhed on the bed, his eyes staring madly about him. Still in his wet clothes, a rough blanket had been thrown across him for warmth, the only concession to kindness that Graves had noticed. The dray had been provided by Lord Melville and Cooper the groom directed to meet the detectives on the drive to collect his most unusual cargo. He had slung a makeshift awning across a simple frame to protect its contents from the elements. Its floor was strewn with straw and discarded tools. Graves hung his head at the indignity of it all.

Hicks had requisitioned a carriage from The King's Head and led Whitlock and Prescott away at gunpoint, Constable Corrigan by his side for surety. Graves was certain Whitlock's journey to the gallows would be undertaken in a stubborn silence. Given his adherence to the Lodge, he would never implicate his fellow freemasons. Looking beyond the row of trees that separated the manor from the causeway, Graves squinted into the low sun as it sat, heavy on the horizon, lending a red hue to the evening sky. Lifting a hand to his head, he unravelled the wet bandage that Maude had tied there. Aside from a dull ache around the bruise beneath his hair, he felt sufficiently recovered from his ordeal. Graves would spend the next few days in Larton with support from Reading Police Station, mopping up those suspected of having a direct hand in recent events. For now, he stood alone on the drive to Larton Manor, watching as the horses were prepared for the journey. Perhaps, he mused, this was how it was always going to end. Since the affair of the head in the ice, Bowman's condition and general health had been in decline. The wonder was he had prevailed for so long. Graves sighed as he rubbed his eyes. In some intangible way, he felt he had failed the inspector.

Without acknowledging the sergeant, Cooper lifted the rear door to the carriage to secure it, whistling through his teeth as if he had been engaged upon nothing more than a mundane errand for his Lordship. Climbing aboard his seat, he gripped at the reins and clicked at the horses in their harness. With a tap from his stick, the two bay mares turned in the drive and started on their way, passing Sergeant Graves where he stood near the gatehouse. As the carriage rattled clear of the drive and onto the road beyond, Graves stood in silent contemplation. If he had been a religious man, he might well have offered up a prayer. Breathing deeply to steady his nerves, he watched as Bowman's makeshift ambulance clattered away into the distance. Finally, running his fingers through his curls and allowing himself another sigh, Sergeant Graves turned his heels towards his room at The King's Head and the solace of an understanding barmaid.

Bowman was falling. He had been falling for so long, he thought he might never hit the bottom. Around him, the wind whistled in his ears. Beneath him, he could see the alleys and passageways of Southwark. He was alive to every moment. He was the hard ground beneath and the clear sky above. At first he thought he must be dead, and with that thought came the attendant relief he had craved for so long. All too briefly, he survived in a state of grace beyond himself. He was beyond Time, able to exist in any moment. He pulled at the strands of his life with his mind, struggling to find the thread that would lead him there. To where he longed to be. As last, he found it, a delicate silver weft that shone like a cobweb heavy with dew. A gentle tug was all that was required and slowly, sedately, he began his descent.

Hanbury Street was all too familiar. From where he was delivered on the path outside the Women's Refuge, he could see the shops, sawmills and workhouses he had come to recognise. A squabble of urchins stood in line to accept their charity with outstretched hands.

Bowman turned his head, fully expecting to see the carriage on its grisly progress, but the road ahead was clear. By now, he knew, he should have been within sight, standing alongside Graves and Williams, his revolver raised in anticipation of the shot. By now he should have heard the shout and seen the passersby scattering in the carriage's path. He should have heard the hooves. Instead, there was silence. A light, bright silence such as one might experience on a crisp winter's morning. The world seemed held in ice, the air clear about him. There, as he turned his head to where he knew she would be, stood Anna. Bowman was flooded with relief. At last, once more, he could see her face. The slope of her nose enticed him, the arch of her brow beguiled him. It was as if he beheld her for the first time. From across the road, she dazzled. In her eyes he saw the world and every possibility it might afford.

In a moment, he was in a house he did not recognise, sitting in an armchair that he sensed was his favourite. A fire blazed beside him and, on his lap, he held a child. A beautiful boy gurgled up at him, his eyes full of wonder. The child reached up for Bowman's moustache and tweaked it playfully between his chubby fingers. Bowman smiled. He felt such love for the child that he could not doubt but that it was his son. And then he smelled her perfume.

"Be gentle!"

Anna sat on the arm of his chair, her skirts arranged about her. Reaching out, she took a tender hold of the child and lifted him into her arms. "Let's leave your father to his thoughts," she said, gently. "Time for bed." She kissed the infant on his forehead, glancing back at her husband with such a look of love that Bowman caught his breath.

"Hello, George."

He was back on the roadside. Anna stood opposite, unmoving. For a moment, Bowman was fearful she would step into the road, unleashing a chain of events to unfold as they always had. But not this time. The world had stopped. There was no carriage. No shot had been fired.

"Anna," he breathed. He lived within the confines of that little word. He placed it on a table to complete a jigsaw and he was whole. He had forgotten how it felt to be complete. "Anna," he said again. "I am sorry."

She nodded, slowly. "Me too."

The grass grew long here, and Bowman traced his fingers along a stem, releasing the seed from the palm of his hand into the breeze. He could hear the river gurgling nearby and, turning, he saw them. The young girl hitched her skirt above her knees, laughing gaily as she splashed the water towards her older brother.

"A rainbow!" She squealed in delight as the summer sun arced through the spray, leaving a daub of colour in its wake. Their joy was unconfined. The young boy waded through the water with a stone, a flick of his hand sending it skimming to the other bank.

"Did you see?" he giggled, turning to Bowman in triumph.

"I saw," he heard himself say. "Well done!"

The girl flashed him a gap-toothed smile. Her hair was lighter and curlier, but the curve of her neck and the slope of her nose marked her out as her mother's daughter.

"A penny for your thoughts?"

He felt a hand curl around his, warm and inviting. Anna stood beside him, watching their children at play. He noticed the fine tracery of laughter lines around her eyes and a fleck of silver in her hair. He reached up to hook it behind her ears.

"If I could live in a moment forever," he said, quietly. "I would choose this one."

"Oh, George," she laughed, smoothing his frown gently beneath her thumb. "Nothing lasts forever."

Bowman caught his breath, aware the scene was fading. "Can I stay here?"

He was back on Hanbury Street, caught between moments.

Anna shook her head, sadly. "You know you can't."

"Why not?"

"You are sick, George." Her eyes were wide with concern. "You are broken."

Bowman was full of pain. "I cannot live without you."

He was old now, older than he had ever expected to be. The fire crackled and spat before him. He knew he did not have long. Drifting in and out of sleep, he felt her hand upon his shoulder. Her face was lined about the eyes and mouth, her almond eyes a rheumy blue. Her hair, a steely grey now, was tied back behind her head. Her lips were as full as they had ever been. She lifted a hand to his face, smoothing his moustache. Bowman's breath was coming in fitful gasps. She looked deep into his eyes as if to find some connection there. He swam in her gaze. He wanted to speak. Shifting in his chair, he licked his lips.

"I am here, George," she soothed. "What is it?"

His voice cracked as he spoke. "My god," he began, the words stilted and raw. He held her face in his hands, marvelling for a moment at the translucent quality of the skin stretched over his knuckles. Leaning forward to rest his forehead on hers, he felt her skin against his. He gasped for breath. The fire was fading, the room growing cold.

"My god," he said as tears pricked at her eyes. "You are beautiful."

Bowman's eyes snapped open. The swaying of the carriage confused him for a moment. The air felt chilled, the light fading. Feeling the straps around his body, holding him fast against the wooden bench beneath, he struggled to make sense of his surroundings. He was in motion, that much was certain. His heart raced and his mind whirled. He could not settle on a single, coherent thought. He was both here and not here. He could hear the sound of horses" hooves and somehow, in his confusion, reasoned he was being taken somewhere. He grasped for meaning. His sense of self abandoned him and Bowman felt his lungs fill with air. Feeling a pressure behind his eyes as if his head would burst, he gave himself to the swell of his grief. Heavy tears traced their course down the sides of his head. He wept until he was empty, slept, then wept some more.

At last, he sensed the carriage was slowing. Bringing his horses to a halt, the driver rapped at the wooden sides of the dray to be sure he was awake. A cold terror gripped Bowman by the heart. It squeezed and squeezed as if every drop of life would be taken from him. He already knew where he was. He heard footsteps around the side of the carriage, the unsteady gait of one who has been too long seated. With a grunt, the driver released the bolts that secured the wooden door to the rear of the dray. Bowman lifted his head to see beyond the awning.

The building loomed before him. Bowman opened his mouth to scream, flexing his limbs against the leather straps that secured him.

"Careful now," the driver called, a note of fear in his voice. "Don't make it worse for yourself."

As Cooper stood aside to accept the help of the two men who had joined him from the imposing entrance beyond, Bowman was afforded a full view of the building before him. There, crouching low on the drive as if poised in anticipation of its new arrival, stood Colney Hatch Lunatic Asylum.

~

End Note.

To live a village life in Victorian Britain was to live a life concerned with the basics. There was a shift throughout the nineteenth century towards greater industrialisation and urban living, which saw many rural workers out of work. The enclosure of land led to unemployment and hardship for many farmers, particularly where a rent was paid to the local country estate. As with Lord Melville in The Body In The Trees, the landowner would provide land for the tenant farmer who is then bound to provide his labour. By the nineteenth century, nine out of every ten acres of farmed land in England and Wales was tenanted. Farm labourers lived in small, overcrowded cottages, spending most of their wages on rent and food.

Under such harsh conditions, suicide or 'self-murder' amongst agricultural workers was by no means uncommon. In fact, it was far more common that homicide. As the century drew on, however, attempts were made to understand the phenomena as something more than an agitated state of mind. Sociological and financial matters were considered to be of import and, although a stigma remained, the English criminal justice system largely abandoned a punitive approach towards the act of suicide. Whilst the bodies of those who committed suicide were no longer buried at cross-roads (in the belief that any resurrected spirit would be confused by which direction to take) it was not unheard of that burial within Holy ground should not be admitted.

The fictional village of Larton is based on Cookham in Berkshire, a village in which I lived for almost twenty years; so much so that, should the reader ever visit, they might well recognise certain landmarks from The Body In The Trees. Like Larton, it sits on the Thames and is made up of three disparate parts; the Village, Cookham Rise and Cookham Dean. Unlike Larton, the inhabitants are welcoming and friendly to a fault.

Richard James, April 2020

SUBSCRIBE TO MY NEWSLETTER

If you enjoyed the third book in my Bowman Of The Yard series, The Body In The Trees, why not subscribe to my newsletter? You'll be the first to hear all the latest news about Bowman Of The Yard - and I'll send you some free short stories from Bowman's Casebook!

Just visit my website **bowmanoftheyard.co.uk** for more information. You can also search for and "like" Bowman Of The Yard on **Facebook** and join the conversation. I would love to hear your thoughts.

Finally, I would appreciate it if you could leave me a review on Amazon. Reviews mean a lot to writers, and they're a great way to reach new readers.

Thanks for reading *The Body In The Trees*!

Richard

Printed in Great Britain
by Amazon